In Praise of *Waterproof Justice*

From the author of *Shorter's Way*, comes another accomplished novel of memorable characters, compelling plot and pitch-perfect dialogue. Grace Hawthorne captures the spirit of New Orleans and Waterproof so completely I could retrace the steps of the characters and even taste Bitsy's lemon meringue pie.

Betty Hanacek, Director of Capacity Building at Park Pride

Loved loved loved *Waterproof Justice*. Could not put it down. The multiple story lines play nicely in sync. *Waterproof Justice* has a little bit of everything: romance, suspense, history, lots of humor and even poetry. I fell in love with all the distinctly Louisiana characters.

Beth Nowak, Regional Manager Pernod Ricard Wines and Champagnes

Typically I'm anxious for a novel to end. With *Waterproof Justice* I bonded with the characters and didn't want to let go. Fascinating. I'm hoping for a sequel.

Philip Kaplan, First Vice President, Morgan Stanley Wealth Management

She sits patiently. Throws a tempting line. Waits for itty-bitty tugs on the line that make small ripples. Before you can say, "Mon Dieux!" Hawthorne has you, hook, line and sinker.

Bob Wells, Filmmaker, Owner of Wells Communications, Inc.

Growing up in Louisiana designing projects for Angola, I recognized the shocking conditions at Louisiana State Penitentiary in the 1940s. *Waterproof Justice* captures that gloom and the fear of an arriving inmate along with the compassion of the sheriff who is delivering him. Grace Hawthorn nails it.

Fred Grace, Founder of Grace Hebert Architects

Also By Grace Hawthorne

Shorter's Way

Yes, there is a town called Waterproof on the Mississippi River in north Louisiana. However, for this book I borrowed the name and moved it down river to the part of the state where I grew up.

Waterproof Justice

Grace Hawthorne

For Freeman

Acknowledgments

My profound thanks go to Cynthia Pearson, Judy Burge, Jan Allen, Barbara Briscoe, Sharon Stulting, Pat Lindholm, Fontaine Draper and Barbara Valentine Pennington, who made up my readers' group. Their insights and comments were invaluable in shaping this book.

I also want to thank Gen. Harold Dye (retired) Army, 59th Field Artillery Co, Germany; Robert Harris, Jr., Army, 78th Infantry Division, France, Belgium, Germany; and Alec Morris, Army 1st Cavalry Division, Philippines and Japan for sharing their World War II memories with me.

Neal J. Kling, Partner at Sher Garner Cahill Richter Klein & Hilbert, L.L.C., New Orleans was most helpful in explaining the Napoleonic Code of Justice and helping me sort out the intricacies of the Louisiana legal system.

I was fortunate to meet Ricky, a trustee working at the Louisiana State Penitentiary Museum, who gave me an insider's view of life at Angola today. The information about conditions in the 1940s came from "Angola, Louisiana State Penitentiary a Half-Century of Rage and Reform," by Anne Butler and C. Murray Henderson.

Special thanks to Beth Nowak and Philip Kaplan who found two glitches in a final draft the rest of us all missed.

As always, my eternal gratitude to my husband, Jim Freeman, who has been part of this process since we bounced ideas around on a 12-hour research trip to Louisiana.

And finally, a special thanks to all the wonderfully cramped, cluttered little book stores in the French Quarter that still look and smell like book stores. Their owners supplied information, books, dictionaries, and maps that helped me round out my reference library.

CHAPTER ONE
(Waterproof, Louisiana 1946)

The pale winter sun came through the glass in the top of the front door and wrote "Waterproof Sheriff's Office" in shadows on the floor. Nate Houston braced his hands on the arms of his chair and carefully shifted his position. Then slowly he opened his desk drawer and looked down at the bottle inside. He hesitated several minutes pretending he had a choice. Finally he took the heavy, brown bottle out and set it on the edge of his desk.

So this is what I've come to, not my proudest moment.

The pain persisted, working its way up from a dull ache to a knife edge. Not to worry, he knew how to take care of that, at least for a while. He hated to admit that he needed the doses more often now than when he first began using, but he still had the situation under control. He opened the bottle and poured out a generous amount. The fumes burned his nose, but that was a small price to pay for the soothing warmth to come.

Horse liniment.

The only thing that tamed the pain in his knee. A little souvenir from Germany. A fragment so tiny the doctors missed it, but big enough to get his attention on a daily basis. He massaged the liniment into his knee and relaxed as the heat began to drive out the pain. Nate put the top back on the liniment and stashed it in his desk.

When he first got home, he thought taking the job as sheriff was a good idea. But he soon found out that having seen war and death up close, it was hard to take a Saturday night bar fight seriously. It was harder yet to deal with what "normal" folks considered threats of life and death. As if on cue, the phone rang.

"Sheriff, come quick! Bud Garvey's got Luther up a tree and he's threatening to kill him." Nate recognized Lucy Castle's voice although it was pitched several octaves higher than usual.

"Does Bud have a gun?"

"No Sir, but he's got a baseball bat. I'm tellin' you it's a matter of life and death, Sheriff. You've gotta get over here right now."

Nate shook his head. He didn't see how Bud Garvey on the ground with a baseball bat posed any immediate danger to Luther up a tree. Oh well, welcome to law enforcement in Waterproof.

He grabbed his cane and headed for the door. The patrol car was a pre-war Chevy that smelled of cigarette smoke, Burma Shave, and Old Spice. It was a little past its prime but well suited for patrols through the rolling hills of West Feliciana Parish. A stranger—if ever there was one hanging around—would have had no reason to suspect he was looking at law enforcement. There were no markings on the car, not because of stealth, but because Nate had never found anybody to paint it.

Similarly, he refused to wear a uniform ever again. Instead, he wore a khaki shirt and pants, and an ancient Panama hat with a sweat-stained hatband. His one concession was the small sheriff's badge pinned to his left shirt pocket, which was totally unnecessary because everyone knew him.

He'd lived in Waterproof most of his life. His father had worked a small farm on the edge of town and his mother had worked at Parchment Products, which canned Grade A Louisiana yams—not to be confused with ordinary sweet potatoes. The culls of the yams were ground up, roasted, and mixed with cottonseed meal to make animal feed. Waterproof always smelled like a sweet potato pie that had overflowed and burned on the bottom of the oven.

Out of habit, Nate reached for a Chesterfield from the half-full pack on the dash, turned on the radio, and sang along with Hank Williams. "Your cheatin' heart, will tell on you ..." When he arrived at the Castle farm, he found the usual suspects, Bud, Beauregard, and Rutledge.

Bud had gotten the two bloodhounds as puppies. "Make great huntin' dogs." In addition to that, Bud and the dogs were on call to help track prisoners who tried to escape from Angola. Just 20 miles north of Waterproof, it was the largest maximum-security penitentiary in the country and by far the most infamous.

Nate had seen more than enough prison camps overseas, but because his oldest friend and mentor Ezra Landry was on staff there, he occasionally made the trip to that officially sanctioned hell hole.

As Nate turned into the driveway, Lucy Castle met him talking a mile a minute. "Sheriff, you gotta stop him. Bud says Luther done broke into Blackburn's Hardware. If Luther done that—and I'm not sayin' he didn't—it's because some of them other boys put him up to it. Luther's not smart enough to think up something like that on his own. He's a good boy and ..."

"It's all right, Lucy. I'll take care of it." Nate maneuvered his long legs out of the car. When he was fifteen, he was a respectable 5'11." Then in one summer he grew four inches. His mother threatened to put a brick on his head to keep him from getting any taller. It obviously worked because he crested at 6'3" and spent the rest of his life ducking under doorjambs, and trying to fit in.

Sure enough Beauregard and Rutledge were sitting at the foot of an ancient magnolia tree and Bud was sitting on the fender of his old Ford pickup, his baseball bat propped against the front bumper. He smiled and waved. "He's up there with the squirrels, Sheriff. I've been keeping an eye on him just waitin' for you to get here."

"What's with the baseball bat, Bud?"

"Nothin'. I was just messin' with the kid. I wasn't gonna hurt him."

"What exactly do you think Luther did?"

"I was down drinkin' Co'Colas with the fellers in back of the hardware store and Blacky happened to mention that somebody broke in and stole a bunch of junk out of his storeroom. Now who else would steal junk but Luther? I figured the dogs needed a workout, so we come over here to have a look see. It's all in the shed over there." He slid off the fender to the ground. "Now that you're here, I'm gonna head back to town." He threw the bat into the cab of the truck. "See you 'round, Luther."

Bud whistled for the dogs. They came slobbering over, obediently put their front paws on the tailgate of the pickup and waited. Bud gave each of them an affectionate pat, lifted their hindquarters into the truck, snapped the latches of the wire cage, and took off in a cloud of dust.

Nate went to investigate the garden shed. Inside, he found an old, dented watering can with the nozzle missing, four rusty pulleys, a coil of new rope, a hammer with a broken handle, a partial roll of Duck tape, and a handful of assorted screws.

"Luther, is this stuff yours?" he yelled across the yard. Luther said yes and admitted he'd gotten it from Blackburn's Hardware Store. "Did you pay for it, Luther?"

"I couldn't, 'cause it wasn't for sale." Luther called down. "Wasn't nobody usin' it. It's been lying around in the back where Mr. Blacky puts the broke stuff. I know 'cause I straighten up for him every Saturday."

"That new rope lying around there, too?" No answer from the tree. "Luther, come down here."

"I'd rather not."

"Bud's gone. Now come down here, I'm getting a crick in my neck."

Reluctantly, Luther climbed down. He hated to leave the magnolia tree because he always felt safe there. Luther loved trees in general, but not all trees were equal when it came to climbing. Pine trees were no good because their trunks grew straight and tall a long way before they branched out. Live oaks were for sissies. Their branches fanned out and then lay down on the ground. A baby could climb them. Magnolias were the best. Their branches started close enough to the ground to reach easily and then grew up the tree like a stepladder. The leaves were thick and green. A perfect place to hide.

Nate looked at the boy and shook his head. He remembered a time when he looked like that. Tall and skinny with big hands and feet. His dad used to laugh and say all his parts would catch up with each other someday. "What are you doing with all this stuff, Luther?"

"I was gonna rig up some pulleys to make it easier to water the ferns Miss Nell's got hanging in the windows. I didn't mean nobody no harm."

Nate shook his head. Luther was in the same grade as his daughter Carrie. The difference was, Luther had been in Miss Nell's sixth grade class as long as Carrie had been in school. "Luther, you can't take things that don't belong to you. Why didn't you just ask Mr. Blacky if you could have them?"

Why did adults always ask questions that didn't make any sense?

Luther frowned, but he patiently answered, "'Cause he mighta said no."

Nate tried to explain the concept of paying for things, but he wasn't sure that was getting through to Luther. As they walked toward the house, Nate took in the scene. A poor place. The small house was weather-beaten gray, the porch swing was broken, and the dogs' ribs stuck out like railroad ties. Luther's beat-up old bike leaned against the concrete blocks that were doing their best to hold up the front porch.

A central fireplace was the only source of heat inside the house. The linoleum floor was covered with kids and a few old toys. Luther's father, Archie, sat in a chair in the living room, his legs covered with an old quilt. His skin was nearly as gray as the outside of the house. Nate took off his hat and hung it on a nail by the door. He nodded to Archie. Luther followed him in the door.

Lucy called out from the kitchen. "Coffee, Sheriff?" Nate accepted the chipped cup and sat down. "Luther, you ever think about leaving school and getting a job?"

Before Luther could answer, Lucy spoke up. "When Archie took sick, Luther went 'round to the plants and stores 'n all, but wouldn't nobody hire him. If you're worried about that stuff out there, we'll make good on it some way."

"Actually, Lucy, I was thinking maybe Luther could come to work in my office. I need somebody to clean up the place, keep things straight. Luther, you think you could do that?"

"Oh yeah, I'm good at cleanin'."

"How does $25 a week sound?"

"Twenty-five dollars a week!!" Lucy's eyes widened with excitement. "Oh Lord, Sheriff, that would be the best Christmas present ever. It would help pay for Archie's medicine and tide us over 'til he gets back on his feet. Luther, what do you say?" she prompted.

"When do I start?"

"Why don't you finish out the week with Miss Nell and take those things back to Mr. Blacky tomorrow."

"Why? They're junk to him."

"Just take them back, Luther, because it's the right thing to do. Then *ask* him if you can keep the old stuff and tell him I'll pay for the rope."

When Nate got into the car, he lit a cigarette and ran his hand over his short-cropped brown hair. When he left the office, he had no intention of hiring anybody, let alone hiring Luther. He hoped there was some money in his budget to cover his salary.

On the way back to town, Nate took a side road that led to the river. For no reason he had ever been able to explain, he'd always felt a kinship to Ole Man River. Sometimes he sensed the weariness of the river, always on the move, and yet never moving. Always in the same place, dependable, predictable.

Guess that's what I am these days, dependable, predictable. I remember when I couldn't wait to leave this town, travel, see the world. Well, I did that and it turns out the world is no bed of roses.

Nate watched the river for a while. He wondered if maybe there was a reason the river flooded occasionally. Broke out of its banks and ran helter-skelter over the land. Not with the intention of destroying anything, just to remind people that it could be free. That idea pleased him.

He lit another cigarette. He was glad to be home, but not only had *he* changed, so had everything else. Before the war, his daughter Carrie was a happy eight year old, now she was about to be a teenager. Before the war, he had a wife, but she died of pneumonia two years after he enlisted. Before the war, Miss

Laura was just his mother-in-law, now she was the anchor of his family.

At supper that night, he told Carrie and Miss Laura about his visit to the Castles. "I didn't go out there to hire Luther, but when I saw the way they were living, it just seemed like the right thing to do."

"I think it's a great idea, Dad. I know Luther better than most people and he's not nearly as dumb as everybody thinks he is. I bet he'll do real good."

CHAPTER TWO
(New Orleans, 1946)

"Basin Street is the street
Where the elite always meet
In New Orleans, the land of dreams ..."

"You're right about the land of dreams, Louis," Minnie Tucker tilted her head back and let a large swallow of B&B trickle down her throat. She remembered when Basin Street was *the* street of Storyville, the Park Avenue of Prostitution. Grand old townhouses standing side by side offered the best food, the best booze, the best music, and the best girls in New Orleans, all in sixteen wonderfully, sinful square blocks of The District.

Storyville was long gone, but the customers were still there. The elite politicians, underworld bosses, businessmen, law enforcement officers, high-rollers from out of town all still came to the land of dreams and Minnie and the girls were there to serve them.

Thank goodness winter had finally rescued the city from the summer heat. Minnie lingered a few more minutes listening to Louis Armstrong's trumpet, then she turned off the big Philco radio standing against the wall. Six o'clock, time to get ready for the evening's business.

Originally, Storyville was set up to confine prostitution to one area, make it legal, and thus protect the servicemen returning from World War I. After World War II, the boundaries of Storyville were dissolved and it became illegal again, once more with the idea of protecting the returning servicemen. The landladies just laughed, the same way their predecessors had laughed when Alderman Sidney Story rounded them up twenty-four years earlier. "You can make it illegal, but you can't make it unpopular." They found other accommodations and continued business as usual.

Minnie was proud of her house. She owned it free and clear, all twelve rooms, antique furnishings, wrought-iron balconies, and patio. As she walked down the back stairs, crossed the walled garden, and entered the main house, she breathed the cool evening air and listened to the familiar sounds of New Orleans, the music from street musicians, kids tap dancing on the sidewalk, boats on the Mississippi just over the levee.

When she passed her large cheval mirror, she tilted it slightly forward and checked her reflection. Not bad for forty-five. She'd maintained her figure, had some professional help keeping her hair strawberry blonde, and made sure she was always stylishly dressed. She favored Joan Crawford shoulder pads because they made her waist look smaller.

Appearances were important and Minnie demanded high standards from her girls. No sloppy-looking loungewear in the house and no suggestive clothing on the street. Minnie ran a high-class establishment that attracted a better class of customers.

Her house often catered to two generations in a family. It was almost a New Orleans rite of passage for a father to take his son to be initiated into the world of sex by his favorite girl. Minnie encouraged the tradition. Some loyal customers had even earned the privilege of having a charge account.

"Evenin', Professor," Minnie said as she passed through the parlor and heard her piano player tuning up. Jazz set the tone for the evening. The bar looked well stocked, hors d'oeuvres were ready, the crystal chandeliers were gleaming, everything was in order. She stepped into the little alcove beside the front door and saw a line of men stretching down the block. She recognized most of the faces. It promised to be a good night.

At 7:00 on the dot, the doors opened and the house filled with men, most of whom knew the routine. Speak to Minnie first, get a drink from the bar, sample the food, have a smoke, relax, and then meet the girls. The girls mingled with the guests and then, one by one, took their "gentlemen callers" upstairs.

Along about eight o'clock, the maid came into the parlor and told Minnie someone outside wanted to see her. "Tell him to come on in here, no need to be shy."

"Ain't a him, Miss Minnie, it's a her."

"A girl looking for work?"

"I don't think so."

Minnie was a bit puzzled. Why else would a girl be knocking at her door? "All right, put her in the little office, I'll come see what's goin' on."

When she opened the office door, a tall female was standing by the desk. She had clear sun-tanned skin and thick dark hair which she wore in a long braid down her back. She wore a nice pair of slacks and a white shirt. Minnie watched her for a moment. Although she stood perfectly still, there was an air of sadness about her.

"I'm Minnie Tucker, the landlady here. What's your name?"

"Ruby."

"Well, sit down, Ruby, and tell me what I can do for you."

The girl sat, ankles crossed, back straight, hands clinched tightly in her lap. She looked straight ahead. "I need a job." She hesitated and Minnie wondered if she were going to cry. "I'm staying at the boarding house over on Burgundy ..."

Minnie interrupted, "We call it Bur-*gun*-dy."

"Bur*gun*dy. The room's paid up 'til Saturday. Then I have to leave."

Minnie noticed the wedding ring. "Where's your husband?"

Ruby looked down at the slim gold band. "Gone."

Minnie was beginning to get the picture. Fast-talking city man meets innocent country girl in her late twenties, bordering on being an old maid. Never a good combination. "Are you sure he's gone?"

Ruby nodded. "He left a letter."

Minnie had heard the story before, many times. Although she felt a little bit sorry for the girl, she couldn't take in every brokenhearted woman down on her luck. As gently as possible she said, "Honey, go back home. You don't belong here." No response. Minnie tried another approach. "The truth is, I can't use you. Don't get me wrong, it's not because of your looks, although you are a little on the tall side, but that don't matter. I had a gal in here once who only had one arm. Customers loved her. It's just that you're ... Men come here looking for a good time, for fun, energy, excitement. I can tell already you're not too exciting. You're... quiet. You got no sizzle."

It took Ruby a minute to figure out what Minnie was talking about and the kind of business she was running. She knew she ought to leave, but where would she go? Instead she sat and waited.

In exasperation, Minnie got up and poured two glasses of brandy. "Here, drink this."

Obediently, the girl downed the contents in one gulp and that caused a bout of coughing and watering eyes. "It's best if you sip it."

Minnie watched Ruby. It was obvious she was making a real effort to hold it together. Push through. Never, never cry. Minnie could identify with that.

"It's against my better judgment, but I'll try to help you. First I need some information. Are you in trouble with the law? You pregnant?"

Ruby shook her head twice.

"So, where did you come from and how did you get here?"

Ruby swallowed several times, but otherwise remained still. "I grew up on a farm in Mississippi. We had nut orchards."

Minnie started to ask for clarification but decided against it.

"My mama died when I was fourteen. Then I ran the business for my dad. My brothers got drafted. I don't know where they are now. The company sold the orchards. My dad had to leave to look for work. Then I met this man," her voice nearly broke, "and we fell in love. We came here and got married. Now he's gone."

About what Minnie expected. She should stay out of this, but there was something about this girl ... "You said you ran the business for your father. What did you do?"

"Kept the books, did payroll, bought stuff, paid bills."

"Were you any good?"

"Yes."

"Are you honest?"

"Yes."

Minnie couldn't remember when she'd had a conversation with more information and fewer words. "Listen, tell you what, I'm gonna take a chance on you. I got a room upstairs and I sure could use an honest bookkeeper to keep track of all the payoffs and bribes I gotta make to run a legitimate business. You reckon you could handle that?"

"That's all I have to do? Manage the office?"

The relief in her voice was so clear, Minnie almost laughed out loud. "Don't worry, Honey, I got plenty of girls to take care of the rest. By the way, what's your whole name?"

"Ruby Bladder."

"Mon Dieu! I can't have a girl working for me with a name like that, even if you're not seeing customers. I got a reputation to uphold. I'm almost afraid to ask, but what was your maiden name?"

"Smith."

"Half my customers are named Smith. That won't do either. Let me see … OK, from here on out you're gonna be … Ruby … Ruby Canelle. It's French. *La canelle,* it means cinnamon 'cause you kinda smell like cinnamon.

"I'm gonna send my handyman, Big Joe, over to Burgundy to get your clothes. You do have some other clothes don't you? I mean the slacks are all right, I wear them myself when I'm off duty. You'll need a nice dress in case I ever need you to collect the cover charge, the entrance fee. Five dollars. Helps pay for the free booze and food and cuts down on the horny country boys and the drunks coming over here from Bourbon Street. I don't allow drunks in my house. It's $20 to take a girl upstairs and they collect that in their rooms. You'll need a dress for church too. You do go to church."

"I can."

Minnie was usually good at reading people, but this one was beyond her. "Well, we don't work on Sunday, so I encourage my girls to go. Lots of tourists, so we pick up customers that way. Most of the girls go to Mass at St. Louis Cathedral in Jackson Square. It's not far. You can go with them."

Ruby seemed to be perfectly content to sit quietly and listen to Minnie, but all that stillness was beginning to make Minnie nervous. "Come with me, I'll show you around. You know anything about New Orleans?" The girl shook her head. "You're in the French Quarter, the Vieux Carre, it sits right on the river. Canal Street, a couple of blocks over, divides uptown from downtown." She glanced at the girl to see if she was following. "Think about it like this, Uptown is upriver from Canal Street and Downtown is downriver from Canal. Easy."

Minnie realized she was talking too much, but she couldn't seem to stop herself. Somebody had to fill up all that silence. "Streets have a different name on the uptown and downtown side of Canal. Like St. Charles Avenue is Royal Street below Canal. If you wanna get somewhere you take the streetcar. Don't call it a trolley. The grassy part in the middle of the tracks, we call that the neutral ground."

It had been a long time since Ruby had had a woman to talk to. Back home, the men left in the morning and didn't come back until sundown. In the meantime, she washed clothes, cleaned the house, fed the chickens, worked in the garden, cooked, and did the bookwork. Sometimes she read from the set of books on the shelf. Silent, alone with her thoughts.

She listened to Minnie, but it was the house she was really paying attention to. Ruby was used to bare walls, braided rugs made out of strips of rags, windows with shades not curtains. Minnie's house was very different. There were black marble fireplace mantels edged in gold leaf, red velvet drapes, thick Oriental carpets, leaded crystal barware, antiques, pecky cypress paneling, comfortable chairs, and sofas. It was overwhelming. Even the small patio was exotic with huge palm trees, hanging ferns, and a couple of parrots that shouted foul things at anyone who walked by.

Finally, Minnie stopped talking. In an effort to get a rise out of Ruby, she pointed to a bronze plaque over the door that led in from the patio. "Know what that says?"

"No."

"Well, it's French. *'Lache Pas! Lache Pas la patate.'* It means 'Don't give up! Keep it up!'" Minnie laughed. Ruby studied the plaque. Minnie tried to explain. "I'm the landlady so I don't give up on the business, and the men, well, they got to keep it up. Get it?" She waited for a response. Ruby smiled slightly.

Minnie rolled her eyes toward heaven. When she got exasperated, her Cajun accent slipped out. "Actually it means, don't drop da potato, but we're not too finicky about da real meanin'." She shook her head, let out a loud sigh and walked into the parlor leaving Ruby on her own. She walked straight to the bar, "Sam, pour me a double B&B." She looked through the French doors out to the patio where Ruby stood. Minnie downed half the drink in one swallow. "I may have just made a bad mistake."

Ruby stood silently looking up at the moon thinking the same thing.

CHAPTER THREE
(Mississippi 1918-1946)

Ruby's education started before she was born. When her mother was six months pregnant with Ruby, a man came to the door selling encyclopedias. Since the young mother wanted the very best for her children, she agreed to buy the set of books and pay for them on the installment plan. As each book arrived, she unwrapped it with great care and put it on the only bookshelf in the house. As soon as Ruby was born, her mother started reading to her. She would hold the baby up and let her point to a volume, then she'd pick a subject at random and start reading. The two older boys had too much energy to sit and listen.

Ruby's mother was part Choctaw. The majority of the tribe had been relocated to Oklahoma, but a remnant stayed in Mississippi. Like most of the Choctaw people, her mother was mild, quiet, kind, and practical. She was Christian, but she also held to some of the old ways. The Choctaws believed all life and power came from the sun. Therefore, they never negotiated on a cloudy day and Ruby's mother taught her to only make decisions when the sun was shining. Ruby grew up hearing equal portions of verified facts from the *World Book Encyclopedia* and Choctaw myths from her mother's heritage.

Her favorite was the story of Redbird. All her mother's stories began the same way. "Once, when time was not quite old enough to be counted ..." In the story, as Redbird flies, he sees a lonely Indian maid who wants someone to care for and someone to care for her. In his travels, Redbird also sees a handsome Indian brave who wants someone to care for and someone to care for him. Redbird brings the two together then flies away, leaving the rest to them.

In addition to her stories, Ruby's mother also passed along to her daughter her strong features and her long black hair. One of Ruby's fondest memories was sitting on a low stool between her mother's knees as she brushed and braided her hair. Her childhood was quiet and peaceful. Following the Choctaw custom, her mother only spoke when she had something important to say, not like the white women they knew who seemed to talk just to hear their heads rattle.

As she grew up, Ruby watched the big yellow school bus stop in front of their house and pick up her two brothers. She stood in the middle of the tung nut trees growing in the yard and dreamed of riding that bus to a place where she could learn new things. By the time she entered first grade, she could already read and write and knew her numbers up to 100. She thought the teacher would be pleased. She wasn't.

Whenever the teacher asked a question, Ruby raised her hand and she always had the right answer. She thought the teacher would be proud of her. She wasn't. She stopped calling on Ruby and the kids made fun of her. They called her smarty-pants and wouldn't play with her. So Ruby learned to be silent.

Like most families in the area, kids were expected to help out on the farm. Her father worked on land owned by a large northern company. The tung nut trees he raised produced hard, black nuts which were harvested to make oil-base paint. In spring, the trees were covered with white blossoms. People often mistook them for dogwoods.

Ruby loved listening to her mother read, but she also loved working outdoors. As soon as they were tall enough to reach the peddles, her dad taught the children how to drive a tractor and how to tend and harvest the tung nuts. Her dad, like her mother, didn't waste words, but he did pray for each of his children by name when he said grace at night before supper. They never doubted that he loved and treasured each one of them.

Despite her early experience at school, Ruby loved to learn. She was good with numbers and often sat and watched as her mother did the bookkeeping for the farm. Since they rented the land, careful records had to be kept. Ruby was fascinated that numbers could mean totally different things depending on which column you put them in.

When Ruby was in the ninth grade, her mother died suddenly. As the only girl, Ruby was expected to stay home and take care of the family. Reluctantly she quit school, but she continued to read her encyclopedia whenever she got the chance. However, she didn't have much free time, what with the cooking and washing and mending and keeping the house and the books. The family worked together and worked hard, but money was always tight.

When the war started, lots of folks left their farms and went to the towns where they could get better paying jobs. The nearby paper mill was hiring and Ruby knew girls who got jobs there. Talking to them, she was sure she could do the work, but she passed up the opportunity because she had to hold things together at home. Shortly after Pearl Harbor was attacked, her two brothers were drafted. She and her father couldn't work the farm without them and there wasn't enough money to hire help. While her father was trying to figure out what to do, the owners notified him that the land had been sold and they would have to move out of the house.

Ruby was stunned. Everything she had counted on was disappearing. The little house they lived in was surrounded on three sides by orchards. The other side was a large, unexplored woodland. It was the playground for Ruby and her brothers growing up. It was her mother's source of herbs and medicinal plants. It was also Ruby's secret place to walk and dream.

When things began to unravel, Ruby went there to try to think. As she walked, she saw a redbird and smiled. An omen? She remembered her mother's story and thought about happier times. Then she saw him. He was standing less than twenty yards in front of her. At first she thought he was a spirit. But he turned out to be very real.

His name was Henry Bladder. He was like a movie star, tall, handsome, and charming. He had a good job as a surveyor and traveled wherever his company sent him. He talked to Ruby and she loved the sound of his voice. He seemed to know exactly what to say to make her feel better. He came to the house to meet her father and they talked about different places where jobs might be available.

Ruby had dated some local boys, but this man was different. He was educated. He had traveled. He listened when she talked about things she had learned from her books. In spite of herself, she was falling in love with him and even more amazing, he seemed to return her feelings.

On a bright sunny day, Henry told her he had to return to New Orleans and asked her to go with him. He said they would get married when they got there. She talked to her father and he said it might be the best thing and gave her his blessing.

They took a train to New Orleans. Ruby wanted to bring the encyclopedia, but Henry said the books were too heavy. They could send for them later. They arrived in the city in the afternoon and took a room in a boarding house in the French

Quarter. That night they were married in the parlor by a judge with two other residents as witnesses.

After the ceremony, they went to Arnaud's for dinner. Ruby had never been in a restaurant with chandeliers and a tile floor. In fact, she'd never been in a restaurant at all. Henry ordered for her and insisted they have a bottle of wine to celebrate. When Henry told the owner they had just gotten married, he insisted on giving them another bottle.

Later, back in their room that night, Henry proved to be a knowledgeable but gentle lover. Ruby had never been so happy. Henry said they would stay in the boarding house for a month while they looked for something more permanent. In the meantime they explored the city. Ruby loved the noise, the crowds, the music, and the excitement.

Then it was over.

Ruby woke up Monday morning a week later and Henry wasn't there. She assumed he had gone out and would be back soon, but she waited all day and he never returned. Finally she went downstairs to talk to the landlady to see if she might know where he had gone.

The landlady patted her hand. "I wish I didn't have to tell you this, Honey, but he's gone. He paid for the room through the end of the week and left this for you." She handed Ruby an envelope. The note inside was short and to the point. "Dear Ruby, I'm sorry, but I have to leave. Please take care of yourself. Henry"

Ruby was shocked. "But he said we'd find an apartment. He said we'd be fine. He said ..." For the first time in her life, she burst into tears.

"Honey, I've known men like him all my life. Handsome, charming to a fault. They're not bad men, not evil. I think they actually believe everything they say, when they say it. They just can't deal with the reality of life. For them it's a game, they're just playing."

"But what am I going to do? I don't know anyone here. I don't ... I can't ..."

The landlady sighed and wrote something on a slip of paper which she handed to Ruby. It was an address on Basin Street. "Maybe this will help."

CHAPTER FOUR
(New Orleans, 1946)

It took a couple of months, but Ruby settled into the routine of the house with relative ease. The hardest part was learning to sleep late. She'd always been up at 6:00 a.m., but since Minnie didn't close up shop until 4:00 a.m., getting up early was out of the question. Nobody stirred until around noon. Breakfast was the main meal of the day. For Ruby, the best part was that she didn't have to cook it. Tee Jean took care of that.

In addition to eggs and bacon and grits, there was fruit from the French Market, and there were always fresh beignets. Tee Jean kept a pot of hot oil bubbling on the stove. When she dropped in the tiny rectangles of spicy dough, they immediately puffed up like pillows, hollow on the inside, crispy on the outside. As soon as she scooped them out of the oil, Tee Jean sprinkled them with powdered sugar. Beignets always came with café au lait.

None of that store-bought crap for Tee Jean. She made coffee the way her Cajun grandmother taught her. First, sprinkle sugar in a cast iron skillet, stir it until it melted and started to caramelize, then add boiling milk. Once it was well mixed, she poured it into one of her two café au lait pots. The other pot was full of hot French roast coffee and chicory. Finally, the magic happened.

With a practiced hand, Tee Jean poured from both pots together into an extra large china cup for each girl. The higher the pots, the more the foam. Coffee always jump-started the conversation around the big oilcloth covered table. The girls shared small talk, gossip, and information that might be helpful to Minnie. Being surrounded by women was a new experience for Ruby. Usually she just watched and listened, but one morning when the girls were sharing funny stories, she took a chance.

"I have one."

"Well, Ruby, have you been talking to the clients?"

"No! I just heard this guy say that the man he worked for was so crooked," she paused a second to make sure she got the words right, "he was so crooked he would steal Christ off the cross and go back for the nails."

The girls clapped their hands and hooted with laughter.

"Must have been one of the older clients. I haven't heard anybody say that in years," Minnie said. "I'll bet it was Boots."

"Yeah, he's one of mine," Fern said. "First time he's with me, he's standing there naked as a jay bird and he wants to keep his boots on in bed. I told him I wasn't gonna put up with that, so he took one off and the smell was so bad it nearly knocked me over. I told him to put the boot back on." Laughter. "He's been wearing 'em in bed ever since." More laughter. The group finally broke up and everyone went their own way. Ruby headed upstairs.

She had a room to herself on the second floor, with a small balcony overlooking the patio. Lola, one of the older girls, helped her decorate it with a thick, white chenille bedspread, a Tiffany lamp she borrowed from another room, a throw rug, a rocking chair she found somewhere in the attic, and sheer curtains for the window and French doors. Ruby couldn't believe she was living in such luxury.

As to her office work, ordering supplies and paying bills was straightforward and easy to keep track of. The bookkeeping was a little more complicated. Minnie kept two sets of books. One for herself, one for anybody who might want to check up on her.

Bribes and payoffs were another part of Ruby's job. Minnie decided on the amounts and Ruby laid out the brown envelopes and stuffed each one with the required amount of cash. Some of these were kept at the house and the beat cops picked them up. Ruby delivered others to the precincts where Minnie's contacts were assigned, the rest went to the police department building on Broad Street. Once Minnie was sure that Ruby understood the system and that she wasn't trying to skim money off the top, she left her pretty much on her own.

The only part of the operation Ruby was not involved in was the Big Black Book. Minnie made no secret that she kept track of the regulars who visited the house, real names, and nick-names, identifying marks, how much they owed, how much they paid, the days they visited, and which girls they liked.

Because Ruby continued to wear slacks and a simple blouse. The other girls in their bright colors and fancy dresses provided enough distraction for her to circulate among the customers almost unseen. Over the months, Ruby came to recognize most of the regular clients.

The various underworld visitors were a frequent topic of morning coffee conversation. One striking older guest was Giuseppe Scapesi, head of the New Orleans crime family. He ran the city with an iron fist. He considered it a personal insult if a member of any other Mafia family came to his city without asking permission.

"It's true," Minnie said. "I heard that one of the guys who worked for Vito Genovese in New York City wanted to come down here for Mardi Gras and Genovese had to call ahead to get permission from Scapesi. Otherwise, they wouldn't have let Genovese's guy leave the airport."

Someone else brought up a well-known legend about Al Capone. According to the story, Capone came down from Chicago and demanded that the New Orleans don supply his outfit with booze at a cut rate. Seems Capone was tired of dealing with the Sicilian Mafia boss operating in Chicago. The New Orleans don, some of his boys, and a couple of policemen, met Capone at the train station. They disarmed Capone's bodyguards, broke all their fingers, and sent Capone back up to Chicago empty-handed. True or not, the story went a long way in establishing the rules when it came to dealing with the New Orleans Mafia.

Morning gossip was fine, but there was work to do. It was the holiday season, lots of tourists were in town and business was good. Minnie and the girls were working overtime. One night there were a lot of new faces around and Ruby pulled Minnie aside. "That's the one! That's the judge who married me and Henry. Maybe he knows where he's gone to."

Minnie looked across the room. "You mean the guy with the mustache?" Ruby nodded.

"Honey, he's no judge, he's an actor. If he's the one who performed the ceremony, you're no more married than I am."

Ruby looked as if someone had slapped her hard. "But the ring, Henry gave me a wedding ring." She held out her hand.

"Ruby, let it go. You're not the first woman to get her heart broken. Think about it. Did you have a marriage license? Oh, Cher, don't take it so hard. If the wedding had been on the level, you'd be in a real mess. You'd be a married woman without a husband.

"Seems to me, he did you a favor. He let you keep the fairytale without having to deal with the reality. This way, you're a free woman. Trust me, I've had several husbands and

I've been on my own without any husband. You'll be fine and, for what it's worth, I'd keep the ring. It might come in handy, you never know." Minnie patted Ruby's hand and went back to her customers.

Later that night, Giuseppe Scapesi's son, Anthony, showed up. He had been a regular since the don first brought him to the house at fourteen. Tony took to sin like white on rice. But unlike his father, who was good company, a big spender, and well mannered, Tony was arrogant.

Because Minnie didn't want any trouble with the don, she sometimes bent the rules for Tony. However, on several occasions, she met him at the door with her sawed-off shotgun and told him if he didn't straighten up, she was going to blow off his kneecaps or call his father. His choice. Each time, Tony settled down for a while.

However, this particular night he was showing off to some of his out-of-town friends and he figured he could talk his way past Minnie. When that didn't work, he forced his way in the door and demanded to see Lola, who was already upstairs with a client.

Minnie offered him and his friends drinks and suggested they have something to eat while they waited, but Tony was too drunk to be reasonable. He stormed upstairs and barged into Lola's room before Big Joe could stop him. When Tony saw Lola was with another man, he went crazy, grabbed the fellow, and dragged him naked and screaming into the hall where he started beating him with his fists.

The girls all knew the routine when there was trouble. Stay out of sight, be quiet, keep the doors closed, and let Big Joe and Minnie take care of the situation. Ruby didn't know the rules. Having broken up many fights between her brothers, she instinctively opened her door just as Tony plunged his knife into the man. Tony was as shocked to see Ruby as she was to see him. Time stopped as they stood less than a foot apart and stared at each other face to face.

Ruby heard Big Joe and Minnie running up the stairs and closed her door just as they reached the landing. Tony dropped the knife, turned and fled down the back stairs.

"You want me to go after him, Miss Minnie?"

"No, Joe, we know where to find him." Then Minnie turned her attention to the man on the floor and the puddle of blood spreading over the rug. Clearly he was dead.

"This feller's gone, Miss Minnie," Big Joe said softly. "Nothing to do for him now."

"Lola, open the door," Minnie said quietly. "Check the guy's billfold and see who he is."

Lola took a look. "There's nothing here but a few dollars. I reckon he didn't want to take a chance on being identified in a raid."

Minnie nodded and told Big Joe to roll the body up in the bloody rug and take it down to the garden shed. Her next thought was to protect her business. In a matter of minutes, she had thrown down a new rug and shifted a table and chairs to cover up any trace of the crime. She walked into Lola's room. "You all right, Honey?" Minnie recognized the beginning of a black eye. Otherwise, Lola seemed to be fine.

Next, Minnie straightened herself up, made sure there was no blood on her clothes, and went quietly along the hallway knocking on doors and reassuring the rest of the girls and their customers that there was no cause for alarm. Everything was all right.

It took a great deal of self-control, but Minnie finished out the night being the perfect hostess. When the house finally closed, she called a meeting. "Y'all need to know that Tony Scapesi killed a man here tonight." She could tell from the subdued reaction most of them had already gotten the word.

"I've got to be very careful how I handle this, so I need to know exactly what happened."

Lola described how Tony had broken into her room all red in the face, cursing, and calling her a whore. "When he came over to the bed, I thought he was gonna kill me. I tried to talk to him, but that's when he hit me. Then the guy I was with spoke up and Tony grabbed him and started hitting him. I've never been so scared in my life. Once they were out in the hall, I locked the door and hid under the bed."

Minnie took her time. "Did anyone else see what happened in the hall?" No one spoke. "Good." She let out a big sigh then squared her shoulders. "OK, the next thing I gotta do is call the precinct. Then I gotta tell the don my side of the story before Tony gets home."

Everyone held their breath. Calling the police was the last thing any landlady ever wanted to do. If the policeman on the payroll could be trusted, it might all go away. But if not, there was no way to predict what might happen. "Just remember, nobody saw nothin.' You didn't see anything so you can't answer any questions. Now go back to your rooms and try to get some sleep. I'll do what I can to take care of this."

Minnie went to her office to make the calls and the girls disappeared into their rooms. Ruby went to her room and locked the door. Suddenly she realized that although the room was warm, she was shivering.

I should have spoken up. I should have told Minnie what I saw. But what good would that have done? They already know who did it. Why did I have to open the door? Well, at least nobody knows I saw him.

Then it hit her, Tony knew. He had seen her as clearly as she saw him. He knew where to find her. Ruby knew she was in deep trouble and there was no one to ask for help.

Minnie took time to compose her thoughts before she dialed police headquarters. She knew the night shift would just be leaving and she wanted to catch the one person she thought had enough juice to handle the situation. It took her a while, but she eventually found the officer she was looking for. "Captain Boudreaux, we've had some bad trouble over here tonight. Tony Scapesi came in drunk, dragged a guy out of Lola's room, beat him up pretty bad, and then stabbed him. Left him in the hall upstairs."

"What do you mean 'stabbed?'"

"I mean stabbed, like dead. Like blood-all-over-the-rug dead."

"Jesus, Joseph, and Mary!! Where's the body?"

"It's in the tool shed. I had Big Joe wrap it up in the rug and take it down there."

"You called the don?"

"Not yet. I wanted to talk to you first to see if we could keep this quiet. Can you take care of this?"

"Godalmighty, Minnie, this ain't no little thing you are askin' me to do."

Minnie was only too well aware of that fact. If word got out that a client had been murdered in her house, it could ruin her business. Minnie had worked too hard and made too many sacrifices to let that happen. Compared to losing everything she had worked for, the idea of getting threatened by Tony or the don didn't seem so frightening.

Captain Boudreaux had his own problems. Tony Scapesi was a mean SOB and as much as he would have liked to lock him up, it wasn't worth getting on the bad side of old man Scapesi. On the other hand, he knew Minnie would make it worth his while. He might be able to afford that fishing camp at Lake Maurepas after all. "I'll take care of this myself. I'm headed over there right now."

"God love you, Boudreaux. I'll owe you for this."

"Yeah, Minnie, that goes without sayin'."

Minnie hung up the phone, breathed a sigh of relief, and reminded herself to substantially increase the money Boudreaux was getting. True, she had enough on him to expect some help, but still, as he said, this was no small thing. She opened her Black Book and made a note by Boudreaux's name. Then she found Giuseppe Scapesi's phone number. She knew the old man would be at his compound out in Metairie near Lake Pontchartrain. She just hoped Tony was staying at his apartment in town.

When the phone rang, it startled the don out of a deep sleep. He glanced at the clock. Five thirty. Not a good sign. "*Pronto?*"

"Mr. Scapesi, I am sorry to call you at such an early hour. This is Minnie Tucker. I'm afraid I have some bad news. Tony was here tonight and … No, no, as far as I know, he's all right." Minnie took a deep breath. "But you see he came here drunk, then he demanded to see Lola. She was with another client and he barged into the room and there was a fight and he beat up this fellow and pulled a knife … and killed the man."

"I see."

"Now I want to assure you there were no witnesses and I had somebody take care of the body, but you know I had to report this to the police."

"You've already called the police? I have police on my payroll."

"I do too. That's why I called them first, to keep a lid on this. I thought if I handled things, it would keep your name out of it. Of course, if you want to handle it …"

"No, it is better your way. I appreciate that you are willing to handle this. I am in your debt. Now it is my responsibility to handle Tony. Do not worry. He will not bother you again."

"Thank you, Mr. Scapesi." Minnie hung up and reached for her bottle of B&B. It was just after six o'clock, but she needed a drink. "Hell, it's early, but I deserve a drink," she said out loud and poured herself a double.

When he hung up the phone, Giuseppe Scapesi grabbed his robe. With his slippers slapping the hardwood floor at every step, he marched down the hall to the other wing of the house where Tony's room was. The door was closed. He didn't knock.

The inside of the room smelled of stale beer, vomit, and the unmistakably metallic odor of blood. Tony's clothes lay where he had discarded them and he lay face down across the bed, wearing nothing but his shorts. His father grabbed the sheet and jerked it with enough force to roll his son out of bed and onto the floor.

"What the hell???" Tony's eyes were bloodshot, his head hurt, and his hands were bruised and throbbing.

"Where were you tonight?"

"Nowhere. I just…."

Tony didn't see the blow coming and somehow the open-handed slap was more insulting than painful. "*Zitto!* Don't open your mouth and lie to me," his father growled through clinched teeth. "You know what happens to people who lie to me. Now tell me what happened."

Tony sat up the best he could and leaned his head back against the mattress in order to bring his father's face into focus. "I was down in the Quarter at Minnie's. There was a fight. I had a knife. I think I might have killed somebody."

"Think!?!"

"I didn't exactly stay around to find out."

Very quietly the older Scapesi asked, "Were there any witnesses?"

Tony found his father's controlled rage far more frightening than being screamed at. Tony's head was pounding and he felt the bile rising in his throat. He wanted to lie, oh God, how he wanted to lie, but he knew that was not an option. Not if he wanted to live.

"Was there a witness?"

Tony lowered his head. "Yes."

"One of the girls?"

"No. That big tall one. I don't think she's one of the whores."

"Can she identify you?"

"Yes."

"*Dio mio! Attenzione, cretino.* I've rescued you for the last time. If you don't wanna end up in jail for murder, you better take care of this. *Capisci?*"

"*Si,*" Tony said and threw up on the floor.

***

Tony wasn't the only one in fear for his life. The reality of the situation had set in and Ruby knew she had to disappear. She started to write a note and then thought better of it. The safest thing for everyone was for her to say nothing. She'd been looking forward to going to midnight Mass Christmas Eve with the girls. But that was never going to happen.

Sadly, she pulled her suitcase from under the bed and began to pack her clothes. She took all the money she had saved, quietly left the house on Basin Street, and headed for Airline Highway.

CHAPTER FIVE
(Waterproof, 1946)

Nate poured himself a cup of coffee, the aroma thick and black as the chicory he mixed into the French roast. He put the pot back on the stove. Miss Laura kept it over the pilot light where it stayed hot and ready twenty-four hours a day, summer and winter. He took a sip and sat down to breakfast.

Actually sitting down to three civilized meals a day had been one of the hardest adjustments when he came home. After four years of eating K-rations or going hungry, the abundance of food at each meal still surprised him.

His wife, Eunice, had not been much of a cook, but her mother, Miss Laura, was a different story. That woman could turn pokeweed into an edible dish, although, thankfully, they had managed to avoid *that* necessity.

Miss Laura kept a small garden that was sufficient for their needs and usually produced enough to swap with the neighbors for vegetables she didn't grow. Secretly, Nate had to admit she was easier to live with than Eunice. Even with her white hair framing her face with soft, grandmother waves, Miss Laura was more of a free spirit than Eunice had ever been. Perhaps her attitude was the result of having lived eighty years.

Eunice had tried to control everything, including her daughter. From the start, she was determined to make Carrie a proper Southern lady, even if it killed both of them. Nate still remembered one hot summer day shortly before he left for active duty, when he heard the two of them in the kitchen. Eunice decided it was time for Carrie to learn how to make pound cake, a necessary skill for any Southern hostess. She took out a pound of butter, a pound of sugar, a pound of flour, ten eggs, and a bottle of vanilla extract. "We'll cut the recipe in half, so if you ruin the first one, you can do it over. No need to waste precious ingredients."

Carrie sulked. "What's so hard about pound cake? You just stir it up and pour it in the pan, don't you? It doesn't look so complicated."

"It's all in the mixing. Fold, don't stir. Fold, never, never stir."

When Carrie's cake came out of the oven and cooled sufficiently to remove from the pan, it looked perfect, for five minutes, then the middle started to settle. The result was a cake dense enough to stop bullets.

"Do it over," Eunice said.

Carrie knew that tone of voice. No point in trying to get out of it. By the time Nate made an appearance in the kitchen, there was more than one ruined pound cake and Carrie was close to tears. However, the last one looked fine, held its shape and Eunice pronounced it an unqualified success. Smiles all around. The cake, topped with fresh strawberries and whipped cream, was given pride-of-place at supper.

Miss Laura's method of child rearing was a lot more relaxed. She settled for raising a happy, independent child, with just enough Southern to add a little charm and finesse. Nate approved.

He and Miss Laura had formed a strong bond and a division of labor that worked for both of them. He appreciated that they shared the occasional off-color story, that Miss Laura found humor in most of her fellow human beings, and only gave advice when she was asked for it. On top of that, she made the world's best biscuits. In every way, she was a treasure.

"I think you did a good thing to hire Luther," Miss Laura said as she sat down opposite Nate. "Luther's not a bad kid, he just needs something to keep him busy, and Lord knows you could use some help around the office. He might even get the place cleaned up. Now if we could just find you a good woman to keep you company ..."

That was the one area where his mother-in-law did not hesitate to voice her opinion, frequently. "Laura ..."

"I know, I know. It's not any of my business. I just hate to see a good man going to waste. In my day ..."

Nate smiled. The subject of his love life—or the lack of it—seemed to bother Miss Laura a good deal more than it bothered him. He wasn't ready for a woman in his life yet, which was just as well since to his knowledge there wasn't an unattached woman in Waterproof. A couple of widows with children, but that was not for him. He had his hands full trying to raise Carrie.

"Sugarfoot," he called, "if you're ready, I'll give you a ride to school."

"I'll meet you in the car," Carrie answered.

Nate treasured every minute he had with his daughter knowing his time as her hero was limited. She was about to turn thirteen and he had no idea how he was going to cope with the reality of her going to parties, and dances, and dating. He knew what Miss Laura would say, "Sufficient unto the day is the evil thereof." One day at a time, he'd just have to take it one day at a time.

After dropping Carrie at school, Nate decided to stop by Blackburn's Hardware and square things with Blacky. Behind the store, was a big open area where Blacky stored lumber. A bunch of old wooden chairs, which Blacky had probably intended to sell at one time, were drawn up in a semicircle. Any man in town looking for a place to sit, smoke, and swap stories knew he was welcome. When Nate walked in, Bud Garvey was sprawled out with a Co'Cola in one hand and a cigarette in the other.

"Hey, Sheriff, come on over. I was just tellin' the fellers about that time me and some other ole boys was out workin' with my John Deere and we bet that oldest Walker kid, Possum, that he couldn't stand three feet away and piss on the magneto in that tractor. Well, Possum knew he could piss a lot farther than that, so he hauls off and lets her fly. The tractor's still runnin' and when he hit that magneto coil, the electricity climbed right up that stream, hit Possum and knocked him on his ass. I'm telling you, we liked to died laughin'. And you know what Possum said when we finally got him conscious and stood him up? He rolled his eyes kind of wild like and said, 'See, I told you I could do it.'"

They had all heard the story before, but Nate laughed along with the rest of the men. Before he left, he talked to Blacky a minute, then drove over to his office.

One of the first things Nate did when he took over as sheriff was to replace the standard metal desk with his old wooden desk from home. It had escaped Miss Laura's dusting routine—if I can't see it I don't dust it—in the far corner of a storage area. As Nate was going through the drawers, he found a manila folder with some type-written pages inside. He glanced at the top one and although it had his name on it, he couldn't for the life of him remember writing it. He sat on top of the desk and started to read.

```
Old Man River
Ninth Grade History Report
Nate Houston


    In the beginning it was just
the two of us. One of us tall and
```

skinny, the other one long and wide. I was just a sapling but I understood the old man. I knew nobody could tame him and that was fine with me.

For hundreds of years he had lived on his own, ebb and flow, give and take. He went where he wanted to go. I put down roots and stayed put.

Then the people came. They cut down the elders and left the babies for later. Great growing things were sliced into boards and nailed into boxes of all sizes. I wasn't big enough to count, so they left me alone. They also left him alone because he was too big for them to control.

Eventually they got curious, plucked up their courage and ventured toward the old man, just testing the waters. They drove poles into the soft edges and the old man just waited and watched. When they stopped the cutting, and stripping, and building, they began filling the boxes with things they wanted and began to trade with one another. They multiplied and filled the boxes with more of themselves.

Then one day a boat came by. The old man was familiar with boats, liked to have their paddle wheels scratch his back down the middle where he couldn't reach.

And so they settled in to stay. Unlike them, I knew what was coming. One day the old man got restless. He decided to visit the nooks and crannies where he hadn't been for a long time. When he tired of that, he went looking for new worlds to conquer. He came unannounced and left when he got good and ready.

The people were afraid. They moved away. But when the old man finally went back to his familiar home, they came back. They cursed his muddy footprints instead of accepting them as the gifts they were. They cleaned away all traces of him and then it began again.

It went on that way for years. I looked down and thought they would never learn. It took a long time, but finally, they gave up. The last time they went away they didn't come back.

Their boxes fell apart. I was glad they were gone. The old man was glad too. They moved up onto higher ground. They are somebody

else's problem now. Once the
trees knew the cutting was over,
they started to come back. I was
glad to have the company. The old
man nourished us and watched us
grow tall and strong.

That is how the town of
Waterproof, Louisiana, was
established permanently on the
high ground safely away from the
periodic floods of the
Mississippi River.

*Ninth grade. That must have been Miss North's history class.
The writing's a little over the top but not too bad for a high school
kid. Wonder what else is in here?*

Twin Bill

What an act you are
Cool saxophone man
Sharing the bill
At Bourbon and Toulouse
With a hot-tamale cart.

Instead of smoky-blue bar haze
You blow through misty-gray
clouds
Of corn-shuck steam.

Your horn is always muted
Not by choice, but by the paper
cup
That collects the bread

```
That pays the bill
For hot tamales.
```

That brought back some memories. Nate and Eunice had driven to New Orleans for Mardi Gras. On Ash Wednesday following Fat Tuesday the tourists went home, but they stayed the rest of the week at a little hotel in the French Quarter. It was before Carrie was born, they were young and although it was an unusually cold February, they didn't mind. Nate immediately recognized the last page in the folder. He had written that shortly after his father died.

```
Nate Senior

My dad rolled his own
    from a tin of Prince Albert
    he kept in his overalls pocket.

He laughed a lot
    and drank a little
    whiskey he made himself.

He appreciated a good woman
    and a good mule.

He cherished his children
    and cursed the federal
    government.

He was a yellow-dog Democrat
    and a blue-tick-hound hunter.

He never went to church
    and never broke a promise.
```

```
My dad was a man
   who rolled his own life.
```

Nate straightened up the papers, closed the folder, put it in the middle drawer of his desk, and forgot about it.

***

Half way up the driveway to his office, Nate slammed on the brakes. The side door was wide open, the windows were up, and all the screens were missing. "I'll be damned. Somebody's broken into my office," he said aloud. More puzzled than angry, he went to investigate.

A fleeting thought crossed his mind. What if someone was still inside? He had a gun at home and his Army rifle was on top of the storage cabinet. He didn't carry a sidearm and hoped he'd never be called on to shoot a gun again. He'd had enough violence for one lifetime.

At the door, he caught the unmistakable odor of ammonia. When he walked in, he saw Luther up on a ladder with a spray bottle and a handful of old newspapers. "Luther, what are you doing?"

It was clear to see what was going on, so Luther waited for the Sheriff to get around to asking what he really wanted to know.

"Why are you washing the windows?"

"They were dirty. I mopped the floor; it was dirty too. I got the coffee going. Half and half just like you like it." Luther beamed. "I had to leave the windows open for the fumes, but it'll warm up soon as I close 'em again."

Nate shook his head as if to shake this new state of affairs into place. "How'd you get in here?"

"Used the key."

"How'd you know where it was?"

"Everybody in town knows that."

Of course, why not. People didn't lock their houses, left keys in their cars and trucks, sent their kids off to play all day without a worry in the world. Nate wiped his feet, crossed the room to hang up his hat, then laid his cane on the desk, and poured himself a cup of coffee. It was surprisingly good, and he had to admit having coffee waiting was a nice touch. But working with Luther was going to take some getting used to.

Nate soon learned that anything Luther did three times in a row became permanently fixed in his mind. Early on, Nate had shown him how to use the police radio. The next day when he came to work, Luther was proudly sitting behind the metal desk Nate had discarded. He had set up the radio and microphone on the desk and further staked out his territory by adding an empty tomato soup can filled with pencils, a stapler, and Scotch tape dispenser.

From then on, every morning Luther sat down and checked in with the neighboring towns. At first, the other sheriffs were surprised to hear his formal announcement. "This is Sheriff Nate Houston's office in Waterproof, Louisiana, calling the sheriff's office in Tunica, Louisiana. Luther Castle speaking. Over."

Sometimes there was official information to relay, but more often the reply was, "Hey, Luther, what's up? Say, did you hear the one about ..." Luther would listen, giggle, and then pass the joke along to the next sheriff on his list. As a rule, he repeated them to Nate. It became part of the morning routine.

Mid-afternoon, Nate decided to take a walk up to the Greyhound Bus Station. Leon Harvey, who ran the place, always knew who was leaving town and who was expecting someone to arrive. Highway 61 was a straight shot from New Orleans to Baton Rouge, to Waterproof, to Natchez, Mississippi. Lots of tourists passed through on the Natchez Trace, but other than stopping to get gas, or grab a bite to eat at the Firehouse Café, they didn't linger. Staying overnight—unless you had family—was out of the question. Waterproof didn't have a hotel or even a tourist court.

The bus station was the hub of social life in Waterproof. It had the town's only Coke machine, a nickel slot machine, and the Baton Rouge *State Times* and *Morning Advocate* and the New Orleans *Times-Picayune,* which came every day on the Greyhound bus.

Nate started walking slowly, using his cane, but the farther he walked the better his leg felt. He knew he needed the exercise. If he worked at it, he might be able to manage without the cane soon. He stepped into the bus station, bought a Baton Rouge paper, and passed the time of day with Leon. Then he headed over to the Firehouse Café, owned and operated by Bitsy Varner.

He glanced around the dining room and took his usual seat at the counter. Bitsy came out of the kitchen with a pot of coffee in one hand and a piece of lemon meringue pie in the other. "Lord, I've got to cut down on the coffee," Nate said under his breath as he reached for the pie.

"Hey, Sheriff, I was wondering if I'd see you today. How's Miss Laura and Carrie? That young lady getting ready for the Valentine's Day Dance?"

"Don't remind me. Her birthday's coming up in February. She'll be thirteen. I can't believe it. A teenager in my house. God help me."

When Nate finished his pie, he swiveled around to take a closer look at the room. He pointed to the woman sitting by herself staring out the front window. "Who's that?" he asked Bitsy.

"Don't know. I saw her get out of a car with an older couple over at the bus station. I thought maybe they were gonna switch drivers, but when they left, she stayed behind. Had a suitcase and walked over here, sat down and ordered coffee. Didn't say much. Nothing, actually."

For some reason, Bitsy decided to leave out the part about seeing the woman remove what looked like a wedding band and drop it into her purse. Nate started to get up, "Now don't you go asking her a lot of questions."

"That's my job, Bitsy."

"No, it's your job to keep the peace and, as you can see, she's not disturbing it. Why don't you just go over there and talk to her, and be nice."

Bitsy believed in two things, love and food. As far as she was concerned, all the ills of the world could be cured with a generous portion of one or both of those elements. She was ten years Nate's senior and had watched him grow up, go to work, get married, become a father, go to war, lose his wife, and come home. The war changed him. It changed everybody, but she could see him fighting his way back to the easy-going man he was before.

To help the process along, Bitsy was administering her piece-of-pie-a-day cure. So far it was working pretty well. But it wasn't enough. Nate needed a good woman in his life or maybe even a bad one. Trouble was, there wasn't either one available in Waterproof. Until now. There she sat, right there in the café, an unknown quantity who just might be the one. Bitsy had been thinking about the possibility since the woman first walked in and sat down.

Maybe it's a sign. Maybe she was sent to my café so I could bring the two of them together. Maybe it's destiny. Fate. Whatever it is, I'm not letting that woman escape without giving it my best shot.

Nate leaned his cane against the counter and walked over to the woman's table. He smiled and extended his hand. "Hello, my name's Nate Houston." The woman looked up at him but didn't respond. "Welcome to Waterproof."

Ruby saw his badge and hesitantly offered her hand. Nate noticed her eyes, deep brown with flecks of gold. "Nate Houston," he said again.

She continued to look steadily at him. "I'm Ruby ..."

Oh God, what name do I use now?

Then her eyes fell on an advertisement. *When It Rains, It Pours.* "Morton," she said softly, "Ruby Morton."

Her hands were soft, but her grip was firm. For a moment they looked at each other and Nate got the strange image of water flowing around a stone. Then she lowered her eyes and removed her hand. Oddly, he found himself at a loss for words, "If I can help you in any way," he gestured toward the counter, "Bitsy knows where to find me."

What's the matter with you, Houston, you're acting like you've never spoken to a woman before.

Nate nodded to Ruby and walked back to the counter. Bitsy was standing there smiling. "What are you grinning at?" he asked.

"To tell you the truth, Sheriff, I'm not rightly sure, but I aim to find out. And I aim to find out about that woman over there. I don't suppose you'd be interested in knowing what I learn about her, would you?" Nate picked up his cane and headed out the door.

Still smiling, Bitsy walked over to Ruby. "That was our sheriff. Nice feller, pretty low key. Mind if I sit down? I've been on my feet all day. You'd think I'd be used to it by now; I've been doing it all my life. Name's Bitsy Varner, I own this place. Used to belong to my parents. When they passed, it came to me. The café and that big old house over yonder. Can't hardly see it from here, behind all the trees and moss."

As Bitsy talked her hands were always busy, straightening menus and condiments, wiping the table. "You headed anywhere special? I'm just asking because the last bus just left and there's not another one due out until noon tomorrow. Waterproof's not big on accommodations, if you know what I mean. By the way, I didn't catch your name."

"Ruby Morton."

For a moment the two women looked at each other. "Listen, Honey, I know it ain't any of my business, but you look like ... well, like maybe you're coming from a bad place. Believe me, I know about the kind of man a woman needs to get away from. Some men think being married gives them the right to do anything they want.

"Anyway, you don't have to tell me nothing if you don't want to, but there's just me in my big house and you're gonna need a room for the night. Why don't you order yourself some supper, we got a good meat-n-three. Pork chops tonight. When you're finished, I'll walk over with you and get you settled in. Terry, my cook, can keep an eye on this place for a few minutes. You'll have the house to yourself 'til I close up, which is usually about 8:30."

Ruby realized she was hungry. She hadn't eaten since the old couple she caught a ride with stopped in La Place.

Well Ruby Morton, I guess this is as good a place as any to hide.

CHAPTER SIX
(New Orleans, 1946)

While Ruby was getting settled in Waterproof, Minnie was doing her best to erase all traces of her from Basin Street. When Ruby didn't show up for breakfast the morning after the incident, Minnie went to her room to investigate. At first glance, nothing was out of the ordinary, but the minute she opened the chifforobe, she knew something was wrong. The only thing hanging there was Ruby's church dress. Next, Minnie looked under the bed and sure enough, her suitcase was gone.

It didn't take Minnie long to put two and two together and realize that Ruby must have seen more than she let on. If she had seen Tony, then it was a pretty good bet he had seen her and that wasn't good. Giuseppe Scapesi might be a gentleman on the outside, but he was also Sicilian. That meant protecting his family at all costs. He could send Tony to deal with Ruby, which meant she had at least a fighting chance of staying alive. Or the don could take charge himself, which was much, much more serious. Minnie had come to like the tall, silent girl and she was particularly upset about losing an honest bookkeeper.

It took the police a couple of days to get around to questioning the girls. Since there was no body, technically there was no crime. But with a house full of guests when it happened, it wasn't surprising that rumors started to circulate through the

Quarter. A possible murder was just too good not to speculate about.

Keeping up the pretense that the murder was only gossip, Captain Boudreaux delegated the investigation to one of his junior officers. The young man showed up one morning at 9:00 to find everyone in the house still sound asleep. Big Joe answered the door, told him to quiet down and suggested he come back at a civilized time, like 2:00 in the afternoon.

When Big Joe related the information to Minnie, she smiled. The captain had obviously picked the newest kid on the force to investigate, probably some farm boy turned policeman. Folks raised in New Orleans would have known better than to expect anybody on Basin Street to be up before noon. Maybe she could handle this after all.

At breakfast she told the girls to expect the police and to remember to stick to their stories. They were in their rooms, the doors were closed, and they didn't see anything. There was, of course, no way to deny that Tony had been there or that he was drunk, but nobody saw him do anything but storm upstairs yelling and screaming.

When he returned, the young cop asked a lot of questions, but it was clear he was getting nowhere. He checked names against his list to make sure all the girls were present.

"I got another name here. One of the whores is missing."

Minnie bristled. "We don't use that word around here. All my girls are present just like you asked for."

"No, there was one more "girl" in the house. How come she's not here? I wanna question her too."

Minnie made a big show of trying to figure out who he might have in mind. "Oh, that might have been the bookkeeper. I had to let her go, skimming off the top, you know how it is."

"Any idea where she went?"

"Not really. She mentioned having family back on some farm in Mississippi."

"So she wasn't here when it happened?"

"No." The kid was making it too easy.

Just to show he had the authority, the cop wandered around, opening cabinets, and looking into rooms. Eventually he left.

Minnie knew that Scapesi had spies in the police department and she was counting on the story she had just told getting back to the don and to Tony. She hoped they would figure out that she was doing her part to keep things under wraps.

Tony did get the word, but he hadn't really been worried. After all, he was Tony Scapesi. Nobody was going to be stupid enough to mess with him. Besides, it sounded like Minnie had things under control. No need for him to get involved.

On the other hand, there was one person Tony did fear, his father. If the old man said to take care of it, Tony needed to at least look like he was making an effort to take care of the girl. He called a couple of friends and suggested they go juking in some of the dives across the river. That way he could drink, dance, maybe get lucky, and still put on a good show for his father.

The next couple of nights Tony and his gang hit all the bars in Westwego, Marrero, Harvey, Gretna, and Algiers. All he got for his trouble was a first-class hangover. He wasn't sure whether he'd gotten laid or not. Since he still had money in his pocket, he figured he hadn't.

That left the highways, but Tony couldn't think of any way to check those out. There wasn't much south of New Orleans except swamps. It didn't make any sense for her to run that way anyhow. She might have headed back to Mississippi, but he sure wasn't going to try to find her in the back woods.

The most likely road out of town was Airline Highway, U.S. 61. Thanks to Huey Long, the four-lane, divided highway ran straight north, 80 miles from New Orleans to Baton Rouge.

Huey was devoted to the LSU Tigers and he needed a direct route from his headquarters in New Orleans to the university stadium in Baton Rouge. As the saying went, the state could go to hell, but Huey never missed an LSU home game.

In an effort to cover all the bases, Tony made a call to some of his father's men at Moisant Airport. Since they worked in the cargo area, they didn't know anything about passengers, but at least Tony could say he tried.

Although Tony wasn't worried about the New Orleans Police Department, his father was. The newly elected mayor, deLesseps "Chep" Morrison was putting the fear of God—or at least the law—into everyone from the landladies in the Quarter to the bosses in the underworld. Morrison had pledged to reform the city. No news there. Every new mayor promised to clean up New Orleans once and for all. Historically it didn't have much effect, but it did mean everybody had to lie low until the do-good fever ran its course.

CHAPTER SEVEN
(Waterproof, 1946)

Ruby was asleep when Bitsy came home the first night and she pretended to be asleep when she heard her getting ready the next morning. An unusual feature of Bitsy's old house was that it had two bathrooms. One was at the back of the house and the other adjoined Bitsy's bedroom up front.

Bitsy had a morning routine. She was careful not to let herself go like some women her age. She took a steaming hot bath both winter and summer. Then she went into the kitchen and bathed her face in ice water. After that, she got dressed and put on her makeup: foundation, powder, rouge, mascara, eye shadow, and bright red lipstick. She checked to make sure her nails were perfect and added a bit of perfume.

She had a standing appointment at the beauty shop to have her roots touched up every other week. For a final touch, she bought her uniforms half a size too small which gave her a perfect excuse for leaving the top buttons open. A little cleavage was always good for business.

When Ruby was sure Bitsy had left for work, she got up. She took a bath in the big claw-foot tub, washed her hair, and ate some breakfast. Apparently the older woman thought she was running away from her husband and Ruby decided to go with that story for the moment. As she wandered around the old house, she thought about Basin Street. The girls at Minnie's wouldn't be up for hours.

Bitsy's house must have been a real showplace in its day. A wide porch ran across the front and down one side. Like many old Southern houses, it had a central hall with large, airy rooms right and left. To the left of the front door was a parlor, obviously not used very often. The smaller room next to it with more comfortable furniture and a floor model radio was obviously where Bitsy spent most of her free time.

To the right of the central hall was a dining room, with a large table, eight chairs, and a heavy sideboard. It adjoined the kitchen. A wide screen porch dominated the back of the house and looked out on a shady back yard with several old live oak trees draped in moss. Almost without thinking about it, Ruby got a broom and started sweeping.

Meanwhile, Bitsy was busy serving breakfast to her regulars. She had decided to give Ruby her space and see how things played out. Bitsy was a great believer in giving folks their space.

Clearly Ruby had made an impression on the sheriff and that might have some interesting possibilities. Be good for him to find somebody and Bitsy was more than willing to help the process along. Her mind was busy all day working out angles. The more she thought about things, the more excited she got. She decided to let Terry close up and she headed home early.

When she walked in the front door, she knew something had changed. She wandered through the house looking for Ruby. "Something's different," she said.

"I cleaned up a little."

Bitsy walked back through the house. Sure enough the floors were mopped, the furniture dusted, clothes hung up, everything was in order. "Well, damn, the house looks nice and all this time I thought the only thing holding this old place together was the dirt. Brought you some supper," she said and handed Ruby a heavy plate. "Meatloaf and mashed potatoes."

Bitsy sat down and lit a cigarette while Ruby ate. "You have any idea how long you might be staying?" Before Ruby answered, Bitsy continued. "Reason I'm asking is it's coming up on the holidays and I wouldn't mind having some company around here."

"It's nice of you to offer, but I can't just stay here without paying. I'd need a job."

"Yeah, I got an idea about that too, if you're interested. Wait a minute, I got something I wanna show you." When she came back, Bitsy handed Ruby a faded sign. "This thing's been in the window over at the café so long it's most nearly faded out, but what it says is that the town council is looking for somebody to take care of our library. Don't many people use it, but Ole Miz Murphy gave it to the town, building, books, furniture, doodads, and all, so they can't just shut it down.

"Nobody's applied for the job so they're still looking, far as I know. You reckon you can handle that? I don't know what it pays, but I can tell you the rent here'll be real cheap. What'chu think? Wait! Before you make up your mind, let's walk down there and you can take a look at the place."

Ruby finished supper and she and Bitsy started washing dishes. "You know I had a husband once," Bitsy said. "Actually I've had a bunch of husbands, three to be exact. I loved the first one, but he died. TB. Married the second one on the rebound. The war got him. I have no idea why I married the last one. He was a handsome devil, but that was the problem. He was too handsome for his own good. I got tired of him cheating on me with every female on two legs. I gave him a choice. Either shape up or ship out. So he left. That ticked me off for a couple of days, but I got over it."

If Bitsy was hoping that priming the pump would get Ruby talking, she was disappointed. Ruby just listened politely as she put the dishes away. The washing up done, they walked over to the library.

It was the first time Ruby had really looked at the town. It was a pretty typical small town. There was a grocery store across the street from the bus station, then houses and businesses were all mixed up together down the main street, which ran perpendicular to Highway 61. There was a drugstore, a large general store, a picture show, and the sheriff's office and jail. Next to the post office were several large houses with front yards filled with azaleas and live oak trees hanging heavy with moss. Bitsy pointed out the house of the new lawyer in town and the one where the mayor lived.

The next building was the small Baptist church and two doors down was a beautiful old Episcopal church surrounded by a graveyard enclosed by an ornate wrought-iron fence. "Church used to have a steeple, but the Yankees shot it off during the War Between the States. It was the only thing they could see from their gun boats down on the river.

"There was some talk about replacing it, but then the congregation realized that the tourists thought the story was romantic, so they left it the way it was and put up a plaque."

Ruby listened as Bitsy rambled on. "We got more churches than we got people to fill 'em. There's the two you just saw and we got a Methodist church and a Presbyterian church and a Catholic church. Hardly enough sinners to go 'round, so they fight over 'em or bring 'em in from around the parish."

"Do you go to church?" Ruby asked.

"Honey, *everybody* goes to church."

"OK, where do you go?"

"I was raised a Baptist, but when my parents passed, I decided to be a Presbyterian. Episcopalians are too formal,

Baptists have too many rules, Methodists are too boring and you have to be born into it to be a Catholic.

"In this town, being a Presbyterian is your best bet because we don't have a full-time preacher so you only have to go to church two times a month." She paused a moment, "You ever heard of foot-washin' Baptists? Well, I guess I'm what you'd call a *Waterproof Presbyterian*." Bitsy laughed until she cried. She always enjoyed her jokes more than anybody. "That was a good one!"

"What about the sheriff? Is he Presbyterian too?"

"No, Methodist, I think. It's different for men. They're not expected to attend on a regular basis and when they do show up, they mostly just stand out under the trees and talk. It's a trade-off for being available to help out when there's real work to be done around the church."

Bitsy went on to explain that the only time the churches get along was around Thanksgiving when they worked together to collect and deliver baskets to the needy. "I always go to my sister's for Thanksgiving and you're invited, of course."

Ruby hadn't thought about the holidays. Since her brothers left, it had just been she and her father, but they'd made an effort and she would miss being with him. However, from what little she knew about Bitsy's nieces and nephews, she wasn't sure she wanted to be invited. Ruby realized Bitsy was still talking.

"Funny what kinds of things some people do about holidays. Sheriff Houston told me that Miss Laura works with the church ladies to deliver baskets, then she serves her family bologna sandwiches on Wonder Bread. When he asked her about it, she said she cooked 364 days a year, but she wasn't cooking on Thanksgiving."

It was getting dark, the street lights had just come on, but there was no one else on the street. Ruby thought about the Quarter and how alive and busy it always was. Minnie and the girls would just be getting ready to open for business. Ruby felt bad about not saying goodbye, but she knew in the long run it was the safest thing to do.

"There it is," Bitsy said and she pointed to a small brick building wedged between two houses. It looked as if someone had dropped it there by mistake. The building was long and narrow and sat with its short side to the street. "Come on, let's take a look inside."

"Won't it be locked?"

"Nah, nobody ever locks nothing around here." Again Ruby thought about Basin Street and smiled at the contrast between the two places, like two completely different worlds.

The library had probably been a private cottage at one time, but the two front windows had been bricked in. The front room looked as if several walls had been removed to make it look more like a public building. To the left was a high counter, which served as a circulation desk. On top of the counter was a two-foot bronze statue of the Virgin Mary. Ruby frowned and Bitsy was quick to see her expression. "Ole Miz Murphy was a Catholic, it came with the building."

On the right-hand wall was a small fireplace surrounded by book shelves. In the front corner, was a reading lamp leaning over the shoulder of an easy chair. A couch and a coffee table covered with magazines faced the fireplace. Behind the front area was a workroom with a sink, an old icebox, and a hot plate.

Through the work room were several other rooms filled with rows and rows of tall wooden shelves sagging under the weight of ancient, dust-covered books. The heart pine floor was worn, but it was clean. The room smelled slightly like lemons. It seems Miz Murphy also left money for monthly maintenance and upkeep.

Grace Hawthorne

"Well now, what'cha think? I know you wouldn't have much traffic through here, but if you don't mind being by yourself ..."

Ruby waited, expecting Bitsy to keep talking, but apparently she expected an answer on the spot. "I don't know, I ..." At that moment Ruby's eyes fell on a row of books behind the front counter. The *World Book Encyclopedia*! There it was waiting for her. Her first instinct was to say yes immediately, but then she remembered the Choctaw way and decided to wait until the next day and pray for sunshine.

"Oh yeah, nothing permanent. That's fine. Listen, there's a town hall meeting tonight. You wanna come with me and meet the town council?"

"No!" Ruby said with more emphasis than she had intended.

"OK. No problem. I'll find out how much the job pays and tell 'em I've got somebody living at my house who wants the job. I'm sure they'll go along with that. I mean it's not like they're gonna look a gift horse in the mouth. The meeting's at the Parish Hall next to the Episcopal church. We'll walk right by there. But don't worry, you don't have to come in. You can just walk on back to the house. You're not afraid to be on the street by yourself, are you?"

Ruby nearly laughed out loud. "I'll be fine. Thanks for your help."

The women parted company at the next corner and Bitsy walked into the meeting with a broad grin on her face. She greeted friends and neighbors, most of whom were also her customers. She helped herself to punch and cookies, all the time searching the crowd until she found the person she was looking for. Then she made a beeline across the room and "accidentally" ran into the sheriff.

"Why, Sheriff, how are you tonight? Come on, let's get a seat up front so we don't miss anything. Never know when somebody might say something worth listenin' to." They sat down and when the moderator called for new business, Bitsy raised her hand and presented her candidate for librarian.

There were some questions, all of which Bitsy answered easily and having ascertained that the salary was sufficient to Ruby's needs, she made a formal motion. She saw no reason to consult Ruby. So the motion was seconded and carried with no objections. That taken care of, there was no further business and the meeting adjourned. Bitsy sat back in her chair, very pleased with herself. She turned to the sheriff and smiled sweetly.

He looked stunned. "She's staying with you?"

"She is."

"What do you know about this woman?"

"Obviously more than you, but then some of us work faster than others."

"This from the woman who told me not to ask her any questions." Nate stood up slowly shaking his head and muttering to himself. "I will never understand women, I will simply never understand them."

Bitsy was pretty sure she didn't understand what was going on with Ruby either. She was beginning to suspect there was more to the story than a bad marriage. Maybe she should have left well enough alone, but then where was the fun in that?

CHAPTER EIGHT
(Waterproof)

In much the same way she had done with Minnie on Basin Street, Ruby settled into a routine with Bitsy in Waterproof. Because of Bitsy's long hours at the Firehouse, Ruby took over the household chores, and Bitsy brought home food from the café.

The day after their visit to the library dawned bright and sunny and Ruby told Bitsy she had decided to take the job as the new librarian. Good thing, since as far as the town council was concerned, it was already official. Ruby happily went to work each day, safely hidden away in the library and reunited with her old friend, the encyclopedia.

Ruby hadn't had a chance to sit down and read for a long time and she realized how much she had missed that simple pleasure. Although she didn't expect anyone to actually come by the library, she thought she ought to be familiar with what was available—other than her beloved encyclopedia—just in case someone asked.

Straightening up the workroom, she found a hot plate, a kettle, a stoneware teapot, and two heavy white china cups like the ones Bitsy used at the café. There were also two proper tea cups with saucers in the cabinet. More investigation turned up several tins of tea with exotic names like Assam and Darjeeling.

She had no idea how long the tea had been there, so she checked her *World Book Encyclopedia* which said that tea stored in a sealed tin box could last up to two years. That was good enough for Ruby.

After some experimentation, she discovered the teas were better when she mixed them together. A warm, safe place to hide, her cherished encyclopedia to read, and tea to drink, she couldn't believe her good luck.

Monday of the next week Ruby found Sunday papers from Baton Rouge and New Orleans on the steps of the library. Eagerly she looked through the *Times-Picayune* to see if there was any mention of a murder in the French Quarter. Nothing. However, she did find a long story about deLesseps Morrison's pledge to clean up prostitution. Ruby smiled. Minnie must be loving that. She wondered if that meant Minnie's payoff envelopes would have to get fatter.

In the Arts section of the *State Times,* she found a long list of book reviews. However, when she checked the shelves, she didn't find a single one of the best sellers. A quick review of the books on the shelves confirmed there were no current books at all. The bindings were all old and faded. That night when Ruby got home, she mentioned the fact to Bitsy.

"I reckon nobody's ordered any. There's probably a budget or something for the library. I'll check into it."

Late one afternoon toward the end of the week, Nate got a call from the mayor informing him that he was now heading up the budget committee for the library. He was sure Bitsy was behind the call, so he decided to put on his coat, walk over to the Firehouse, and confront her.

"What have you got against the library?" she asked innocently. "Seems like you might want to drop by and welcome Ruby to town or something. Sitting there all by herself all day, she's probably lonely. Now that you're the official head of the budget committee, you've got an official excuse to see her. Why don't you just give her a call and set up a time to go by?"

Having planted the idea, Bitsy walked off to handle other customers. Nate grumbled his way through a piece of apple pie and a cup of coffee and then left the café without a further word to Bitsy.

She smiled. "*Gotcha!*"

Nate *had* been looking for an excuse to talk to Ruby, but he preferred doing things at his own pace, not getting pushed into something before he was ready. Back at the office he hung up his hat and coat, laid down his cane, and bowed to the inevitable. "Luther, find me the number for the library, would you please?" Then, number in hand, he sat down and dialed.

"Hello?"

"This is Sheriff Houston, we need to talk. How about 3:00 Friday afternoon?"

"Is something wrong?"

"No, just wanna talk."

Ruby agreed to the time and Nate hung up the phone.

Damn it. Why did I do that? I sounded like I was gonna arrest her or something. I should have asked how she was settling in. I should have been friendlier. Ah crap!

On top of that, Nate realized his knee hurt, he was out of liniment at the office, he'd smoked his last cigarette, and he had a ton of paperwork on his desk that needed to be done. The walls were closing in. "Luther, I'm going home early."

When he got there, he went straight to the kitchen. Carrie was doing her homework and Miss Laura was busy putting together a casserole for supper. Nate took a spare bottle of liniment from under the sink and started rubbing it into his knee.

"I'm glad you're home a little early," Miss Laura said, "because Lucy Castle called me today. It seems she's so grateful to you for giving Luther a job that she's invited us all to come to their house for Christmas dinner. Now you and I both know there's no way they can afford a big dinner. I don't want to hurt her feelings, but I don't see how this can work."

"Why not invite them over here instead?" Nate suggested.

"No, that's us feeding them, that'll hurt her pride. Some way we have to help without it seeming like we're helping."

A long discussion followed. No workable solution presented itself until Carrie came up with a plan. Her idea was to get everybody involved and to divide up the cooking. First they'd have to see if Bitsy would be willing to have the dinner at the café, which was always closed on Christmas anyway.

The sheriff's family would provide the turkey. They'd ask Lucy to be in charge of the vegetables, which she could probably get out of her garden and Bitsy would be responsible for the desserts. There was plenty of room at the café and Lucy would share an equal part in the meal.

Nate quickly endorsed the idea, knowing that if Bitsy were involved, the chances were very good Ruby would be involved too. In fact, maybe he could salvage his blunder on the phone by presenting this idea to Ruby when he met her at the library.

Miss Laura contacted Bitsy, who was more than happy to be part of the festivities. She loved her sister, but frankly spending time with her brother-in-law and their horde of screaming kids was not her idea of the perfect Christmas.

Miss Laura called Lucy and very diplomatically explained that she had already made some plans with Bitsy, but that if Lucy were willing to help them out, they could combine their plans and make it easier for everyone. She assured Lucy that this way no one would have to cook all day or eat Christmas dinner alone.

For her part, Carrie stayed after school one day and told Miss Nell about their plans. Her idea was to ask Miss Nell to help collect toys, but instead she volunteered to buy toys for all the Castle kids. "All my nieces and nephews are grown up now and I miss having an excuse to buy Christmas presents," Miss Nell said. Carrie didn't know where her teacher usually ate Christmas dinner, but Miss Nell happily accepted when Carrie invited her to join them at the café.

That had turned out so well, Carrie decided to ask Mr. Blacky to donate a scooter or a wagon or something from the hardware store. Blacky wasn't too keen on donating new toys, but he said he'd spread the word, and be a drop-off point for anyone who had old toys to donate. Bud Garvey happened to be hanging around and said he'd fix them up and paint them so they'd be good as new. Then he volunteered to take them by the café Christmas Eve. Carrie invited both men to come to dinner, but they each had other places to be.

Friday afternoon Nate was in the office when he realized it was time for him to meet Ruby at the library. "Luther, where are the car keys?"

"In the car, I guess. Where're you off to in such a hurry?"

"Library." He headed for the door then turned around. "No, better walk, no place to park over there." Once more he headed for the door, then turned around and put the cane across his desk.

It's only a five minute walk; I don't need to show up looking like a cripple. Just calm down, don't go bustin' in like you're breakin' up a fight. Be friendly. Talk about the library committee. Talk about Christmas dinner. No pressure. Just be natural. Who am I kidding? I don't know how to do this anymore. Damn that Bitsy.

Ruby looked at her watch. Three o'clock. He was late. Maybe he wasn't coming. That would be a …well, she wasn't sure how she felt about that.

Calm down. I'm not guilty of anything. There's nothing to be afraid of.

Nate walked up the steps to the library and opened the door. It was bright and warm inside. Ruby was sitting in front of the fire reading. Again he got the image of water flowing around a stone.

"Hello, Sheriff. Come in," she gestured to the couch as she got up. "I was just making a pot of tea, would you like some?"

Nate started to say no, but thought better of it. One cup of tea wasn't going to kill him. He sat and she returned with a pot and two heavy china cups. She couldn't picture Nate drinking tea from a dainty cup balanced on a small saucer. As she poured the tea, she asked, "May I?" and added some sugar. "I think you'll like it better that way." Then she sat, folded her hands in her lap, and watched him.

Nate took a sip; it was surprisingly strong and slightly sweet. "It's good," he said, trying not to sound too surprised. Nate had no practice making small talk with strange women. He talked easily enough with the women in Waterproof, but he'd known them all his life. He had gone to school with them, played ball with their brothers, knew their husbands and children. That kind of talk came easy.

"I guess now that I'm on the library budget committee, we'll be seeing each other more often." Ruby looked puzzled. "You remember, you asked Bitsy about buying new books ... It's the library committee that handles the budget for books and the mayor assigned me to the ..." Nate's voice trailed off. "Bitsy didn't tell you about any of this, did she?" Ruby shook her head. "I see."

You better think of something quick, Houston. You're dying here.

He tried a different approach. "Well, did she happen to mention plans for Christmas dinner?"

"Yes."

Nate breathed a sigh of relief. That broke the ice. They talked about plans for dinner. "This will give me an opportunity to introduce you to my family, Miss Laura, my mother-in-law, and Carrie, my daughter."

The look on Ruby's face told Nate this demanded further explanation. Apparently Bitsy hadn't explained his situation to Ruby. "My wife died while I was overseas, pneumonia. Miss Laura moved in and she lives with us now."

"I see."

To keep the conversation going, Nate explained how he had come to hire Luther and the situation with the boy's family. He told her about Bud Garvey and the bloodhounds and Luther up the tree. Finally he stopped. "I'm talking too much."

"No," Ruby said.

"What about your family?" he asked.

"There isn't anyone."

Nate wasn't quite sure how he was supposed to respond to that so he concentrated on his tea. "It's nice here. Quiet." Ruby sat still and watched him. Normally that kind of attention made him nervous, but somehow with her, it was all right.

Ruby realized Nate was like some of the guests at Minnie's. He just wanted someone to pay attention, someone to talk to. She relaxed a little. As long as she kept him talking, she didn't have to divulge anything about herself.

Nate drained his cup and held it out for a refill. "Bitsy told me not to act like a sheriff and ask you a lot of questions, but how else am I going to get to know you?"

"There's not much to tell." Counting on the fact that the sheriff was observant, Ruby touched the empty spot on her ring finger, making sure he saw the motion. "I needed a change. Nothing I want to talk about. What about you, did you grow up here?"

"I'm afraid so. My folks owned a small piece of property outside of town. After they passed on, I sold it. Used the money to buy the old Wilcox house here in town and made some improvements. That's where we live now."

He fell silent. With Luther in the office and two women at home, Nate didn't hear a lot of silence. He stretched his legs out and sipped his tea.

It was getting late in the afternoon and Ruby asked if perhaps he were hungry. "I have some sandwiches in the back sent over by…." she smiled at him, "by Bitsy, of course. She seems to have thought of everything."

"No surprise there," Nate said. Together they unpacked Bitsy's basket and Ruby made another pot of tea. Nate told her about Bud Garvey volunteering to fix up the used toys. "Just about the time I think I have a handle on that guy, he does something completely out of character."

"Tell him if he wants to drop the toys by here, I'll wrap them and store them until he picks them up Christmas Eve."

They talked for a while longer, then Nate left. He walked all the way home before he realized his car and his cane were at the office.

In the next weeks, Thanksgiving came and went, then it was Christmas. Bitsy closed the café on Christmas Eve and Nate dropped Miss Laura and the turkey off very early Christmas morning. Bitsy and Ruby were already there, so Nate made the necessary introductions.

Bud Garvey was the next to arrive. He had a cup of coffee and unloaded all the toys he had picked up from the library. There was something special for Luther, which Bud hid in the pantry. His next stop was to pick up the Castle family.

Mid-morning, Nate brought Carrie over and introduced her to Ruby. Then he went to pick up Miss Nell. Luther rolled up on his old bike. The turkey was roasting in one oven and Bitsy had pies going in another. Bud pulled into the parking lot and the Castle family poured out of the pickup. Each child carefully carried a large bowl of homegrown vegetables. To everyone's surprise, Archie Castle came too.

Lucy proudly announced, "Luther's been buyin' Archie's medicine and he's got so much better, the plant foreman said he could come back to work after the first of the year. Ain't that grand?"

Archie helped Ruby set up tables and chairs. Then she decorated the tables with Mason jars of camellias from Bitsy's front yard. Bitsy was glad to share her flowers, but she insisted they were japonicas, not camellias. It was beside the point since they were the only flowers blooming that time of year.

It was after 3:00 before they sat down to eat. After dinner, Miss Nell read *Twas The Night Before Christmas*, and Nate passed out the presents. Instead of exchanging gifts, the adults had decided to concentrate on the kids. Carrie got a set of rhinestone earrings and a necklace she'd wanted forever. The Castle children got not just one toy each, but lots of packages.

Luther couldn't decide if he'd been counted as an adult, or if he had been overlooked. Then Nate came out of the pantry wheeling a bicycle. Bud had done a great job and it looked brand new. "Merry Christmas, Luther."

Luther was overjoyed. He threatened to ride the bike around the café but Bitsy shooed him out the door. After several laps around the parking lot, he came back in beaming. "You guys can have my old bike," he said to his little brothers. They were as pleased to get the old one as Luther was with his new one.

At the end of the day, Nate made two trips to take the Castle family home with more toys than the kids had ever seen and enough leftovers to eat for a week. It had been a great Christmas all around.

CHAPTER NINE
(Waterproof, 1947)

No sooner had they gotten through Christmas and New Year's than it was February 1, Carrie's 13th birthday. For a special treat, Nate and Miss Laura took her to Baton Rouge for dinner and a movie. Carrie chose the Piccadilly Cafeteria and then they walked down the street to the Paramount to see Danny Kaye and Virginia Mayo in "The Secret Life of Walter Mitty." When they got home, Carrie proclaimed it her best birthday ever. However, if Nate thought he could rest on his laurels, he was sadly mistaken.

The next morning at breakfast, Miss Laura reminded him, "You realize the Valentine's Dance is just two weeks away and this is Carrie's year to cross over the rope. That's a very big deal for her." The tone of Miss Laura's voice told Nate trouble was brewing.

The only place in Waterproof large enough to host a dance was the American Legion Hall and it was actually too big. So the dance committee invited all the kids in town and then divided the hall with a rope. Little kids on one side, teenagers, low lights, a mirror ball, and the jukebox on the other. You had to be a teenager to cross over the rope.

Miss Laura continued, "The problem is Carrie's been talking about Teddy Bradshaw since school started this year. She's convinced he's going to ask her to the dance because last summer he said something about being there when she crossed over the rope. She took him seriously, but I think it was just chatter. He hasn't called her or anything since then. I think she's headed for a big disappointment."

"Well, if he doesn't call, I could always send Luther over to shoot him."

"Nate Houston, don't you dare tell Luther Castle to shoot somebody unless you want to find them dead on your doorstep! Luther tends to take everything literally."

"OK, I'll keep that in mind."

Nate thought that Miss Laura was probably blowing the situation with Carrie way out of proportion. However listening to his daughter at supper, he realized Miss Laura was right.

"Dad, I can't wait for you to see the dress Nana and I are making for the dance. It's gonna be soooooo beautiful. It's red taffeta and it's kinda off-the-shoulder and it fits tight at the waist and has this real full skirt, but I don't want you to see it until it's all finished."

She took a bite and rushed on, "I wonder if Teddy will bring me a corsage, he might not be able to afford one, but I don't care. Did I tell you about my shoes? Black patent *heels.*" Another bite. "I wonder if I should wear my hair in a pony tail or leave it down? Down, I think. Definitely down."

Nate looked across the table at his daughter. Her face was flushed, her eyes shining, and the eagerness in her voice broke his heart. What if that knucklehead didn't call?

The week before the dance Carrie waited by the phone every night willing it to ring. She came home from school every day with a new excuse for why Teddy hadn't asked her to the dance yet. Wednesday night—the last night a girl with any pride would accept a date for the weekend—came and went without a call. "He's got plenty of time to ask me in person, I mean, the dance isn't until Saturday. I'll probably see him somewhere at school tomorrow."

When Carrie got home from school Friday, Miss Laura knew she hadn't seen Teddy. No one talked much during supper. Carrie pushed food around her plate then asked to be excused, went to her room, and closed the door.

Nate didn't see her the next morning, but when he got home in the afternoon, Carrie was curled up on the couch. Her eyes were red and puffy and he sat down and put his arms around her. "Listen, Sugarfoot, just because that stupid boy didn't call you doesn't mean you can't go to the dance. All your friends will be there."

Wrong thing to say. "That's just it, Dad," Carrie sobbed. "Everybody'll be there tonight but me and I can't go."

Miss Laura glanced up from the *Saturday Evening Post* she was reading. "Carrie's right." Nate opened his mouth to protest, but she silenced him.

"You're right, Sweetie, you probably shouldn't go. On the other hand, it's a shame to let the dress go to waste. Why don't you just try it on and let Dad get the Kodak and take some pictures? Then we'll drive over to Jackson and go to a movie. How's that?" No response. "Go on now, take a quick bath, and wash your hair. When you're done, come in the bedroom."

Miss Laura looked at her granddaughter. She had her mother's red hair and blue eyes, but she was going to be tall like her father. Carrie was already 5'4". According to her, that meant she was the tallest girl in her class.

Fresh from her bath, Carrie shuffled into the bedroom where everything was laid out: a pink satin garter belt, a box with a pair of sheer silk stockings, a fluffy petticoat, and high heels. It was too much to resist.

When Carrie was dressed, Miss Laura handed her the rhinestone earrings and necklace she'd gotten for Christmas.

"Let's put your hair up so these will show a little better and maybe some perfume." She handed Carrie her prized bottle of Chanel Number 5. "A little behind your ears and at your wrists. No need to overdo it. Maybe a little lipstick too. Now turn around and take a look at yourself."

Carrie could hardly believe her eyes. "Nana, I'm pretty!" She ran her hands over the dress and twirled around once or twice. "I'm really pretty."

"Indeed you are. Too bad nobody but your dad and I will see you. Come on, let's go take some pictures."

When Carrie walked into the living room, Nate was stunned. He grabbed the Kodak and used up all 24 shots on the roll of film. By then Carrie was smiling from ear to ear. "Maybe," she said shyly, "I could go to the dance for just a little while."

Nate acted as her chauffeur and Carrie rode to the dance like a princess. When they arrived, he helped her out of the back seat and she leaned over and kissed him on the cheek before she disappeared in a swirl of red taffeta.

She hesitated a moment at the door, slid the shoulders on her dress down so that it looked more like a strapless dress, stuck out her chest, and walked into the dance on the grownup side of the hall.

It took Carrie's eyes a minute to adjust to the dim light inside. The mirror ball sent little prisms of light fluttering around the room like a thousand fireflies. Nat King Cole was singing "I love you for sentimental reasons..."

It's beautiful. I just know he's going to be here and he'll ask me to dance and everything will be perfect.

No one was dancing yet. The girls were lined up on one side of the hall, the boys on the other side. Finally, at the chaperones' insistence, they started to mingle and that was when she saw him.

Teddy was standing across the room and he smiled and waved. Carrie's heart stopped. She smiled and waved back. Then in slow motion she watched as he walked across the room and went right by her to put his arm around Dixie Cox, the most popular girl in school. Carrie was shocked. All she wanted to do was disappear.

Oh God, please don't let him see me now. How could I have been so stupid? He never liked me; he doesn't even know I exist. What am I going to do? I can't go home and I can't visit anybody 'cause all my friends are here.

Jimmy Westmore talked to her for a second, but she was too upset to stop and pay much attention. When she got to the front door, she slipped out into the darkness and started to walk. She had no idea how long she walked, but finally she realized she was getting cold. Bitsy's house was nearby so she knocked on the door. Ruby answered.

"Carrie. What are you doing out so late?"

"Hello, Miss Ruby. Is Miss Bitsy here?"

"Ahh no, she's gone to visit her sister. Come in, it's cold out there." A fire crackled in the living room fireplace. "I was just going to make tea. Can I offer you some?"

"I guess so."

"I'll be right back." Ruby stopped in the hall and phoned to let the sheriff know where Carrie was. The girl was sitting quietly when Ruby returned with a tray and a beautiful tea set. "I just got this in the mail. It's called Royal Albert Old Country Roses."

As miserable as she felt, Carrie was intrigued. A tea party. Just like in *Alice in Wonderland*. Miss Ruby picked up one of the dainty cups and poured the tea. "Would you like cream and sugar?"

"I guess so."

Ruby stirred the tea and handed it to Carrie, along with two exotic-looking cookies. No homemade oatmeal-raisin here.

"Did your mamma make tea like this?" Carrie asked

"Oh no, we were much too poor. My mother died when I was about your age ..." Ruby stopped abruptly. "I learned a lot just reading books. You should come by the library some time."

"Can I bring Luther with me? You know, everybody thinks he's dumb, but he's not. He just ... he just kinda sees things in a straight line. He doesn't read too well. You think you might be able to help him?" Carrie held out her cup for a refill.

"Maybe Luther has been trying to read the wrong books. I'll see if I can find something he might *like* to read. I'm sorry Bitsy isn't here," Ruby said gently. "I'm a good listener, if you want to talk to me. Did something happen at the dance?"

Carrie had just been waiting for an invitation and the whole story came pouring out between sobs and sniffs. "He said he'd be there when I crossed over the rope."

"Carrie, I don't understand what that means."

Carrie explained. "I know I shouldn't have gone, but Nana and I had worked so hard on this dress and I'd never had a garter belt or stockings before ... I thought I looked pretty 'til I saw that Dixie Cox," she spat out the name. "She had on a strapless dress and she looked all grownup and glamorous—and she's got boobs." Carrie dissolved into more tears.

Ruby lowered her eyes to hide her smile. "Do you want to stay here until the dance is over?" Carrie nodded. "Good. Come with me." Carrie followed Ruby into the dining room and sat down at the table. Ruby opened a well-worn box about the size of her two fists. "Dominoes, a double nine set. My dad used to play this with us. He said it was a good way to learn math."

"Do you have brothers and sisters?" Carrie asked.

"I have two brothers. They got drafted. I don't know where they are now." Ruby flipped the box over so the pieces came out facedown. She explained the rules and they started to play. Carrie had planned to spend the rest of the night feeling sorry for herself, but surprisingly she started to get interested in the game. It went slowly at first because she had to count all the dots, but then she started to recognize shapes. The one that looked like an "H" was a seven. A dot in each corner was a four. If all the spaces were full, that was a nine. Adding the dots on the ends of the tiles that had been played took longer, but Ruby gave her time to do it by herself.

At 11:00 Bitsy pulled into the driveway. Ruby met her at the door and quickly explained the situation. Bitsy walked into the dining room. "The dance was breaking up when I came by the American Legion Hall, so Miss Carrie Sue, I think we better get you home."

When they stopped in front of Carrie's house, she got out of the back seat and was almost to the front door before she remembered her manners. She turned around and came back to the car. Ruby rolled down her window. "Thank you for teaching me to play dominoes and for the tea party, Miss Ruby. I had a nice time."

Ruby smiled. "So did I."

As they were driving home, Ruby glanced over at Bitsy. "What are you smiling at?"

"Nothing, nothing at all."

Miss Laura and Nate were listening to the radio in the living room when Carrie came in. "Did you have a good time at the dance, Sugarfoot?" Nate asked.

Carrie plopped down in a chair. "I didn't go to the dance. Well, I did go, but I didn't stay. Teddy was there with that stupid Dixie Cox, in her strapless dress. You know what? I always thought he was so tall up there on his lifeguard stand, but he's short! I could never wear heels with him. Anyway, I left."

"I'm so sorry," Miss Laura said. "Didn't you dance at all?"

"No," she brightened slightly, "but Jimmy Westmore, he's in the grade ahead of me, he said I looked really pretty and asked me to meet him at the picture show on Saturday. He's tall and a lot nicer than that stuck-up, ole Teddy Bradshaw.

"Anyway I didn't want to hang around the dance, so I went over to see Miss Bitsy. Only she wasn't home. So I talked to Miss Ruby and she taught me how to play dominoes and we had a tea party with a real china tea set." Carrie babbled on about her evening until she finally ran out of steam. "I'm going to bed. 'Night."

Miss Laura looked at Nate. "So, it sounds like Carrie and Ruby got along pretty well. That's nice, don't you think?"

Nate sensed that was a loaded question. "I'm going to bed too." As he walked upstairs, he had a vague feeling Miss Laura attached some special significance to the tea party, but he wasn't sure what.

It's a secret conspiracy, I know it. Some kind of confounded female conspiracy.

CHAPTER TEN
(Waterproof)

They had all lived through "the dance fiasco" with no more than minor injuries. So without a crisis looming on the horizon, Nate decided to leave home early one morning and drive down to the levee before going to the office. Six o'clock was the best time to watch the mist burn away and imagine what the town must have been like in the old days.

Cotton wagons would have been lined up for a mile waiting to unload their cargo onto the riverboats. Store keepers would be opening up, sweeping off the board walks in front of their stores, hotels employees dusting off furniture, putting out flowers waiting for the tourists who would come from the river. Maybe there would even be a showboat docking.

It was all gone now, not a trace left behind. The river had seen to that long ago. Everything was different now. The only thing that was the same was the Mississippi itself. Like the song said, it just kept rolling along. Nate breathed a sigh, started the car, and headed for work.

The town was relatively peaceful for a month or two, and then one blustery March morning Nate arrived at the office to find Luther making coffee and Bud Garvey pacing up and down, anxious to report that his pickup, with the dogs in the back, had been stolen.

Since, in Bud's mind, he was a part of Waterproof law enforcement, he volunteered to ride along to search for the truck. Nate agreed because it was easier than arguing about it, but he insisted on having his coffee first.

A short way out of town headed north, Bud spotted the pickup nose down in a ditch. The two men got out to investigate and as soon as the dogs heard Bud's voice, they started to howl. There were beer bottles all over the floor of the cab and a boy slumped over in the passenger seat. He was apparently sleeping it off completely undisturbed by the noise or the cold wind blowing through the open windows.

Bud calmed the dogs down. "Look at them dogs, Sheriff. If we hadn't found 'em they coulda starved to death, sure enough. That's kidnappin', ain't it? And my truck, that's gotta be grand theft auto and that's a felony. You be careful now. I'll keep my eye on the perpetrator and if he tries anything, I'll jump him."

The sleeping teenager looked perfectly harmless to Nate. "You've been listening to too many cop shows on the radio, Bud. Let's just wake him up and see what he has to say for himself."

The boy was Arlan Walker, younger brother of Possum, of magneto-pissing fame. The Walkers were a large family who lived on the edge of town. Arlan was obviously a little worse for wear, but otherwise unhurt.

On one binge or another, Bud had driven his truck into almost every stationary object in Waterproof, so it was difficult to determine if there was any new damage. "Tell you what, Bud, I'll put Arlan in a cell until he sobers up. How's that."

"That's good, Sheriff. Lock his sorry ass up. Kidnappin' dogs, it just ain't right."

Nate woke Arlan up and put him in the front seat of the patrol car. Then he told Bud to get in the pickup and see if it would start. The engine seemed to be fine so Bud backed the truck onto the highway and headed home to take care of the dogs.

On the way to his office, the sheriff tried to find out what happened. It was clear someone else had been driving but Arlan wouldn't elaborate.

"You want me to call your mamma and tell her where you are?" Nate asked.

"We don't have a phone, but if it's not too much trouble, can you run by the house so I can tell her. I don't want her worrying about me."

Nate left Arlan in the car and went in to talk to his mother. When he came out he saw Possum walking away from the car. The boy turned around and shook his finger at his brother, "You remember what I told you, ya hear!"

"What was that all about?"

"Nothin', Sheriff."

When they got to the office, Nate explained the situation and Luther showed Arlan into the cell. It was clear the boys knew each other. Arlan was on the football team and everybody liked him. No wonder, he was handsome, smart, and always willing to help out a friend.

"Arlan, I gotta lock you up, soon as I get the keys. You just stay put 'til I do." Luther turned to Nate, "How long are we gonna keep him, Sheriff?"

"I don't know. I was planning on holding him until Bud calmed down and then sending him home."

The cell was just a room with bars across one wall. It had been added to the back of the sheriff's office as an afterthought. It had one window, a cot, a toilet, and a sink.

"Sheriff, if I'm gonna be in here a couple of days, can Luther go out to the house and pick up my books and maybe get my assignments from school?"

Luther left to run the errands while Nate searched the office for the key to the cell door. Then he remembered how Luther had started filing everything. He opened the top file drawer and checked under the K's. No luck.

On a hunch, he checked the drawers in his desk. He didn't find the key, but he did find his Purple Heart. In an instant, he was back in the war, lying in an evacuation hospital, his mind addled with drugs, watching some faceless general pin the medal to his pillow. He heard a voice and realized Arlan was trying to get his attention. Carefully he slipped the medal into his pocket.

"Try the O's," Arlan volunteered.

Sure enough that's where Nate finally found an envelope containing the key. He looked at Arlan.

"O for open. That's what you needed to do, so that's where you'd find the key. It's just the way Luther thinks. I was trying to teach him to play chess a while back and I got to where I could kinda follow the way his mind works."

By the time Luther got back with the books and the assignments, it was mid-afternoon. "Reckon we ought to feed the prisoner, Sheriff? It's kinda late and didn't none of us get any dinner. I could run over to the Firehouse and see if Bitsy's got anything left," Luther said hopefully. Nate waved him out the door.

Bitsy sent over cheeseburgers and Dr. Peppers for all three of them. They ate, then Luther cleaned up, took out the garbage, swept the floors, and headed for home. Not long after, Nate started to leave too. He'd found the key, but he hadn't actually seen fit to use it. "Arlan, I guess I oughta lock the cell door. You reckon you'll be OK locked up in here by yourself tonight?"

The boy was propped up in bed, doing his homework.

"Yes Sir, I think so. You know, I never had a room all to myself before. It's nice and warm and it's got a toilet, so I don't have to stand in line or pee off the porch. I got plenty to do since

Luther picked up my books. I'd feel better though if you'd leave the key where I can reach it, you know, just in case there's a fire or something?"

Nate left the key in the lock on the cell door. "Just turn out the lights in the office when you get ready to go to sleep." When he got home, he told Miss Laura and Carrie about the situation.

Miss Laura just shook her head. "Nate, don't ignore Bud Garvey. He's likely to be up to something. He generally is. I swear that man makes a habit of stirring up trouble. You haven't heard the last of this, you mark my words."

Later that night, Nate took the Purple Heart out of his pocket and looked at it for a long time. He hadn't gotten the medal for bravery, he had—like all the others—gotten it for being wounded. Almost without thinking he picked up a pencil and started writing. After a number of false starts, he had something he thought might be worth saving.

```
Hind Sight

Medals
Wrapped in plastic
Locked away in boxes
Forgotten.

Like bodies
Wrapped in plastic
Locked away in boxes
Almost forgotten.

Another war to end all wars.

We did our bit, but bit
By bit
By bit
```

```
By bit
Another generation will long for
Medals
Wrapped in plastic.
```

Getting the thoughts out of his head and down on paper calmed him. He sat for a moment longer, then undressed and went to bed. He slept well.

His first thought the next morning was Arlan. Nate was anxious to get to the office to make sure everything was all right. When he opened the door, he got a shock. All the file drawers were open and all the files were gone. He immediately headed to the back to see if Arlan was OK only to find the two boys sitting in the cell surrounded by stacks and stacks of files.

"Hey, Sheriff," Luther said. "Lookie here, Arlan's helpin' me straighten out the files. He says things ought to be filed under what they are, not what they do. Like wanted posters ought to go under the W's for *wanted* instead of under the C's for *crooks.* His system's kinda hard, but I'm gettin' the hang of it."

While the boys worked, Nate decided Miss Laura might be right, so he wrote an official memo saying he was holding Arlan Walker for ten days for stealing Bud Garvey's truck. If Bud came in, he hoped that would be enough to get rid of him.

A week later, Nate walked into the office a little late one morning and Arlan wasn't in his cell. "Luther, where is Arlan?"

"His brother, Possum, came in first thing this morning, paid his bail, and took him home."

Nate took a deep breath and then decided it was not worth the trouble to explain to Luther that a judge had to set bail. "Just for curiosity sake, how much was the bail?"

"Ten dollars and I got it right here. A five-dollar bill and five ones. I made Possum sign a paper so it's all legal." Luther proudly handed a roughly typed page to Nate.

"To Whom It May Concern, Possum Walker has paid $10 bail for his brother Arlan. This is an IOU for one brother to be delivered to Sheriff Houston whenever he needs him." It was signed by Possum.

"We couldn't just leave Arlan sitting there in the cell. Helpin' with the files was fine, but he needed to get outside sometime and I was runnin' out of things for him to do. He cut the grass, trimmed all the hedges, and painted the cell." Clearly Luther considered that a proper explanation.

"And you trust Possum to turn him in if we ever need him?"

"Oh yeah 'cause he'll want his money back." Luther seemed confident that the situation was under control, so Nate let it ride. The whole thing might blow over, and if not, he was sure Arlan wasn't going anywhere.

Starting with the gang of men hanging out at Blackburn's Hardware, Bud related the story of his stolen pickup and the mistreatment of Beauregard and Rutledge to anyone who would listen. Egged on by the response of his initial audience, Bud began to embellish the story and the more he told it, the more serious the crime became and the madder he got. Bud soon became a hot topic of conversation in Waterproof and he liked the attention. In fact, it was addictive. The more he got, the more he wanted.

Then he happened to see Arlan walking around town, fancy free. That did it. Bud convinced himself he was entitled to his day in court, so he drove over to talk to the District Attorney in Belle Chase and demanded justice.

"That kid stole my truck and kidnapped my dogs. Now the sheriff's let him go. Can't you make him re-arrest the kid? Stealin' a truck's grand theft, ain't that right? My dogs are part of my livelihood. Don't that count for something?"

When Bud left, the DA phoned Nate. "Garvey's on his high horse. He says the boy stole his truck. If it's true, Bud's right, it is grand theft. The last thing I want to do is make trouble for this kid if he's innocent, but you know Garvey. He's got a big mouth and he can stir up a lot of trouble if he puts his mind to it. You got any ideas about this, Nate?"

"You're right about Bud. He likes to blow things out of proportion. Arlan is from a poor family, but he's a bright kid. Might have a future ahead of him if his older brother doesn't screw him up. In this case, he just got caught doing something stupid. Far as I can tell, he wasn't the one driving. I'm not sure he even knows how to drive. Which brings us back to his older brother."

"What's Arlan got to say about that? He admit anything?"

"It's more like he didn't *deny* anything. Bud and I found him passed out in the cab of truck, so he was obviously there. Somebody'd been drinking, there were beer bottles all over the place. Thing is, I know he wasn't alone, but he's refusing to confirm that. I thought keeping the boy in jail a while would satisfy Bud. How'd you leave it with him?"

"I told him I'd have to talk to you before I decided whether there was a case here. But just between you and me, I don't think Bud's going to give up on this. He's told the story so often, he's convinced himself he's the injured party seeking justice. Do you know if there's some history of bad blood between the Garveys and the Walkers?"

"Not that I know of, but it wouldn't surprise me. Folks can have long memories when it comes to family. See if you can talk some sense into him and let me know what happens. It would be a real miscarriage of justice if that boy goes to jail." Nate hung up the phone.

Looks like Miss Laura was right. This could turn into a real mess.

Nate needed some time to think. It never failed, the more he worried, the worse his knee hurt. He reached for the bottle of liniment, rolled up his pants leg, and started massaging his knee. Although he didn't want to admit it, he was afraid. Not the kind of fear he felt in combat, but the cold fear that something bad was about to happen and he didn't know how to stop it.

It boiled down to two outcomes. As a kid, if Arlan were convicted, he could be sent to a juvenile detention facility for who knew how long. But if things really got out of hand and he was tried as an adult, Nate had to face a remote possibility that Arlan might end up in Angola.

The mere mention of the name was enough to scare grown men. Located in the Tunica Hills at the very end of Louisiana Highway 66, Angola was known as the bloodiest maximum-security prison in America. About 20 miles north of Waterproof, the 18,000 isolated acres held thousands of inmates who worked in the fields under the supervision of unpaid and untrained convict-guards on horseback armed with rifles and shotguns. If anyone tried to escape, the order was shoot to kill.

In the years before the war, Nate and Eunice had often visited Ezra Landry and his wife at their house on the prison grounds. In fact, Carrie had walked for the first time at their house. Carrie thought that was a great story. How many kids could say they took their first steps in Angola State Penitentiary? When Eunice got wind of what Carrie was telling everyone, she was appalled. She made it perfectly clear *no one* was ever to mention that incident outside the immediate family.

The living conditions for staff at Angola were strange to say the least. They were locked in like the inmates, but they lived a privileged existence in a separate compound with free rent and all the free food and servants they wanted. The Landrys had a white frame house on the edge of Camp B. Inmates cleaned their house, worked in their vegetable garden, tended Patsy's flowers, cooked their food, and even took care of their children when they were young.

Now that Patsy was gone and their children had moved away, Ezra lived there with Doc, the trustee who had been with him for decades. In all his visits, Nate could never reconcile the rows of flowers and the sound of children's laughter that were so out of place against the background of guard towers and barbed-wire fences.

The previous spring when Nate went to Angola, he found Ezra sitting on his front porch with Doc. "Good to see you, Nate, come on up here," Ezra said. "You want a cold drink?" Before he answered, Doc appeared with two Co'Colas. As always, he kept his head down, his eyes averted. Nate knew Doc's story and he understood.

When Doc was nineteen, he killed his father to keep him from beating his mother. He was sentenced to life without parole. He had tried to escape twice and the last time he was beaten so severely, he never spoke again to anyone except Ezra. Doc had been in Angola for fifty years. He would die there.

Nate and Ezra exchanged family news. "So Carrie's turning thirteen. Lord, how time flies," Ezra said. "You know we've got a couple of kids her age in here. It's a shame, but they're just thrown in with everybody else. Doesn't matter how young they are, if they run, there are only two choices, shoot them or bring them back, which means they'll be flogged or shut up in The Hole. I'd hate to be responsible for that ever happening to anybody."

Nate had never forgotten that conversation. Before the war, he thought Angola was the worst place in the world. That was before Buchenwald. The U.S. Third Army liberated Buchenwald on April 11, 1945. Nate was part of the 80th Infantry Division that took control of the camp the next morning. Men with barely enough skin to cover their bones and no clothes to cover their bodies surrounded the American soldiers as they tried to walk through the camp. Prisoners reached out with hands that looked like claws. Hundreds of men were too weak to stand.

Nate and his buddies were told the camp had run out of coal to fire the furnaces, so corpses were piled like cord wood behind the crematorium. The smell was overwhelming. Nate could still feel the wave of hate that rolled over him. The survivors, who were strong enough, did their best to stand tall and salute the Americans. They greeted the U.S. soldiers like angels sent from God.

In an effort to escape the awful stench, Nate and his buddy, Charlie, stumbled out the main gate. Just as they reached an open field, they heard a click. Nate would never forget that sound. Land mine. A Bouncing Betty. Soldiers feared them the most because they rose out of the ground and exploded about chest high. That one cut Charlie's body in half and blew deadly pieces of shrapnel in all directions.

The noise was deafening. It took Nate a moment to realize he was bleeding from a number of wounds on his left side. He managed to call for a medic and was aware of being loaded onto a stretcher before he passed out. He woke up in a hospital in England. For him, the war was over.

However, before he was shipped back to the States, he had a lot of time to think. A lot of time to try to come to grips with the sadistic brutality that some men—and women—were capable of inflicting on their fellow human beings. Nate made a promise to himself, no matter what the circumstances, he would never be involved in anything like that again. Yet, here he was.

Luther broke in on his thoughts when he came into the office carrying two hanging baskets filled with ferns. "These are from Miss Nell. She said her room was gettin' to look like a tropical jungle and she was pretty sure we didn't have any plants in here. Miss Nell says every room ought to have something livin' in it, something besides people." He stopped long enough to actually look at Nate.

"What's the matter, Sheriff? You look kinda green. I know what you need, a nice strong, hot cup of coffee." Luther fanned the air in front of his face, "You been using that horse liniment again. Smells kinda like Vicks. My mamma used to rub it on my chest when I had a cold. Lord, I hated that stuff."

Luther dumped the grounds in the garbage and started a new pot. When the coffee was ready, he carried a cup to Nate, and set it down on the edge of his desk. "You wanna talk about what's botherin' you? Miss Nell says when you got something on your mind, it always helps to talk to somebody about it." He waited expectantly.

Nate took a sip of coffee. "Bud's making trouble about Arlan being out of jail, so I guess we're gonna have to pick him up again. Things may get a little complicated, so just in case, can you find the name of that new lawyer, the young feller who just moved here a couple of months ago?"

"His name's Neil Hebert, he says it's a-bear, French. I'll look up his number for you."

When Nate got Neil on the phone, he explained Arlan's situation as best he could. "Can you act as the boy's public defender? I imagine we ought to have some funds around here somewhere for that kind of thing. Bud's demanding that I put him back in jail. Can you come by here and talk to him?"

Neil was just starting his practice and he was glad for the work. The case might be interesting and the boy sounded like he deserved a good defense. He made arrangements to visit Arlan after Nate picked him up.

Nate should have felt relieved, but the situation had stirred up too many bad memories. He felt a needle of ice growing in the middle of his chest.

CHAPTER ELEVEN
(Waterproof)

The trial of Arlan Walker was the biggest thing to happen in Waterproof in years. In the weeks leading up to the opening day, Neil Hebert made numerous visits to the jail to talk to his client. It should have been an easy defense. All he needed was for Arlan to tell him whose idea it had been to steal the truck and who was driving, but Arlan steadfastly refused to do so.

"I'm up against a brick wall, Sheriff. If he won't cooperate with me, I don't know how I can help him."

Arlan was the topic of conversation during supper at the Houstons every night. Finally one evening, Carrie said, "Why don't you talk to Luther? He knows Arlan real well, maybe he knows what's going on."

Nate didn't put much stock in that approach, but in truth he didn't know where else to turn. So the next morning, he called Luther outside where they could talk without Arlan overhearing. "Do you know what's going on with Arlan? Why won't he talk to Neil?"

"Don't let on to Arlan that I told you, but you know, pretty much everybody can figure out Possum was behind all this. He was probably drivin', but Arlan can't tell you that."

"Why in the world not? Doesn't he realize he could spend a lot of time in jail if he doesn't tell the truth?"

"That's just the point, Sheriff, *somebody's* gonna go to jail. The way Possum figures it, he's over eighteen and he's been in trouble before. So with Mr. Bud on a rampage, if *he* went on trial, they might send him up for a long time. Arlan's just a kid, so he'll probably get off light, you know, reform school or somethin' like that."

Nate was running out of patience. "It's too bad Possum is such a sorry SOB, but that's no reason for Arlan to take the blame."

"Yes it is. Arlan can't let Possum go to jail, 'cause he's the only one in the family workin' and bringing in any money. Their daddy's gone most of the time and when he *is* home, he's drunk. If Possum ain't around, them kids might starve. Ain't no way Arlan's gonna tell what really happened."

They walked back into the office. This was worse than Nate had imagined. He knew the weight of the family responsibility Arlan was carrying and he knew Luther was right. The boy was truly between a rock and a hard place and Nate didn't see any way out.

He walked over to Neil's office and related what Luther had told him about Arlan's situation. "Neil, I know how it is with these sharecroppers. They're dirt poor, surviving by the skin of their teeth working somebody else's land on the halves. Without cash coming in from some source, they won't make it. The parish welfare department will split the family up, put the kids in foster homes and without the kids there to help with the farming, the owner will throw the old folks off the land."

The longer they talked, the more the icy fear in Nate's chest spread. He wasn't sure there was anything Neil could do. Neil wasn't sure either. Without Arlan's testimony against Possum or Possum's confession, all Neil could possibly do was to try his best to convince the jury that Arlan was a good kid who deserved another chance. Neil also suggested that they pray for an understanding judge.

Luckily, Judge Albert Rivers was due to hear the case. He lived in Waterproof and knew almost everybody in West Feliciana Parish. Nate saw a glimmer of hope; things might work out after all. Without his noticing it, another source of hope had been arriving in the mail every day. Apparently every girl at the high school had sent a good-luck card to Arlan.

On the night before the trial, Neil called the sheriff. "Nate, I've got some bad news. Judge Rivers has been called out of town on a family emergency. Stub Swetman is taking his place."

Louisiana no longer hung convicted criminals, but Stub Swetman was still known as the hanging judge. He was eighty-five years old and had lost his right arm below the elbow in a hunting accident when he was a teenager. He'd been "Stub" so long no one remembered his given name.

He was definitely old school. Although he was retired, he was called in on an *ad hoc* basis from time to time. Prosecutors loved him, defense attorneys feared him, and criminals hated his guts.

On the day of the trial, the courtroom was packed. Although it was only May, the room was hot and the ceiling fans didn't help much. Neil Hebert had on a dark suit. Arlan was wearing a white shirt open at the neck because it was too tight to button and a brown suit that smelled of mothballs. The entire Walker family, minus the father, of course, was sitting in the front row. Nate, Miss Laura, and Carrie sat just behind the defense table.

In an unprecedented move, Bitsy closed the cafe and she and Ruby sat with the sheriff. Luther sat on the end of that row. Bud was strutting around shaking hands like a Southern politician on Election Day.

The DA got right down to business. He laid out the facts. The truck was stolen and yes, the dogs were in the back. The sheriff had found Arlan in the truck. He had been drinking and he didn't deny any of the facts. Clearly, Arlan Walker was guilty of being in the wrong place at the wrong time.

Neil admitted that Arlan had done something foolish, but he presented Arlan as a very bright boy who did well in school and helped out with the younger kids at home. He called a number of character witnesses, including the sheriff, the principal from Arlan's school, and Brother Reed, from the local Baptist church.

Then Judge Swetman decided to get involved. Clearly he was overstepping his authority, but when Neil tried to point that out, the judge overruled him and took over altogether. "I want to hear what that boy's got to say for himself. Come on up here, Son."

Arlan hesitated. He looked to Neil for direction and all the lawyer could do was whisper, "Just answer his questions and tell the truth." He tried to look encouraging but he felt helpless as he listened to Arlan being sworn in.

"What's your name?"

"Arlan Walker, Sir."

"You swear to tell the truth, the whole truth and nothing but the truth, so help you God?"

"Yes Sir."

"You go to school?"

"Yes Sir."

"What grade you in?"

"I'll be a senior next year."

"So you plan to graduate?"

"Yes Sir."

"All right, you understand you're under oath. So mind your P's and Q's. Had you been drinking on the night in question?"

Neil stood. "Objection."

"Overruled." The harshness of the judge's voice caught everyone's attention.

Arlan heard it too. He looked at Neil. "Tell the truth."

"Don't pay attention to him. Look at me, Boy. Were you drinking on the night in question?"

"Yes Sir."

"Now we're getting somewhere. Did you steal that pickup truck?"

Arlan looked at his mother and Possum sitting in the front row. "Yes Sir. Sort of."

"Sort of? Does that mean you had help? Who else was with you?"

Possum shook his head just once, a movement so slight only someone paying close attention would notice. Arlan saw it and so did Nate and Neil.

"Objection."

The judge turned on Neil. "Sit down and stay out of this! Did you hear my question, Boy?"

"Yes Sir."

"So, who was with you?"

"I can't tell you."

"You don't have a choice. Now who was with you?"

Arlan shook his head. "I can't tell you, Judge. I just can't."

"You can't or you won't?" Swetman hadn't been called for a trial in a long time. His blood was up and he was enjoying himself. "Don't trifle with me, Boy. I'm not gonna put up with this stubbornness in my courtroom. You better understand there are gonna be some serious consequences if you don't tell me what I want to know."

Neil spoke up again. "Your Honor, my client is from a very poor family and he's just..."

The judge snapped. He stood up and shouted at Neil. "Sit down! I don't need a lecture from the likes of you about being poor. You and your fancy suit and your rich daddy and your Tulane education. You're nothing but a pampered little titty

103

baby. You see this?" he waved his stump around, spit flying from his mouth with every word. "I didn't get this in no huntin' accident like everybody says, nosiree. When I was thirteen, I was working in a sawmill to help support my family and it got cut off. They bandaged it up, sent me home with a ten-dollar bill for my mamma, and fired my ass.

"I know more about poor than anybody in this courtroom. I never asked anybody for pity or help and I'm not about to start passing it out now. All right Boy, your lawyer says you deserve another chance, well here it is. *Tell me what happened!"*

Tears rolled down Arlan's face, but he clenched his teeth and shook his head.

"So be it. Just remember you brought this on yourself." The judge then turned his rage toward the jury. "The evidence clearly shows this boy is guilty. That right?" No one moved, no one disagreed.

"Your Honor..." Neil began.

Without taking his eyes off the jury, the judge cut Neil off. "For the last time, sit down and shut up. Now I say this boy is guilty. Is that right?" The foreman glanced at his fellow jurors. No one moved. "Since you have nothing to say, I'll take that as consent and I'll render the verdict for you. I say he's guilty.

"Now let's get this over with. Arlan Walker, stand up and face me. As judge of this court, I hereby sentence you to five years for being drunk..." the audience gasped, "...five years for stealing the truck..." Mrs. Walker began to sob. "...and five years for contempt of court. Fifteen years in Angola State Penitentiary!" He banged down the gavel, rose abruptly, knocked over his chair, and walked out of the courtroom.

All movement stopped. Even the dust particles hung in suspension. The smell of fear rolled through the courtroom. After a moment of impenetrable silence, all hell broke loose. Mrs. Walker started to scream, "No, no, no, no, no!" Possum ran up to the judge's stand, grabbed the gavel, and threw it at the plate-glass window. Arlan slumped in the witness chair and covered his face with his hands. He was sobbing.

Always on the lookout for a good story, Hines Lomax from the *Waterproof Chronicle* had wandered over to the courthouse with his Speed Graflex camera. He handled the big camera with ease and was able to change the film sheet, focus, cock the shutter, and shoot with amazing speed.

He had hoped for a shot of Arlan and his family, but this was the kind of story every small town editor prayed for. This story was going to be front page news not just in Waterproof, but all over the state.

CHAPTER TWELVE
(Waterproof)

As quickly as possible, Nate and Neil converged on Arlan and swept him out of the courtroom and into the sheriff's car parked half a block away. Nate got behind the wheel, backed out, and turned left at the corner. He headed for the river and as he crested the hill, the ferry was taking on the last car in line. He stomped on the accelerator and drove onto the ferry just before the deck hands pulled in the gangplank.

The captain blew the whistle and the boat headed out across the Mississippi. It took about fifteen minutes to cross the river. No one was allowed to sit in their cars, so the three men stood silently on the deck.

As he watched the water, Nate felt the power of the river momentarily soothe his soul. It was as if for the duration of the trip, they were floating free of the mainland, free of the law, free of the consequences that awaited them when they returned. Once again the river offered him a short reprieve.

When they docked, Nate turned down a gravel road and about half a mile farther on, he pulled to a stop in front of a small country church. He'd never been inside, but the little church had always looked safe and peaceful. Two huge live oaks protected the building with their long leafy arms. A slight breeze fanned the moss. There were no sounds other than distant bird calls and an occasional tug boat on the river.

A water trough and a pump stood to one side of the church. Nate walked over, picked up the Mason jar of water sitting on the ground, and primed the pump. In a minute, cool water spilled from the spout into the trough. He motioned to Arlan to cup his hands, drink, and then wash his face and hands. Neil followed suit. Arlan pumped water for Nate and refilled the Mason jar. Then they sat down on the church steps.

Nate put his arm around Arlan's shoulders. "This was never supposed to happen. Judge Rivers would have understood your situation. I am so sorry. Luther told me about your family, so I understand why you didn't answer the judge. There was nothing else you could do."

"That man is a disgrace to the legal profession and I'm going to do everything I can to get him removed from office and disbarred as well," Neil added. "As soon as I get back in my office, I'll start working on your appeal. We'll get this thing straightened out." The words were meant to be encouraging, but they hung limp as rags on a bush.

Finally Arlan asked the question none of them wanted to deal with. "What happens now?" His voice broke, "Do I have to go to Angola?"

"I'll keep you here as long as I can, but eventually, yes, you'll have to go. I'll take you myself and I have a good friend there who is one of the captains," Nate said. "I'll talk to him and do my best to get you assigned to his camp."

"Will they put me in a cell?"

Nate didn't know whether his answer was going to make things better or worse. "Not exactly. There are large buildings, with bunks lined up in rows. Everybody is in there together."

He didn't want to use the word dormitory because it sounded civilized and there was nothing civilized about the cellblocks at Angola.

Nate was pretty sure Arlan would end up in a two-story building that housed as many as 600 inmates on the top floor. The kitchen, eating space, showers, and toilets were on the main floor. The conditions were crowded, security was impossible, and physical violence was the order of the day. Ezra Landry said some of the inmates slept with Sears Roebuck catalogues taped to their chests to protect themselves from the threat of nightly stabbings.

When it started getting dark, the men headed back to Waterproof. Bitsy saw the sheriff's car and started packing up food. She had never been very good with words. Oh sure, she talked all the time, but when it came to saying something important, she was at a loss. Bitsy's language was food.

She'd learned something important watching her mother at the café. There was a time when her mother decided the café ought to offer some fancier dishes. She started reading recipe books and putting new items on the menu. Like Chicken Kiev. She pounded the meat thin, rolled it around butter, dipped it in flour and eggs, then in bread crumbs, and fried it. Just a touch of a fork and a fountain of golden butter would spurt out.

The problem was people didn't know how to eat it. They'd look at it for a while, then gently poke it like a kid poking at a frog. When the butter came out, they'd jump back and look ashamed because they thought they'd done something wrong. That's when Bitsy figured out that fancy food tended to make people uncomfortable.

When she took over, she threw out all the cookbooks and the expensive McCormick spices, and went back to butter, salt, pepper, vinegar, Cajun spice, and Louisiana Hot Sauce. All the flavors anyone ever needed.

No fancy-schmancy presentation either. Just big pieces of golden fried chicken along with a mound of mashed potatoes with a pond of butter in the middle. That's what made folks smile and dig in.

Bitsy didn't know of any scientific reason why potatoes or macaroni and cheese made people feel better, they just did. So she concentrated on dig-in food and let that do her talking for her. Bitsy knew after what had happened in court, the three men would need some kindness. So she met them at the office and started unloading food from her car.

Nate and Neil stopped in the front office, but Arlan walked directly into his cell and sat down on his cot. Luther caught the sheriff's eye and motioned for him and Neil to move chairs into Arlan's cell so they could keep him company.

Bitsy followed with the food. It was a little crowded, but there was some comfort in being together. At first, they ate in silence, but then they began to talk. Bitsy smiled. She knew their hearts were hurting, but their stomachs would be happy.

After supper, Neil left with a promise to be in touch with Nate the following morning. The sheriff looked at Arlan and couldn't bear to leave the boy alone. As if Luther had been thinking the same thing, he volunteered to stay the night.

Nate called Blacky who brought over an Army cot he had in the storeroom. Luther opened all the windows to let the breeze flow through. Bitsy cleaned up and then made a quick trip to her house to pick up a pillow and a set of sheets, which she dropped off before she went back home.

Nate clapped Luther on the shoulder. "Be sure to call your mamma and let her know where you are." Then he headed home too. Luther might not be the smartest kid in the world, but he had a knack for doing the right thing at the right time.

***

When the *Waterproof Chronicle* came out later in the week, the front-page banner headline read, *Local Teenager Sentenced to Angola.* In an effort to remain objective, at least in print, Hines had carefully selected pictures to tell the story.

In the upper right hand corner, a remarkably sharp photo of Judge Swetman showed his face contorted with rage, waving his stump and screaming at the jury. Another showed Mrs. Walker reaching out to her son, her tear-stained face caught in a random patch of sunlight. Hines congratulated himself out loud. "That's a Madonna shot if ever I saw one."

Arlan looked small and helpless slumped in the witness chair. The final front-page shot caught Possum in full swing and the gavel headed toward the plate-glass window. The cutlines simply provided identifications. The story followed.

Without a confession and over the objections of Public Defender Neil Hebert, Judge Swetman sentenced Arlan Walker, 17-year-old son of Mr. and Mrs. Clarence Walker, to 15 years in Angola State Penitentiary.

The article went on to lay out the facts. Hines saved his outrage for the editorial page.

In all my years of covering courthouse news for Waterproof and West Feliciana Parish, I have never seen such a blatant misuse of power as I did at the trial of young Arlan Walker. If this kind of misconduct on the part of Stub Swetman and judges like him is not brought to an immediate halt, I fear we shall see the demise of justice in our time.

For anyone reading this who may not be familiar with the laws in our fair state, let me illuminate you. A major distinction between Louisiana and the other 47 states is that while common law courts tend to rule based on precedents, judges in the great state of Louisiana rule based on their own interpretation of the law.

Since April 30, 1812, when we became a state, we have functioned under the proud tradition of the Napoleonic Code of Criminal Procedure. Judge—and I use the title with extreme reservation—Judge Stub Swetman made a mockery of that Code and everything it stands for.

Swetman rode roughshod over the public defender, bullied the jury, and in short, hijacked the trial. He is an embarrassment to this parish and a detriment to the legal profession in general.

It is my sincere hope that the Judiciary Commission will take whatever steps are necessary to expunge, yea verily, to obliterate this man from our courts before he can do any more damage.

Over the next few days, the news story, pictures, and Hines' editorial were picked up by the Baton Rouge *State Times* and *Morning Advocate,* the New Orleans *Times Picayune* and the *Item,* as well as the Associated Press wire service. A teenager sentenced to Angola was unfortunate, but a rogue judge was big news.

Neil's original plan was to apply to the First Circuit Louisiana Court of Appeal to review and correct Judge Swetman's decision. He double checked to make sure West Feliciana was within the First Circuit's jurisdiction and made sure he followed the letter of the law in presenting his complaint.

However, in light of the widespread press coverage of the judge's actions, Neil saw an entirely different set of possibilities for gaining Arlan's release. As Hines mentioned in his editorial, allegations of judicial misconduct were routinely reviewed by the Judiciary Commission, which was a nine-member panel that then recommended disciplinary action to the Louisiana Supreme Court. Under normal circumstances, the process held out little hope of success because the commission that oversaw the procedure was composed of attorneys and judges motivated to protect their own.

There was, however, one exception. When the conduct of the judge was so blatant and outrageous that it attracted national news coverage, the committee was only too happy to purge their ranks of the offending party. In the face of convincing evidence, it had the power to impose a wide range of sanctions, from a public reprimand to removing the judge from office.

That sounded like a good plan to Neil. On a hunch, he enlisted Nate's help to see if other trial lawyers in the First Circuit might have had similar problems with Swetman. Turned out it was far from the first time the judge had taken the law into his own hands.

The judge's conduct in general and the verdict in particular shocked everyone in Waterproof, even Bud Garvey. He called the sheriff at home, apologized, and said if there was anything he could do to fix things, he was willing to try. Nate said he didn't know of anything, but he would be in touch.

From her vantage point as an outsider, Ruby watched and listened. She remembered the town's excitement before the dance and the buzz of gossip before the trial. Now people were silent, shocked, and angry. It was as if the law they trusted all their lives had turned against them. Even the arrival of spring and the azaleas blooming all over town couldn't dispel the gloom. Then it started to rain.

Although Nate did his best to keep Arlan's spirits up, the boy just sat on his cot with his back to the corner and his knees pulled up to his chest. His family came to visit and they cried together.

Both Nate and Luther moved around the office under the weight of the inevitable trip to Angola. Knowing what was to come made it impossible to talk about anything else, and talking about the reality of Angola wasn't an option either. The office was noisy with the words they were afraid to speak.

Finally Nate did the only thing he knew to do that might help the situation. He called Ezra Landry. "I know it's a lot to ask, but can you please come down here and meet Arlan? He's never been in trouble before and without some help, he's not going to last a week up there. I don't know how the system works, so I can't help him much."

Ezra caught a ride and arrived the next day. Arlan's cell was open, but he remained inside. Ezra understood. He got a chair and sat down by the cot. The older man took his time and when he spoke, his words were harsh, but his voice was kind.

"I'm not gonna sugarcoat this, Son, Angola is a mean place. It can be brutal, it can be deadly. There are inmates younger than you and some who've been there fifty years or more. Lots of 'em will die there. You'll be on a work gang, you'll work from can see to can't see. It'll be hard labor, but you're young and strong. Some of the old ones can't keep up."

Nate had a flashback to the bodies at Buchenwald, the bodies of men who had literally been worked to death. *Vernichtung curch Arbeit*, extermination through labor.

"You're gonna be in with all kinds. You have to be aware of everybody around you every minute. You need to figure out who to be afraid of and who you can trust. You gotta protect your manhood and try to keep as much dignity as possible. Watch and listen. Don't talk to the guards. Don't make eye contact. Do exactly what you're told. Little by little you'll get to know some of the other inmates.

"We don't have walls at Angola, don't need 'em. Each of the five camps is fenced and there are double wire fences around the perimeter. We're surrounded on three sides by the Tunica Hills. Sounds nice. It's not. Thick undergrowth, wild boars, swamps, quicksand, snakes, and mosquitoes. On the other side is the Mississippi. It's a mile wide with a fierce current. Nobody's ever beaten the river. Inmates who try to escape are hunted down. The searchers will be on horseback, they'll have dogs and guns, so don't try it.

"I'll see what I can do to get you assigned to my camp. But I won't be out there when you're on the work line. We don't have enough money to hire professional guards, so we make do with what we've got and in lots of cases that's untrained, uneducated, unsupervised convicts.

"You'll survive if you keep your head down, do what you're told and keep your mouth shut. Inmates in my camp don't usually make trouble 'cause they know they'll be sent to another camp that's far worse." He extended his hand, "I'm sorry, Son. I wish I could help more."

CHAPTER THIRTEEN
(Waterproof)

After Ezra Landry left, Arlan folded himself into the corner again. Why would anyone *want* to survive in a place like Angola? Fifteen years was almost his whole lifetime. He simply couldn't imagine living that long in prison. He wanted to cry, but he had no tears left.

Luther went to the Firehouse and picked up food for his friend each day, but Arlan didn't eat much. Normally Luther would have been glad to finish the leftovers, but he'd lost his appetite too. At night Luther racked his brain for something to talk about. The future was too scary and the past just reminded both boys of things Arlan would never be able to do again.

Nate was having the same problem. Just being free to come and go seemed like a betrayal of the boy sitting in his cell. The seasons were changing slowly and the days were starting to get longer.

For want of a better place to go, Nate found himself walking down to the library. He didn't expect to find anyone there, he was just looking for a quiet place to sort out his thoughts. When he opened the door, he saw Ruby sitting on the couch reading. She looked up and smiled.

"Reckon I could get a cup of tea?" he asked.

Before Ruby answered, Nate sat down with his elbows on his knees and the heels of his hands pressed hard against his forehead as if he were trying to stop the thoughts racing around in his brain. She went into the back room to make tea. Nate was still sitting in the same position when she returned. She touched his arm and handed him a cup of strong tea.

"I don't know what to do. I hate being the one who has to take Arlan to that awful place, but putting it off just seems to be making it worse." Ruby sat quietly facing him, waiting for him to continue.

"I remember once when I was a kid, our dog, King, got really sick. He was old and his hind legs wouldn't work and he wasn't able to control his bladder. He'd try to drag himself outside, and he looked so ashamed when he didn't make it. My dad was going to put him out of his misery, but my mother couldn't stand that idea. So they called the vet instead. He was due to come in the afternoon of the next day and all morning we had to walk around knowing what was going to happen. Even King seemed to know. It was the worst time of my life. That's exactly the way I feel now."

Ruby hesitated, then she moved to stand behind Nate's chair, and put her hand on his shoulder. He reached up and covered her hand with his. Ruby's voice was soft, "My mother used to say, 'It's worse to dread than to do.' It's the fear of the unknown that makes everything worse." She hesitated. "You just said it yourself, waiting is the worst part. Maybe doing something will be easier than doing nothing."

Nate patted Ruby's hand then ran his hand over his face and his short hair. He massaged his neck and let some of the tension slide off his shoulders. "I've managed to put this off for nearly a month, but you're right. I'm not helping anybody by putting it off any longer. I'll tell Arlan tomorrow, let his family come one more time, and then we'll leave the next morning."

Ruby stood facing him. On an impulse, Nate took her face in his hands. "Thank you," he said and kissed her. Ruby was stunned and Nate was gone before she could react. Safely outside, Nate was equally flabbergasted.

What was I thinking? I just meant to kiss her on the cheek. Hell, who am I kidding? I've wanted to do that since I first saw her. There's something about that woman that makes me want to ... Good God, Houston, what's wrong with you? You're about to turn Arlan over to Angola and all you can think about is Ruby. That's not fair to the boy. Get your head on straight and take care of business.

The morning they were due to leave, Carrie insisted on coming to the office with Nate.

"I've got something for Arlan," she said and planted herself in the front seat. When they picked up Martha Walker, Carrie moved to the back seat. Luther and Bitsy had apparently also decided to be part of the farewell.

When Nate opened the office door, he and Carrie were greeted with the aroma of bacon and coffee. Nate's desk was covered with plates of fresh biscuits, scrambled eggs, grits swimming in butter, jelly, and more coffee. Arlan was sitting with a plate of food in front of him. He wasn't eating. Martha went to sit by her son.

"Grab a plate, nothing worse than cold breakfast," Bitsy said. "Now your mamma's here, you better eat," she said pointing her finger at Arlan. "I know this is a sad occasion, but that's all the more reason to take advantage of what you got while you got it. Eat!" she pointed to Arlan again. When he didn't move fast enough, she thumped him on the head. "Eat!"

In spite of himself, Arlan managed to smile. "See? You're feeling better already and you ain't even tasted my crabapple jelly." As if she didn't trust them to serve their own plates, Bitsy heaped great portions of everything on plates and passed them around. "You waitin' for the blessing? OK, here goes. 'Good food, good meat, good God, let's eat.'" They did.

When it was time to go, Nate got everyone out so Arlan and his mother could have a moment alone. They came out with their arms around each other and Nate motioned for Arlan to sit in the passenger seat. Carrie ran over to the car and through the window she handed Arlan a New Testament with a metal cover. "I gave Dad one of these when he went overseas. It can stop bullets, just in case you might need it."

Then they were gone.

Some situations in life are so painful that even when they are shared by a family or a group of people, it's still too much to carry. Everyone looks for a way to escape. Some people cry, some work, some get angry. The little group at the sheriff's office went their separate ways, each one looking for a place, as the old spiritual goes, to "lay their burdens down." Bitsy offered to drive Martha home.

Nate could feel the weight of his responsibility as they headed toward Angola. He had postponed the trip as much for his own sake, as for Arlan's. Strangely enough, it turned out that Ruby was right. Rather than the silence Nate had dreaded, Arlan started talking. He asked about what it was like in the war and Nate told him things he hadn't discussed with anyone else.

He admitted to being scared and so homesick it hurt and being cold and wet and hungry most of the time. "All we had were K-rations, nothing hot. The boxes they came in were waxed and they would burn, but we weren't allowed to have a fire. Too afraid the Germans might see it.

"One night we slept in a barn. It was pretty rough, but at least it was out of the rain and the hay smelled clean. In the morning, this old woman came out with a skillet of scrambled eggs and what was left of a loaf of brown bread. That was the best food I have ever tasted. Later we realized she probably used all the eggs she had been saving for her family to feed us. I thanked God for that woman every day of the war after that."

When Arlan asked about his injury, Nate hesitated. Then he realized the boy was on his way into a war zone of sorts and the least he could do was to tell him the truth. "Do you know what Buchenwald was?"

"Yeah, I saw it in a newsreel at the picture show. It looked awful."

"It was, worse than you can imagine. My unit went in the day after they liberated the camp. The smell was something I will never forget. Burned and rotting bodies. A bunch of us were coming out the main gate trying to find a breath of fresh air, and suddenly I heard this little snap followed by an incredible noise. It was so loud I felt it in my chest. I thought it had burst my eardrums and maybe even my heart.

"That's when I saw my buddy Charlie lying to my left. He had this stunned look on his face, but I didn't think he was wounded. Then I realized the top of him looked perfectly normal, but there was nothing left from the waist down. He took the full force of a land mine, a Bouncing Betty, that's what we called them. They didn't just blow up when you stepped on them, they were like a beer can filled with razor sharp pieces of steel. When you hit the trip wire, they would shoot up about three feet and then explode waist high. It cut Charlie in half. I threw up.

"I didn't feel any pain at first, but my left side was all wet. Charlie's blood and my blood all mixed up together. I stood there thinking I was going to die. I may have I called for a medic and I remember reaching down to Charlie. Then everything went black. I woke up in a hospital in England. They patched me up pretty good, but I still carry a reminder of that day in my knee."

For several miles, neither of them said anything. "Sheriff, I'm scared."

"I know, Arlan. I wish I could help. The only thing I can tell you is take it moment to moment. Don't make it worse by worrying about what might happen. I saw it in the war, guys making themselves crazy thinking about all the horrible things we saw in the death camps. Worrying about what might happen to us if we got captured. Just concentrate on the fact that Neil is working hard and I will be too. We'll do everything we can to get you out of there."

About half a mile from the entrance, Nate pulled over to the side of the road. Reluctantly he put Arlan in the back seat, like any other prisoner. He didn't want to take a chance that some inmate might see them arrive and spread the word that Arlan was getting special treatment or that he was a friend of the sheriff. They finished the trip in silence. Louisiana Highway 66 came to a dead end at the main gate of Angola.

Nate stopped the car and for the first time he really looked at the gate and the guard with a rifle looking down at them from the tower close by. Ezra was right, there were no high walls, only double barbed-wire fences as far as the eye could see. Framing the gate were two pillars and an arched sign reading, "State Penitentiary." The actual gate was only about head high. Everybody called it the Tunica Gate. It was the only official way in. For inmates, there was no way out.

Nate had been through that gate many times, but he'd never had to deliver a prisoner before. Within the next hour, he would drive back through the gate headed toward home and freedom. He would be alone on one side of the wire fence and Arlan would be alone on the other.

He handed the guard his identification through the open window. Then he parked in front of the administration building. Without turning around, he said, "Arlan, from here on, we're both going to do exactly as we're told because I don't know what's involved. You just remember what Ezra told you."

Arlan wasn't in handcuffs, but he did walk ahead of Nate as they entered the building with its rows and rows of identical barred windows. For Nate, there was very little involved in turning over the prisoner. He filled out and signed several papers. Then a guard appeared and led Arlan through an ordinary-looking door. But Nate knew nothing was going to be ordinary from that moment forward.

CHAPTER FOURTEEN
(New Orleans)

Both the political situation and the weather were heating up in New Orleans. June had been hot and July and August were promising to break records, even for the Crescent City. Like every politician before him, deLesseps Morrison, the newly elected mayor, was threatening to clean up the Quarter. When he finished *that* chore, he was going to expand his campaign and move on to crime and corruption in the city in general.

That meant he was going to be looking closely at don Scapesi and his bookmaking, loan-sharking, gambling, slot machines, and even his legitimate businesses, which were all suspected of being nothing more than money-laundering fronts. Political threats like those came around about as often as hurricanes and folks usually just hunkered down until they blew over. The difference this time was that the mayor sounded deadly serious.

No politician had caused as much concern among the landladies and the criminal element since the 1930s when Governor Huey Long threatened to put the city under military law to search out prostitution in the "cesspool of iniquity," which is what he called New Orleans. Back then, lots of Minnie's predecessors closed up shop for a while, but in 1935 Long was assassinated and life went back to normal.

With Morrison, Minnie took the precaution of working out an agreement with a Creole woman who lived across the back alley. Whenever Minnie was warned about a police raid, the girls slid a makeshift bridge across the alley from Minnie's to the house next door. Then they crossed over and when the police came, they found no one at home but Minnie.

With his usual arrogance, Tony Scapesi paid no attention to the mayor's latest crusade. Politics was his father's business. He did, however, make it a point to stay out of the don's way as much as possible. He spent a week with friends in Thibodaux and when he was in the city, he stayed at his apartment on Tulane Avenue close to Charity Hospital.

However, occasionally he made an effort to show up at the Scapesi compound in Metairie to take his mother to six o'clock Mass and stay for Sunday dinner afterward. He knew the don wouldn't discuss business in front of the family. So he was safe, or so he thought.

"Tony, you stay a while. I wanna talk to you." The invitation sounded harmless enough, but Tony was on his guard. When they were alone, his father looked at him, "So, what have you done about that business at Minnie's? You found that woman yet?"

Tony explained in great detail all the places he had visited across the river. According to him, no one had seen anything.

"That's it? That's all you've done?"

"Well, I didn't think...."

"No, you never do."

Before Tony could think of anything else to say, the don outlined exactly what he expected to happen. The Scapesi mob controlled gambling in Louisiana. They had slot machines all over the state and an army of men who regularly checked the machines and collected the money. "You gonna use our guys who collect from the slots. They go all over, so tell 'em what to look for. Tell 'em to spend some time listenin' in the local bars. If there's a new, good-looking woman in one of those jerkwater towns, there'll be talk. I got no time to mess with finding this woman. If the guys turn up anything, you go have a look yourself. Don't take nobody's word for nothin'."

Tony nodded and started to leave the room, but the don stopped him. "You check it out first. If it turns out to be her, *then* you come to me. Don't do nothin' on your own. We got people who know how to handle that kind of thing.

"You gotta understand, with that *bastardo* deLesseps poking his nose in our business, we don't need no more trouble. Any sign of weakness and the other families will be out for our blood. Don't forget what Capone did to the North Side Irish and Bugs Moran. We don't need nothin' like that down here. *Capisci?*"

Tony thought the possibility of something like the St. Valentine's Day massacre happening in New Orleans was just ridiculous, but he kept his opinion to himself.

"You understand what I'm sayin' to you?"

Tony knew better than to argue. His father was paranoid sometimes, but that came with the territory. The old man ran New Orleans with an iron fist and Tony understood that. He liked the aura of fear and respect that came from being Giuseppe Scapesi's son.

Because he was Sicilian, most people outside the family assumed Tony was a "made man," but most people didn't have any idea what that meant. To be a made man, Tony would have to carry out a *contract* killing. Personal business like the incident at Minnie's didn't count. Tony knew there was no chance the don was going to send him out on an official job because his father still had hopes of Tony finishing college and becoming a legitimate businessman.

All right, if his father wanted him to use the slot men, fine. He'd get the word out to the crew who picked up money and serviced the slots. He couldn't give them much to go on, just a tall, good-looking woman with long black hair. Somebody who was new in town. It was a long shot, but it was an easy way to cover a lot of territory.

The Scapesi crime family had slot machines everywhere: restaurants, bars, motels, juke joints, dives along the highways, bus stations, car repair shops, pool halls, any place men spent time was a profitable location.

It was hot in the city, so Tony decided to drive north to La Place and check that out himself. It was just a wide spot in the road about halfway between New Orleans and Baton Rouge but everybody stopped there. It was the best place to get gas, grab a bite to eat, and give bus passengers a rest stop. Tony was looking forward to a couple of oyster po-boys and a beer or two.

CHAPTER FIFTEEN
(Waterproof)

Throughout the summer Neil worked hard on Arlan's appeal. Nate and Luther worked equally hard on uncovering other instances of Swetman's misconduct. They had all started out with revivalist zeal, but it soon became apparent that gathering evidence and filing paperwork was a slow and tedious process, like trying to plow a field knee-deep in mud. Every time they thought they were on solid ground, they slipped and had to find a different route.

It was the Army all over again. Hurry up and wait. Nate heard nothing from Ezra and he tried to follow his own advice and not worry about what might be happening at Angola. Then the letter came.

As a rule, Luther didn't like sorting mail, but now he eagerly waited for the postman, hoping to find evidence from another parish to help build their case against Swetman. One letter caught his attention because it was heavier than the others. It was addressed to Sheriff Houston, West Feliciana Parish, Waterproof, Louisiana. There was no return address so Luther looked closely at the postmark. Angola Post Office. He dropped the envelope as if it had suddenly burst into flame.

On the one hand, Luther wanted to rip the letter open, but on the other hand, he was afraid of what he might find. Instead, he picked it up by one corner and laid it in the center of the sheriff's desk. The minute Nate opened the office door, Luther practically dragged him across the room. "It's from Angola. I was scared to open it."

Nate sat down, took out his pocket knife, and split the envelope. He carefully unfolded the letter just enough to see that it wasn't written on official paper. That was a good sign. The handwriting was very small, but readable. "It's from Arlan." Luther relaxed and pulled up a chair with the look of a child waiting to hear his favorite bedtime story.

> *Dear Sheriff and Luther,*
>
> *I'm sending this to you because I don't know our RFD box number at home. Will you please read it to my mamma when you can find the time? Sorry the writing is so small, but I got a lot to say and they only let us send one letter a week. Also paper is hard to get, can you send me some?*
>
> *I'm OK. The food's mostly vegetables we grow here like greens, peas, beans, and cabbage. We get a little bit of meat once a week. Breakfast is usually cornbread with blackstrap molasses made at the sugar mill. You generally have to pick the bugs out of it. It's nothing like what I got in your jail from the Firehouse.*
>
> *They took my clothes and gave me a set of heavy black and white striped prison pants and a shirt. No underwear. The clothes are too big, but Ace (I'll tell you about him later) says too big is a lot more comfortable than too small. I used to see the convict gangs working on the road around Waterproof. Their uniforms had big "LSP" letters on the back. Luther, remember how we*

used to laugh and say that stood for Louisiana Society People? Back then, I never thought I'd be one of them.

Tell Carrie that they let me keep the New Testament. They also let me keep my work boots and my socks. I never take them off for long. Every night I wash out my socks and wash my feet. I put my boots back on before I go to sleep. I put the wet socks under my shirt. It's so hot in here they dry in no time.

I'm trying to do what Mr. Landry said and I've met one guy I think I can trust. He said he was about my age when he was sent up here for stealing a pack of cigarettes! I wanted to ask him how that happened, but asking questions isn't a good idea. His name is Ace and he sleeps in the top bunk across the row from me. He's teaching me how to get by and stay out of trouble.

Everybody likes him because he tells real good made-up stories. Sometimes about cowboys and Indians and sometimes about gangsters. In his stories, the gangsters always win.

Sometimes he can even make us laugh ... a little. It feels real good to have somebody to talk to.

Another guy I met is Tiny. He's a big, mean-looking guy with a scar that runs down the side of his face from his hair to his chin. He's a lifer. The story is, he killed his neighbor's family, but nobody in here knows for sure. He can't read or write but when he found out I knew how, he promised to see that the other inmates leave me alone if I would write a letter to his mamma every week. When he gets a letter it's my job to read it to him. I kinda like him, but everybody else is scared of him.

He's not the only one who can't read and write. The guard who's in charge of us can't count. Can you believe that? What he does is keep a pebble in his left pocket for each convict he's responsible for. When he runs us out to work in the morning, he takes a pebble out of the left pocket and puts it in his right pocket. At night, he reverses the process and puts them all back into his left pocket. That's how he keeps track of us!

They try to get everybody involved in sports, so I play on the baseball team. The trick is to hit the ball over the fence, not to make a homerun, but because none of us can go get the ball. That means one of the guards has to ride all the way around the other side of the fence to throw it back over. They also have what they call self-help groups like Dale Carnegie and a book club and Bible study.

Sometimes I work on the long line in the cane fields. Lately a bunch of us have been working to build up the state levee system. Some of the inmates are trucked out to work on a chain gang, but we've been working around the loading dock here on the river. Barges dock here to pick up vegetables from the farm and sugar from the refinery. Before sunup they run us from the camp to wherever we're going to work that day and then run us back when it gets dark.

After working all day in the heat, some of the old guys can't make it. Us younger ones try to help. If they fall down, the guards will beat them with the strap or lock them in The Hole. That's this little tiny cell with just a grill in the door, no window, no bed, no plumbing. The guards feed them once a day, give them one cup of water, and a bucket for a toilet. It's a real bad place and the guards can put you there for doing anything they don't like.

Sugar cane season is really important here. They ship sugar out and it makes a lot of money for the prison. Once the grinding starts in the late fall, it has to go on twenty-four hours a day to keep the temperature high because that's what keeps the sugar cane juice flowing. If it stops, the syrup will crystallize and gum up the works. Everybody works in twelve-hour shifts. Ace says it's the best time of the year because there aren't enough guards to watch over everybody.

Last year somebody set up a little copper still with a gas burner in the loft of the sugar mill. It made pretty good liquor, but the guards found it and took it all apart. It's easier to make beer. They take cane juice and add some yeast from the kitchen. That makes it ferment. Sometimes they leave it long enough to make rum.

Ace said one time somebody threw a wrench into the gears at the mill and they had to get an engineer all the way over here from Houston to fix it. It was real expensive and a bunch of guys went to The Hole for that one.

Nobody here goes by their real name. I don't even know Ace's real name. My nickname is Chops. One night we were talking about what we missed most and all the men talked about were women. They were pretty crude and I stayed back so they couldn't see I was embarrassed. Finally they asked me what I missed and I said, "Bitsy's pork chops." They thought that was something dirty, but I said no, real pork chops with potatoes and gravy. Anyway, now that's my name.

I've heard a lot of stories about inmates getting beaten by the convict guards, but Mr. Landry—they call him Cap Landry in here—he was right, the men in his camp, even the guards, don't cause trouble or they might get moved to another camp. I haven't seen Cap Landry, but he seems to be respected as a good boss.

Please write and tell me how my appeal is coming. I'm trying to do like Cap Landry said, but it's kinda like holding your breath all the time because you never know when the guards are going to call you out for something.

Don't read this part or the other bad parts to Mamma. Tell her and Possum and the rest of the kids not to worry. I'll try to write again when I get some more paper.

Arlan

Nate carefully folded the letter and put it back into the envelope. Neither he nor Luther spoke for several minutes. "I'm going to tell Mrs. Walker that I have to keep this letter on file and I'll read her enough so she'll know Arlan is all right. I'll give Miss Laura and Carrie the same news. No need to upset the womenfolk if we don't have to."

Then Nate called Neil and shared the letter in its entirety with him. "We've got to get him out of there before something bad happens." They continued to talk for some time trying to figure out ways to speed things up.

When he hung up, Nate walked over to the Firehouse for his afternoon pie and coffee, thankful for a moment of sanity. Bitsy had fans going in every corner of the café trying to keep her customers comfortable. She was making the rounds talking to folks when she saw Nate. As soon as he sat down, she joined him at the counter.

"I'm glad to see you've decided to broaden your horizons, Sheriff," she said as she poured his coffee.

"What are you talking about?" Nate did his best to look both annoyed and innocent.

"From what I hear, you've been droppin' in at the library from time to time. Checkin' out books, I suppose, or is there something else at the library you've been checkin' out?"

Oh my God, does she know about the kiss? No, Ruby's not one to talk. This is just Bitsy being Bitsy.

"Oh, no need to explain to me. Miss Laura and me both think it's wonderful that you're trying to improve your mind." She waltzed over to the juke box, dropped in a nickel and punched F3. Eddy Arnold's, *What Is Life Without Love.* "Nice song, huh, Sheriff?" Bitsy called from across the room. Several men looked at the sheriff, smiled, and gave him a thumbs up.

Nate was headed for the door when Bitsy stopped him. "Listen, Sheriff, I got something serious to ask you about." Nate gave her a skeptical look. "No, this is important, or it might be, I'm not sure yet. Have you noticed that car with Orleans parish plates around town? I reckon it's the guy who tends to the slot machine over at the bus station. Thing is, he's usually in and out pretty quick. You know, stops at the bus station, comes over here for dinner, and then heads out. But this time he's hanging around talking to customers and one of the boys said he'd dropped into the roadhouse out on the highway last night. You know anything about that?"

"Not a thing. You want me to introduce you?"

Bitsy swatted him with a dishrag. "No! It just seems a little strange. Nothing changes around here forever, and then Ruby shows up out of the blue and there's the whole thing with Arlan and now this big-city guy's hangin' around. It's just not normal, that's all."

"OK, I'll talk to some folks around town and see if I can find out anything."

If Bitsy had been paying as much attention to Carrie as she was to Carrie's father, she would have been aware that Nate wasn't the only one spending time at the library. Carrie had taken Luther to meet Ruby so she could help him with his reading. It didn't take long to discover the only books Luther had ever tried to read were textbooks. Carrie explained to Luther that if he had a library card, he could come in and borrow any book he wanted.

Luther looked suspicious. "You mean I can take any of these books home with me and I don't have to pay for 'em? 'Course I could, 'cause I'm workin' now and I get paid every two weeks."

Ruby explained the lending system and got Luther signed up with an official library card. Then she sent him home with *The Hardy Boys, The Phantom Freighter*. "It's brand new, we just got it in yesterday," she said. "You'll be the first person to read it and if you like that one, there are lots more Hardy Boys stories."

A week later, Luther rode his bike over to the library to get another book. "I took the book with me to read at the office when the sheriff didn't have nothin' else for me to do. He's been helping me with some of the words. This is a great story, can I get another one?"

Ruby showed Luther where the Hardy Boys were on the shelf and told him to pick any one he wanted. He picked two. "Miss Ruby, this is a real kind thing for you to do. I know I'm not too smart, but I bet if I learned to read better, I might get smarter. You think that's true?"

She took him into the kitchen, poured him a cup of tea and led the way into the front room. Luther smiled. "The sheriff told me about your tea. He said the first time you gave it to him, he thought it'd be awful, but it wasn't half bad. Now he kinda likes it."

Luther looked at the cup, then sniffed the tea. "You get these from the café? They look like Bitsy's coffee cups. I'm used to drinking tea at home, but it's always ice tea. It's real nice in the summer time." He was trying to put off actually drinking the stuff as long as possible. However, he liked Miss Ruby and he didn't want to be rude, so he finally took a tentative sip. "You know, the sheriff's right, this ain't awful at all."

Ruby smiled. "Luther, there's a whole world out there for people who read books. Books can take you anywhere you want to go."

"Oh, I don't know about that. I'm not smart enough to know what to look for."

Ruby put down her cup. "Now you listen to me, Luther Castle. You are not dumb. People are just smart in different ways. You can learn anything you want to and I'll help you. All right?"

Luther sat up a little straighter, adjusted what should have been a crease in his pants, and crossed his legs the way he'd seen big shots in the movies do. "Yes Ma'am, that would be fine, it surely would."

When he finished his tea, he carried the cup back to the sink, thanked Miss Ruby, and loaded up the books in the carrier on the back of his bike. On his way back to the office, he came across Carrie and told her what Miss Ruby had said.

Later that night, Carrie relayed the story to Miss Laura. "Nana, I like Miss Ruby, can we invite her over for supper sometime?" That was just the opportunity Miss Laura had been looking for and she knew Bitsy would be interested, so she invited her too.

To cushion the blow when she announced her plans to Nate, she promised to make her world-famous meatloaf with Hunt's tomato sweet-and-sour sauce, mashed potatoes, collards, banana pudding, and lots of ice tea. His favorite meal.

Oddly, Nate didn't seem the least bit upset when he found out she had invited Bitsy and Ruby to supper. Miss Laura wondered if there was more going on than she knew about. But no, if that were true, Bitsy would certainly have said something. All the same, she decided to keep a close eye on Nate and Ruby.

Instead of eating at the kitchen table like they usually did, when Ruby and Bitsy came over, Miss Laura decided to use the dining room. Carrie got the tablecloth and napkins out of the sideboard and carefully took the silver out of the chest. This was going to be a real party.

Luther was the main topic of conversation as they sat around with dessert and coffee. Nate had made a point of sitting across the table from Ruby. At first Miss Laura wondered why he hadn't sat next to her, then she realized what was going on. The sparks flying back and forth across the table were hot enough to melt the butter.

"When I hired him, I wasn't so sure it was a good idea, but he's turned out to be … well, let's just say Luther sees the world differently from most of us," Nate said. "It's like the way he files things. Arlan was the only one who understood it. Take the first time we tried to put Arlan in the cell. I couldn't find the keys. Turns out Luther had *filed* them. But they weren't under K for keys, oh no, that would be too simple. They were under O and Arlan explained that was for "open" because that's what keys do."

"Could just as easily have been under L for lock," Miss Laura said.

"Or U for unlock," Bitsy added.

"OK, if y'all think you understand the way his mind works, where do you think he would file traffic accidents?"

Ruby said, "That's easy. Under C for cars ..."

"...unless it was a truck..." Nate prompted.

"Then it would be under T," Ruby said as she finished his thought and they laughed together.

"How about speeding tickets?"

Miss Laura chimed in, "That would be F for fast ..."

"No, T for *too* fast," Carrie said.

More laughter. Carrie was very proud of herself for keeping up with the adult conversation and making them all laugh.

"We have a lot of stolen property reports that come in, know where he puts those?" Before anyone answered, Nate went on. "Under L for lost, because he remembered me saying most things people report as stolen are just lost and eventually turn up."

"That just proves what I told you about the way Luther thinks. Don't joke and tell him to shoot somebody unless you want to find 'em dead," Miss Laura said.

"I'll be sure to keep that in mind."

Bitsy glanced around the table, "You gotta admit Luther's system would save a lot of time and trouble."

"Bitsy!" Miss Laura tried her best to sound outraged. The conversation continued over more coffee and banana pudding. All in all, it was the best night any of them could remember in a long time. Miss Laura was especially pleased.

CHAPTER SIXTEEN
(La Place)

Tony downed the last of his beer and signaled for his check. The po-boys were good, but he'd eaten better in the Quarter. It was the trashy atmosphere of the bus stop at La Place that attracted him. He looked around the room, black and white worn linoleum floors, peeling chrome tables, mismatched plastic chairs, bad lighting, cheap candy displays featuring Heavenly Hash, black fans moving hot greasy air, country girls with bleached hair and big *tette*. Even the passengers who poured off the Greyhound bus could be counted on to look trashy. He was so far above all that and yet ...

He took out a new pack of Luckies, tapped it on the table. He opened the pack, lit one, and slowly blew the smoke toward the ceiling. He flicked his Zippo lighter several times to signal the waitress again. He knew without looking that she had been watching him.

He wasn't really in any hurry. In fact, if the opportunity presented itself, he was more than willing to spend the afternoon sampling some of the local talent. Out of boredom, he picked up a Baton Rouge paper lying on the next table. The words, "Rogue Judge Highjacks Waterproof Trial," caught his attention. He smiled at the picture of a guy throwing the gavel at the window and was just about to lay the paper aside, when he noticed the

137

people in the background. He took a closer look and sure enough, she was sitting right there behind the defendant's table. The tall woman. No doubt about it.

Instead of getting his bill, Tony ordered another beer. He took a long drag on his cigarette. Although it wasn't his strong suit, he had some serious thinking to do. He studied the picture more closely. The woman was sitting beside a man wearing a badge. Never a good sign. Still, now he knew where she lived. The question was, what to do about it?

He hadn't really expected to ever see the woman again. He hadn't given any serious thought to what he would do if he actually found her. What he did realize, was that whatever he did, there would be consequences. It was important to take things slow and get it right.

Although he gave the impression that he was his own man, Tony had actually avoided making decisions his whole life. The don said go to college, so he went to college and then spent most of his time drinking and partying. The don said stay out of trouble, and up until now, he hadn't done anything the don couldn't easily fix.

This situation was different. His father had said to bring all the information to him and he'd have one of the boys handle it. But he had also told Tony to take care of it. The dilemma was that obeying his father—which was usually the best course of action—was not going to get Tony what he wanted. What it came down to, was that he did not want to be a legitimate businessman. That was just boring. Nobody was afraid of a businessman. My God, he might even have to go to an office every day.

No. Tony wanted to be like his father. He wanted to be feared and respected. He wanted to be a made man. But how to make that happen? He and the don agreed the woman needed to disappear, but he couldn't just ask his father to give him the contract. That's not how it worked. There were rules. Contracts were just business, nothing personal. Still his father had said, "Take care of it," that was almost like a contract …

Tony started making plans. First, he'd send one of the slot guys to check it out. See where the woman lived. What she was doing with the sheriff. Once he had those facts, then he'd take care of things. He realized he'd need a gun, but the truth was, he'd never fired a handgun. No, stick with a knife, that made more sense. Knives were quieter, too.

He's always telling me to show some initiative. Well, that's exactly what I'm gonna do.

CHAPTER SEVENTEEN
(Waterproof)

While Tony pondered his next move and soaked up the trashiness of La Place, the summer heat moved slowly into Waterproof trailing the lemony scent of magnolias and the sweetness of honeysuckle. Ladies hid inside or protected their skin from the sun with wide-brimmed hats. Professional men sweated in shirts and ties, laborers poured water over their heads and cursed the heat.

Nate had always hated the cold, so summer was like the return of an old lover, and he looked forward to her arrival. His body relaxed, his knee hurt less, his mind functioned better.

At least, that had been the case in the past. This summer Nate was finding it difficult to stay focused on his job. One minute he was concentrating on the Judiciary Commission of Louisiana and what they could and could not do to remove a rogue judge, and the next minute he was thinking about Ruby and wondering what he should or should not do about her.

It had been a long time since a woman had occupied his thoughts. He hardly remembered the days when he and Eunice were dating. They had known each other since they were children and they had stumbled into marriage more out of convenience than out of passion. Things were all right in the beginning, but after Carrie was born, Eunice turned all her love and attention to their daughter. Nate assumed that was normal and poured his energy into the farm he worked with his father until his parents died. At Eunice's insistence, he sold the land and bought the house in town. He worked at Parchment Products until he enlisted.

Somewhere along the way, he had lost sight of his writing. It had been a while, but occasionally he still jotted down a poem. At one time, he'd toyed with the idea of trying to get some of them published, but life always seemed to get in the way.

Serving in the Army changed his world. It took nearly two months for the letter telling him about Eunice's death to catch up with him. He was ashamed to admit it, but in the middle of battle, it was just one more death. It was far removed, not like the buddies he shared a foxhole with or the blood and gore he saw every day.

By the time he got home, his world had changed again. Miss Laura was running his house and his daughter was turning into a teenager. When he was offered the job of sheriff, he took it. After all, he had a family to provide for and it was his nature to do what was expected of him. He'd never had any grand plan for his life other than that.

Maybe it was time he made a plan. With Ruby. But she was a mystery. He hardly knew anything at all about her. In a society where the first question people asked was, "Who's your family?" his lack of knowledge about her left a serious void. Convention said he should worry about that, but instead he found it intriguing. There was a lot to discover about this woman and he was only beginning to realize how much he wanted to know all of it.

If he were honest with himself, however, he did worry about it a little. Bitsy had said it, Ruby just showed up out of nowhere. Was she in some kind of trouble? Was she running from something, or somebody? Was she married? She didn't wear a wedding ring, but that didn't really prove anything.

Nate pulled himself back to the present. Thoughts of Ruby would just have to wait. Getting Arlan released had to be his immediate priority. Neil said there was still a slim chance they might get him out in time to start school in September. He was afraid to let himself believe that. It was a little like listening to the big-wigs tell you the war was almost over with bullets flying around your head and people still getting killed. He wished he had someone to confide in, someone to ask for advice.

***

Twenty miles and a world away, Arlan was surviving hour to hour. He had included a lot of information in his letter home, but not everything. After Nate left him, he was taken to the receiving station at the main unit, Camp E. He was "fresh fish," a new arrival.

As he had written, he was given shirt and pants but no underwear. He didn't mention that he had no soap, no towel, no toothbrush, no comb. He found out later it was a miracle they let him keep the shoes and socks he was wearing. At night, he could pick out the other new arrivals, because he heard them crying. They all cried at first. But not for long. If the guards heard them, they'd "give you somethin' to cry about."

At first he was assigned to the long line and sent out with a hoe to chop weeds in the cane fields. Inmates couldn't eat weeds, they couldn't be shipped out and sold as vegetables, and they must never be allowed to "catch the crop." Sugar cane made money and was to be protected at all costs.

The inmates were turned out for work at four o'clock in the morning and brought back at eight o'clock at night. Sometimes if Arlan was working on the end of the line out of sight of the guards, he was almost able to forget where he was, but not for long. With a hundred men stretched out along the rows of cane, their hoes eventually fell into a rhythm, a strange, unholy drum beat. Whoosh, chop, chop, whoosh, chop, chop. Hour, after hour, after hour. The sun beat down, his muscles ached, but he kept working and all he could hear was whoosh, chop, chop.

Although Ace told him not to get too excited about what might be happening on the outside, Arlan couldn't help it. He had proof. He had a letter from Sheriff Houston telling him that Neil Hebert was expecting a ruling from the Louisiana Circuit Court of Appeals very soon. "The Louisiana Circuit Court of Appeals," he loved the official sound of the words. Maybe he'd be out in time to go back to school for his senior year after all.

And even better than that, Mr. Hebert said that because of Judge Swetman's "willful misconduct in violation of the Code of Judicial Conduct," the review board had ordered a "psychiatric examination." Arlan wasn't entirely sure how that was going to help him, but it sure would be great if the Judge ended up in the State Mental Hospital in Jackson. Ace said it was even worse than Angola.

On the other hand, maybe he shouldn't get his hopes up too high. Ace knew a lot about the system and it didn't always work the way you wanted it to. He'd been up for parole twice and been turned down. "Don't count on nobody but yourself," he said.

Arlan thought that was good advice, but what could he do for himself? The system told him when to get up, when to sleep, when to eat, when to work. He even had to ask permission to pee. He had precious few belongings and those could be taken away at any moment.

Then one day working on the line, he realized there was one thing they couldn't control, one thing they couldn't take away. His mind, his brain. Mr. Landry had said to pay attention to everything. He could at least do that. So he started to really watch what was going on around him. The difference in the lay of the land when they were working on the levee and the way the cane fields were laid out. The barges that docked on the river. The river itself. The movement of the guards, the paths they used to drive the convicts to work. The horses each guard rode. Who dozed in the saddle. Who was alert, who wasn't. He paid particular attention to Pebbles and the stones he kept in his pockets.

If the opportunity presented itself, did he have the nerve to try to escape? He'd heard stories from the other inmates about failed escapes and what happened to the men who were caught. The lucky ones were shot on the spot.

Arlan was afraid. Afraid to die. Afraid to be beaten. Afraid to survive for fifteen years. When he found himself thinking too much, he'd make an effort to stay in control, to keep his head down and his eyes open. For the time being, that was all he could do. He kept reminding himself that he had a brain and that might be all it took to make a difference.

So, he wasn't about to cause trouble, but he couldn't help daydreaming about escaping. He kept trying to work out an escape plan that wouldn't get him killed or worse. Since it was all just pretend, he didn't ask questions for fear someone would take him seriously or that he might get someone else in trouble. Still, he wished he had someone to confide in, someone to ask for advice.

***

Ruby enjoyed her quiet days at the library, reading the *World Book Encyclopedia* and browsing the shelves for other treasures. She had no idea her life was in danger. She did check the New Orleans papers every week to make sure there was no mention of the murder. She never saw anything about it. As far as she knew, she was safe. She didn't know the old couple who had given her a ride, so there was no way anyone could find her through them.

Still, she made it a point to be aware of the people around her. Although she didn't actually know many people in town, she was beginning to recognize faces and associate them with particular places and so far she hadn't noticed anyone acting suspiciously. Besides, she only went from Bitsy's to the library and back. There had been that one supper at the sheriff's house, but she didn't see how that could make any difference. The sheriff on the other hand, well, he might make a difference, maybe even a big difference.

He hadn't been back to the library since the day he kissed her, but they certainly had connected at supper that night. She had tried to keep her eyes to herself, but every time she looked up, he was looking at her, no, not just *at* her, but more like into her soul. She wondered what he saw. A woman full of secrets or a woman who was willing to meet him half way, if he asked her to.

Suppose he did ask. How much was she prepared to tell him? How much *could* she tell him without putting them both in danger? If Tony ever found her, she was sure he would try to shut her up. Worse still, the don might send someone else to do the job. Someone she didn't know to be afraid of.

Maybe she should talk to Bitsy. She seemed like a woman who had been around and maybe ... No, Bitsy might be a friend, but she was incapable of keeping a secret. Minnie. She would know what to do, but Ruby didn't dare get in touch with her. Reaching out to Minnie would be like drawing a straight line to herself for anyone in New Orleans who might be trying to find her. No, Basin Street was out of the question. She wished she had someone to confide in, someone to ask for advice.

***

Luther, on the other hand, had never been happier. He had lost himself in a world of books. Miss Ruby was right. Books could take you anywhere. Now whenever he got to worrying about Arlan, he'd read another chapter in one of his Hardy Boys books.

He tried to write to Arlan, but soon gave it up as a bad idea. Putting things down on paper was much too hard. First he had to think up what to say, then he had to figure out what to say first and, on top of that, he had to spell everything right. No, writing was out of the question. Besides, he didn't want to remind his friend of all the things he had left behind.

Instead of a letter, Luther decided to put together a box of stuff he thought Arlan could use, but nothing the guards might take away from him. He decided to send nothing but soft things. The way he figured it, that should be OK. Just to be on the safe side, he decided *old*, soft things would be even better.

Luther found some old bath rags and two old towels and put those in the box along with two old T-shirts. He started to put in some underwear, but all he had were the ones his mother made out of feed sacks and Luther was embarrassed to send those. He wrapped up a bunch of half-used pieces of soap, and a tin of tooth powder. No toothbrush because he'd heard some inmates filed those down for weapons.

He got a couple of partially used tablets from Miss Nell at school and a box of old crayons. He wanted to add a pencil but decided that might give the guards an excuse to throw the whole box away.

When he told Carrie what he was doing, she said they ought to get a picture of Arlan's family and put that in too. Carrie talked to her dad and convinced him to go out to the Walker place with the Kodak and take some pictures. Once they were developed, they went into the box.

"Luther, the package is a great idea," Nate said. "I'll take it to the post office and mail it to Ezra Landry. That way we can be sure Arlan gets everything."

"Thanks, but no Sir. I rather you just gave me Mr. Landry's address, I'll mail it myself. I'll put my name as the return person so Arlan will know it came from me. I think it's the right thing to do."

CHAPTER EIGHTEEN
(Waterproof)

Luther opened the envelope with the Angola postmark expecting to see a letter from Arlan thanking him for the package. Instead, a scrap of paper torn from one of the school notebooks floated to the floor. It landed face up and Nate and Luther read the three-word message together. It was written with a red crayon.

They killed Ace.

The icy shard in the middle of Nate's chest was back. It took his breath away. He carried the paper to his desk and sat looking at it in disbelief.

"What'chu reckon happened, Sheriff?"

"I have no idea, Luther." Questions were racing through his mind so fast he wasn't able to grasp any of them. Was Arlan involved? Did he see the killing? Was Ace shot? Beaten? Should he go to Angola? Would that help or make things worse? "I'll call Ezra Landry and try to find out what happened and what the situation is now."

"I'll make coffee."

Strange how a small thing can sometimes have the greatest impact. The sound of Luther going through his morning routine and the aroma of brewing coffee helped to settle Nate's nerves and melt the ice in his chest. He needed to get all the facts.

Foremost, was Arlan all right? The next thing to do was to find out exactly what happened and if there was something he could do to help.

"Is there anything *I* can do, Sheriff?" Luther asked as he set Nate's coffee on the desk.

"Not that I know of right now. We may need to make a trip to Angola, but we can't decide that just yet. Thanks for the coffee."

Nate picked up the phone and dialed Ezra's home number. He knew there was very little chance Ezra would be there, but it was the only contact he had. Doc might be home, but Doc didn't talk to anyone except Ezra. The phone ran a long time, before anyone answered.

"Yeah, this is Landry."

"Ezra! I was hoping you'd be home, this is Nate."

"Glad to hear from you. I thought you might be calling. You hear anything from Arlan?"

"Yeah, we got a note from him but all it said was, 'They killed Ace.' What in the world's going on up there?"

"A tragedy. A damn useless tragedy. The reason you found me at home is that I was gonna call you and I didn't want to make the call from the office."

"We'd appreciate any information you can give us. Did Arlan have anything to do with this? Is he in trouble?"

"No more than anybody else who was there when it started. Lord God, it's an ugly story. Never should have happened."

Nate wanted to scream at Ezra for taking so long to get to the point. But that was just Ezra's way. He couldn't be rushed, especially when it was evident he didn't want to talk about the subject at all. Nate waited.

"Monday morning, the long line was working out in the cane field. It was hotter'n hell and they kept at it all day in the boilin' sun. By quittin' time everybody was draggin.' Had one of my regular guards been on duty, none of this would have happened. He'd have let the men walk back, no need to run 'em to death. But this mean SOB from Camp E was on duty and he figured he'd have some fun."

Nate wanted to put the phone down. He knew enough to know the story was not going to end well. Like most soldiers, he'd heard horror stories about guards in the death camps using inmates for target practice, doctors using them as Guinea pigs. He didn't want to hear any more of those stories.

"Instead of linin' everybody up to run single file like normal, he just yells, 'Run!' At first nobody moved. Then he shot off his gun like a starter's pistol and all hundred inmates started runnin' at the same time. They got no idea which way he wanted 'em to go, so they're running in all directions.

"Seems that's when he got to laughin' and firin' more shots. Then he uses his horse to herd the inmates like they was a bunch of cattle. He's wavin' around this cowboy hat he always wears and cuttin' out men, like he thinks he's in some damn rodeo or something."

Nate had driven around the prison grounds enough to have a pretty good idea of the terror and panic that must have caused. Outside the barbed-wire fences that surrounded the camps, the fields stretched for miles. If the men ran in the wrong direction, the guard was within his rights—in fact it was his job—to shoot them. If they didn't follow his orders, if they stopped, he could shoot them.

"You can imagine, everybody's trying to keep movin' and stay out of his way at the same time. He chased down one old man, and when he fell, the guard jumped off his horse, tied him up like a steer, and started hittin' him with the bat. It's a strip of leather about five inches wide attached to a handle.

"Anyway, from what I've been able to find out, that's when Ace got involved. He tried to shield the old man, so the guard took out his fury on Ace. Beat him pretty bad. It don't take more than about ten blows to open the skin on a man's back. Ace musta got thirty before some other guards pulled the guy off him."

Despite everything Nate had seen in the war, this story brought tears to his eyes. One man trying to help another and getting beaten for it. Why? What in the world fueled that kind of rage, that kind of hate?

"The guard ordered two of the inmates to drag Ace back to camp. When they got there, the guard had them throw him into The Hole. It's not the first time it's happened and unless some miracle occurs around here, it probably won't be the last. Everybody heard Ace moaning, but there was nothing anybody could do.

"Finally, one of the trustees came and told me what was going on. I got my bag together and went over there to do what I could to help. I put some medicine on Ace's back, something to dull the pain and toughen the skin as it healed. I didn't have much to give him other than some aspirin, but I left the bottle with him and I brought him some extra water and a biscuit or two.

"I worked real slow and I talked to him while I was workin' on his back. I've been through this before and I know that sometimes a gentle touch can do as much good as strong medicine.

"Ace passed out a couple of times, but I made sure he understood what I was saying to him. I told him to hold on. I'd do my best to get him out, but he'd probably have to stay a day or two. Guards get to decide how long an inmate stays in that hell hole."

Nate shook his head. Who in God's world had come up with a system that used inmates as guards? Instead of showing some consideration, or having some sympathy, they were always the worst ones. It was almost as if they enjoyed inflicting pain. He'd heard about collaborators in the death camps who turned on their own. Kill or be killed, that was the only rule that applied.

"I went back late the next day to dress his back and take him some food and water, but he was dead. Now Ace was a strong man. There's no doubt about it, The Hole is a terrible place, but it shouldn't have killed him and, as it turns out, it didn't."

My Lord, Nate thought, what could possibly be worse? Did someone poison his food?

"I did some checking and found out that Ace just had five years to go on a twenty-year hitch. He was due for parole again in two years. Seems he still had family on the outside and he was making plans for what to do when he got out. Come to find out, the guard went back over there and told him he'd let him out the next day, but they were tacking another twenty years to his sentence.

"That's what killed him. He just gave up. He'd come so close to freedom and then to have it snatched away, was just too much. A whole lot of what it takes to survive in here is the will to live. Without that, you're a goner.

"And it was all for nothing. Guards got a lot of power, sometimes life or death, but they got no say over a man's sentence. No way that SOB could have added a day to Ace's time. The hell of it is, Ace didn't know that."

Luther had been watching the sheriff's face throughout the conversation and when he saw tears running down Nate's cheeks, he knew that something really terrible had happened. Something worse than just getting killed.

"Men get killed around here all the time," Ezra continued. "Inmates get hardened to the fact. But something about this death has got everybody riled up. Ace was well liked. He told stories and kept people's spirits up. Lots of the inmates looked up to him."

One of the oddest facts about Angola was the funerals. In spite of the inhumane treatment some men received, when an inmate died, he was laid in a pine box, but then the coffin rode to the graveyard in a hand-made, ebony hearse, pulled by two beautiful black horses. Inmates were allowed to attend the burial, if they chose. In the case of Ace's death, almost the entire prison population turned out. The mood was quiet, but sullen, like a pot of grits that quivers just before it boils over.

"We put everybody on lock-down for twenty-four hours, but keepin' thousands of prisoners locked up together in the barracks just makes a bad situation that much worse. Best thing to do is put everybody back to work. I haven't heard anything specific, but tension is way too high for comfort. I have a feelin' there's gonna be more trouble before this is over.

"Might be a good time to come visit young Arlan, maybe bring his mamma with you. Just let me know when you're coming and I'll get Arlan over to the house, so y'all can have a little privacy."

Nate and Ezra talked for a few more minutes, then he slowly hung up the phone and sat staring at the floor. He couldn't look at Luther and he didn't trust himself to speak. He felt the same wave of hate he'd experienced at Buchenwald. He didn't know what would happen to the guard who had lied to Ace, but at that moment Nate couldn't think of a punishment horrible enough to fit the crime. It was bad enough that Ace died, there was no point in explaining the useless cruelty of what really caused his death to anyone else. Nate just swallowed the pain.

Without a word, Luther reached over, picked up Nate's cold coffee, and replaced it with a fresh, hot cup. Then he sat down and waited patiently. Finally Nate looked at him. "Ace was trying to help an old man and the guard turned on him. He beat Ace with a leather strap hard enough to rip open his back. Then they threw him in The Hole. Ezra tried to help him, but he'd lost too much blood. He died. Ezra's afraid there's gonna be more trouble." He wrapped his hands around the hot coffee and drank.

"I didn't ever know Ace," Luther said quietly, "but I feel kinda like I've lost a friend too. Reckon Arlan's gonna be OK?"

"I hope so. Ezra thinks we ought to take his mamma to see him. I'm going to go see Neil and then I'll stop by the Walker's place on my way home."

The last thing Nate wanted to do was to repeat Ace's story, but he knew it was important to let Neil know the mood of the prison and the possible consequences. According to Ezra, Angola was a ticking bomb.

At the end of their conversation, Nate said, "I know it's only been three months and things are starting to move, Neil, but somehow we've got to speed it up. Three months for us must seem like three years to Arlan. Ace was his only friend up there and this kind of thing might tip him over the edge. The inmates are angry and if there is a riot, who knows what might happen."

Nate was exhausted. He wished he were a drinking man because he would have welcomed being unconscious for a while. Instead he got in the car and headed out to the Walker place to talk to Arlan's mother.

He made sure she understood that Arlan was all right, but Ezra had suggested a visit and Nate was prepared to take her to see her son as soon as she could be ready to go. Martha saw the pain in the sheriff's eyes and heard it in his voice. She didn't ask for details, but she knew there was more to the story than he was telling her. She said she'd be ready to go the next morning— early.

Back in the car, Nate searched the glove box and found an almost empty bottle of liniment. He lit a cigarette and doctored his knee before he headed for home. When he got there, he told the story one more time, fixed himself some scrambled eggs and went to bed. He was so tired he was asleep almost before his head hit the pillow.

The following morning, he picked Martha up at 6:30 and headed north. When they got to Angola, Nate drove directly to Ezra's house. "There's flowers!" Martha said as they drove along one of the fence lines. "I surely didn't expect to see no flowers."

Nate was glad Ezra had arranged for Arlan to meet them at his house. Seeing her son in prison stripes was bad enough for Martha, but at least she didn't have to talk to him through bars or behind a barbed-wire fence.

Arlan tried to put on a brave face, but when his mother put her arms around him, he broke down and Nate realized all over again that he was just a scared, lonely kid.

CHAPTER NINETEEN
(The Atlantic Ocean)

Tuesday, September 2, 1947, dawned as another beautiful day in the eight colonial territories that made up French West Africa. As the usual matter of course, the local weather bureau monitored an area of low pressure. When it moved into the Atlantic Ocean, it was classified as a depression and then quickly became a tropical storm with maximum sustained winds of fifty miles an hour. Still, nobody paid much attention, it was nothing much to worry about. Even when it became a Category 1 hurricane, it didn't set off any alarms. It stalled for five days, then it turned northwest across the Atlantic.

By September 13, it had reached Category 4 intensity. It was still moving slowly over the ocean, but it was headed for land, specifically the east coast of Florida. That got the U.S. weather bureau's attention. Hurricane warnings were issued from Titusville to Fort Lauderdale. The National Guard was mobilized. If the hurricane hit in full force, they would have their hands full trying to evacuate the 15,000 people who lived in the path of the storm.

Louisiana authorities paid no attention. Florida was several states away. Nothing to worry about.

Four days later, the storm finally made landfall near Fort Lauderdale with maximum sustained winds near 155 miles per hour. It was the only major hurricane to pass directly over Fort Lauderdale since 1926 more than twenty years before.

Still the hurricane was a long way from Louisiana and no one there gave it a second thought. Eventually the storm moved slowly inland and it diminished to a Category 2 hurricane over the Everglades. The New Orleans weather bureau did begin to watch it, but since it seemed to be heading northeast, they breathed a sigh of relief.

Mother Nature smiled at the gullibility of mankind. The storm began to re-intensify, reaching winds of 115 miles per hour. Just one day later, on September 18, it moved into the Gulf of Mexico and turned west-northwest. On Friday the 19th, it headed straight for St. Bernard Parish, which borders Orleans Parish, the City of New Orleans, and Lake Pontchartrain. Now the weather bureau paid serious attention.

Storms were just part of life in south Louisiana so even with hurricane warnings being broadcast, most New Orleans residents weren't too concerned. Besides, it had been more than thirty years since a major storm had actually reached the city. Just to be on the safe side, some folks boarded up their windows, but they were more worried about flooding from the excessive rain preceding the storm than about the high winds.

Throughout the weekend, WWL, the New Orleans 50,000-watt, clear-channel radio station, broadcast hourly reports and warned residents in the low-lying areas to evacuate. The worst flooding was predicted to hit Old Metairie, portions of Orleans Parish lakefront, Gentilly, and Moisant Airport. The full force of the storm finally hit the city with wind gusts of 125 miles per hour.

The French Quarter was one of a number of the older neighborhoods built on higher ground along the river. Minnie and the girls closed all the wooden storm shutters and thanked the original builders for their foresight. Then Minnie put out the word that the house was officially closed for business until after the storm. Otherwise, they didn't pay much attention.

However, Tony, who was staying at his apartment on Tulane Avenue, heard the warnings and knew his family in Metairie was in danger. He also knew the don would never evacuate. The old man thought he controlled everything in New Orleans, including the weather. Tony tried calling home, but the phone lines were down and the radio said streets were flooded.

High winds and rain pounded the city, but Mother Nature wasn't finished yet. WWL reported that the center of the storm now measured twenty-five miles across. The weather bureau also predicted that if it continued on its present path, it was going to reach Baton Rouge with high winds, tide surges on the Mississippi, and record rainfall.

That set off alarm bells in Waterproof. The history of the town was closely tied to the Mississippi. Originally the founders built on the low-lying areas near the river to make it convenient for the riverboats to pick up the cotton. The fact that they had to contend with frequent floods was just a part of life. However, eventually they moved to higher ground.

The current flood-related problem was loss of power when the electrical lines came down. Everyone kept flashlights and a kerosene lantern or two around in case of emergency. Most people had gas stoves. The real concern was fresh water. Since lots of people still had their own wells, downed lines meant the pumps wouldn't work, and that meant no water for drinking, cooking, washing, or flushing toilets until repairs were made. As soon as Miss Laura heard the radio report, she and Carrie started filling the bathtub and pots and pans and buckets, anything that would hold water.

Nate sent Luther home to be with his family. Then he went by the Firehouse. Bitsy was taping up the glass windows at the café. Because Ruby had grown up on a farm, she knew about storms, and pumps, and water. She filled both bathtubs and any other large pots she could find in Bitsy's kitchen. Finally, Nate and Bitsy each headed for home, prepared to stay in and ride out the storm.

It took an act of God to defuse the situation at Angola. Convicts by the hundreds were turned out in the storm to save as many of the crops as possible. Even in the face of a possible riot, economics trumped security. Thousands of acres of rich, river bottom land were cultivated with crops that were harvested and sold in out-of-state markets. Along with the sugar cane harvest, vegetables, and the herds of cattle were a major source of income for an institution that had little or no budget and was supposed to be self-sustaining. The crops were also the only source of food for the 5,000 inmates.

Some of the fields were already under water, but the crops had to be picked nevertheless. Men stood in knee-deep, cold water blindly salvaging anything they could reach. Along with the guards on horseback, men on foot drove the cattle to higher ground.

Scores of other convicts were dispatched to reinforce the levee. Guards emptied the barracks. Arlan and the rest of the men in his area were lined up in the thunder, lightning, and pouring rain. As usual Pebbles was there trying to keep track of the men under his charge. He was holding a handful of stones when a loud clap of thunder startled him and he dropped them. The inmates froze. Pebbles fell to his knees and started picking up stones as fast as he could. But not quite fast enough.

One small stone fell next to Arlan's boot. With the slightest movement he stepped on it and ground it into the mud. His heart was beating so loud he was sure somebody might hear it over the noise of the storm. No one noticed. When Pebbles was satisfied he had retrieved all the stones, he mounted his horse and drove the convicts to the levee.

The skies were uncommonly dark, the rain was coming down in sheets, and whenever the lightning flashed, it left everyone momentarily blind. Arlan was ordered to work on the river side of the levee packing sandbags into place. In a matter of minutes he was covered in mud, working hard to keep his footing and not slide into the water. Even without the flooding, the Mississippi was nearly a mile wide at Angola and Arlan knew there was no way to swim across. The force of the floodwaters, and the current would drag him under in no time.

In a flash of lightning, he saw a barge outlined against the river. It was tied up at the dock, but until that moment, he hadn't realized how close it was.

The work went on for hours. Finally near midnight the captain called a halt. They had held back the river. Strange that the inmates felt a sense of pride in that. Like Ace always said, "You gotta enjoy the little wins 'cause that may be all you get."

Back at the barracks, the guards had the fire hoses ready. At full force, the water could break a man's back, but this time they were just trying to wash off the mud before they let the convicts back inside. The guards decided not to do a head count. "With the storm and after what we just put 'em through, ain't nobody gonna have the strength to run away." So the day ended.

***

The next morning Miss Laura was up fixing breakfast as best she could in the dark. She was listening to a small battery radio in the kitchen. The news said the eye of the storm had passed over New Orleans and Baton Rouge and was on a diagonal course across the state headed for Waterproof and DeRidder. The winds were down to fifty miles an hour but it was still raining hard. The river was rising and was already near flood stage.

At five o'clock, the phone rang. Miss Laura answered it, listened in silence and said, "I'll tell him." Then she went upstairs to wake Nate up. He took one look at her and knew something was very wrong. She was white as a sheet.

"I heard the phone. What's the matter? Is it Arlan? Is he dead?"

She shook her head and sat down on the bed shaking with sobs.

"Laura…."

"He's escaped. Last night during the storm. They've got the guards and the dogs out up there already and they're putting together a posse. They want you to get hold of Bud and go up there right now." She began to cry again.

Nate put his arms around her. He tried to comfort her, but the truth was, he wanted to cry too. Why couldn't Arlan hang on just a little longer? They were so close to getting him out.

In a daze, Nate got dressed and put in a call to Bud, then got his hunting rifle. "I'll ride up with Bud; they'll give us horses when we get there. Will you call Luther and let him know what's going on? Let's hold off on telling Martha Walker until we know more. God, I hate this job."

CHAPTER TWENTY
(Angola)

Even under the best conditions the drive to Angola was tedious. There was nothing to give the mind a rest, just trees and dense undergrowth on both sides of the road for miles. A natural barrier to anyone who tried to escape. Through the rain on the windshield, the greens and browns ran together like an oil painting.

Out Nate's side window, the details were ominously clear. How could anyone run through that? He felt the bloodhounds' excitement as they moved from side to side in their cage on the back of the pickup. The rain pounding on the cab roof made conversation difficult and Nate thanked God for small mercies.

As they neared the main entrance, Bud raised his voice over the storm noise. "Sheriff, I just wanna tell you again, I never meant for none of this to happen. That judge just went crazy, no kid belongs up here. Listen, don't worry about the dogs."

"I thought about that. The rain will make it harder for the dogs to track Arlan."

"Not exactly. If Arlan's been working out here, his scent is gonna be everywhere, so it'll be hard to pick up the right trail. But the rain ain't gonna make his scent disappear, it'll just hang low to the ground wherever the water puddles. What's really gonna help Arlan is this wind. Strong as it's been all night, it's already blowed his scent away. The hunt'll give the dogs a good run, but I reckon Arlan ain't in no danger from none of these bloodhounds."

With the one exception of cane grinding, attempted prison breaks took precedent over everything else at Angola. No one was allowed to escape. It was bad for business. While the hunt was on, prisoners were either locked in their barracks or herded into stockades guarded by skeleton crews. The rest of the guards formed the core of the posse. Then reinforcements were called in: state police, local sheriffs and their deputies, even armed volunteers.

Men brought their rifles and many of them brought their own horses. Some, like Bud, brought bloodhounds to add to those owned by Angola. Horses were provided for those who needed them. Hurricane or no hurricane, the search for Arlan was on.

When the posse was assembled in the main yard, the warden got on a bullhorn to make himself heard over the rain. "Now listen up men. This here convict is young and far as I know, he ain't caused any trouble before this. But one thing you gotta remember about a convict, you can't trust 'em. They may be in here for nothing more than stealing a box of matches, but once you put 'em behind bars, they get dangerous. So treat him that way.

"If you get close enough to catch him, fine. Tie him up and bring him on back. We'll take it from there. If he's too far away to catch, you are authorized to shoot to kill.

"Now, if you got a flask with you, get yourself one last pull and then put it away. I don't want none of y'all shooting each other. Anybody got any questions?"

Nobody did. Locals had been through the routine before. Most of the time, the convict was caught. Good for the posse, bad for the inmate. Every once in a while somebody got shot, but that was rare. Huddled in his rain slicker, Nate realized the storm was working in Arlan's favor. It would make it a lot harder to spot him. On the other hand, after being out in the elements all night, he would be soaked to the skin and cold.

The posse, a hundred strong, fanned out through the heavily wooded area of the Tunica Hills surrounding Angola. Bud was right. All the dogs were having a hard time picking up a scent, but whichever way they went, men on horseback followed them. On a hunch, Nate joined a group of men headed toward the levee. When they got there, the river was a scene of chaos.

With all the rain, the water was at flood stage running high and fast. Shortly after dawn a 195-foot barge carrying gravel broke free from its mooring upriver at Natchez. When it reached the curve just past the Louisiana line, the current pushed it toward the eastern bank, and it crashed into the barge at Angola, which shuddered and then tore free from its mooring. When the posse arrived, all that was left was the ruined dock and the raging waters of the Mighty Mississippi.

"Reckon that barge broke free on its own?"

"Not likely. Just look at that dock, or what's left of it. I'm guessing something hit it, maybe another barge from up river. I've seen it happen. If more than one of them things gets caught up on a sandbar or sinks in the middle of the river, it can tie up traffic clean down to New Orleans. Hell, it could stop barge traffic on the whole damn river," one of the old hands said. "Thank God it's not our problem. The Coast Guard'll have to sort that out.

"Our best bet is to search along the bank. Most of the convicts who run, come this way. They think the river's gonna help 'em. This ole river just swallows 'em whole. Sometimes it spits 'em out farther downstream, sometimes not."

As the morning dragged on into afternoon, the wind died down, but the rain never let up. The men searching the Tunica

Hills found the remains of several prison uniforms in the bush, but they were old and faded. Leftovers from other failed escapes.

Finally, one of the men in the group searching along the riverbank saw what looked like a black and white prison shirt caught on a tangle of brush. It turned out to be a shirt covered in mud and debris from the river. It was relatively new. Upon closer inspection, the front was stained with blood, partially washed out by the muddy river. They took the shirt back to the main staging area.

It was getting dark by then and most of the other crews had come in with little or nothing to report. The warden examined the shirt, determined that it was about the right size, mostly new. With no other evidence to the contrary, he announced that it was a pretty good bet the convict had drowned. It wouldn't be the first time. He sent the posse home and said the Angola guards were going to continue to search for the body as they cleaned up and assessed the storm damage.

The group broke up and headed for home, glad to be out of the rain. Bud and Nate rode in silence for a while. "We didn't find no body," Bud said. "You know what they say, 'No body, no crime.' Maybe this time it means no body, no problem."

"Let's hope you're right," Nate answered.

"Lots a ways that shirt coulda got there. I seen some strange things happen. I mean without a body, you just never know."

"That's true. No way to be sure. Let's just tell our folks they've called off the search for now. No need to jump to conclusions. Let's give it a couple of days."

The men agreed and slipped back into an uncomfortable silence.

It was nearly 9:00 p.m. when Bud dropped the sheriff at the office. Luther met the sheriff at the door and Nate told him what they'd found—or more importantly—what they didn't find. "It just doesn't feel finished. There was too much confusion during the storm and then with the high winds and rain, and the barge being gone; it was chaos. The official word is that they sent the posse home and from here on Angola will be running their own search. We'll just wait and see."

Luther left and Nate faced up to the thing he had been dreading all day. Finally he couldn't put it off any longer, and although it was late, he drove out to the Walkers to talk to Arlan's family. As gently as he could, he explained to Martha about the posse and what had happened.

"We didn't find a body, so we don't know for sure what happened yet. They'll keep looking up there and we'll keep looking down this way. I don't want to give you any false hope, but I think the fact that no one found anything is probably a good sign. Let's just hang on a couple of days. What with the storm and all, he might have made it. Hold on to that thought."

Nate dragged himself home. He was cold, hungry, tired, and his leg was throbbing. He headed straight for the cabinet under the sink and doctored his leg as he related the whole story to Miss Laura and Carrie.

They listened and then Miss Laura filled him in on what had happened while he was gone. "The power was out most of the day, but it's back on now. That means the pump's working again and there's plenty of hot water. Why don't you take a bath and I'll fix you some supper."

Nate gladly followed her suggestion. He filled the tub and lowered his aching body into its steaming embrace. He closed his eyes and tried to relax, but he kept thinking about Arlan. If he survived, the boy was out there somewhere and he would be cold, wet, and hungry too.

Nate wished he still believed in prayer. But even if he did, what would he pray for? Lord, please let Arlan survive? For what? To be on the run? To be caught and taken back? The water in the tub began to cool and Nate got out and pulled the plug. He put on dry clothes and headed back to the kitchen.

As soon as he sat down, Carrie started asking questions. Nate knew she was concerned, but he didn't have any answers. Finally, Miss Laura came to his rescue. "Carrie, give your dad a chance to eat his supper. Nate, as soon as you finish, why don't you go up to bed? Carrie and I will clean up here and then we'll turn in too. It's been a long day for everyone. Go on."

Nate was tired, but he was too keyed up to relax. He lay down on the bed, but he couldn't sleep. He reached for a cigarette hoping that might calm his nerves. Being out in the cold all day had played havoc with his knee. He hobbled down to the kitchen and without turning on any lights he found the liniment where he'd left it on the counter. He'd washed off the first application so he reapplied a generous amount and slowly massaged it into his knee. He knew there was no use trying to go to sleep, so he went upstairs and got dressed. The rest of the house was quiet.

CHAPTER TWENTY-ONE
(Waterproof)

Nate slipped out the front door and got into the car. Something always seemed to pull him to the river. He parked close to the ferry landing and walked along the levee. The river was still high, but the storm was over, the rain had finally stopped, the sky was clear, and there was a full moon. Instead of its usual muddy color, the river looked silver. Amazing that something so beautiful could also be so deadly.

Nate had known the river all his life. He swam in it as a boy, dreamed of building a raft like Huck Finn and floating down it. He fished in it with his father and once watched a body being fished out of it.

He thought of the river as his friend. Someone to share a lazy afternoon with, someone to listen to things he couldn't say to anyone else. He'd even read some of his poetry to the river which listened, but didn't comment.

It was hard for Nate to realize this was actually a northern river. It was born a Yankee somewhere in the northern part of Minnesota. The headwaters there were part of Lake Itasca and it was shallow enough to wade across. The river flows north at first, but then it turns south and starts its journey to the Gulf of Mexico. Nate preferred to think of the grownup river, the working river, the one Mark Twain described as "sired by a hurricane, dammed by an earthquake."

People find God in strange places and for Nate, the Mississippi was as close to a supreme being as he was likely to get. Instead of the Bible, he had first read Twain's *Life on the Mississippi* when he was a boy and he could still quote from it chapter and verse, like scripture. The river could be a vengeful God or a caring Savior and Nate had seen it be both.

Walking helped his knee and the river sounds were familiar and comforting. No matter how late Nate came to visit, the river was always awake, ready to listen. All he really wanted at the moment was to spend some quiet time with a friend who would understand the sorrow he felt at the useless waste caused by man's cruelty to man.

Suddenly he realized he was not alone. He whirled around and saw Ruby. "What are you doing here?"

"Bitsy's gone to her sister's. I couldn't sleep. Sometimes I walk down here just to watch the river." She came to stand next to him and for a few minutes they stood together in silence.

Finally Ruby asked, "Arlan?"

"Nothing. I thought about calling you but it was late and I didn't want to disturb you. We didn't find him. But we didn't find his body either, so there's still hope. All we found was a prison shirt snagged on some brush in the river. I just can't allow myself to believe he's dead. I know it would be a miracle if he survived, but sometimes miracles happen."

She took a step closer and slipped her arm around his waist. She had never touched him that way before and it surprised him. So there they were, just the three of them—man, woman, and river—silently trying to make sense of the world. Nate could hear the river lapping softly at the bank.

Then very slowly he took Ruby by the shoulders and turned her toward him. He looked down into her face and her dark eyes. "Ruby …"

"Yes."

The moonlight drained the world of color and replaced it with the stark beauty of light and shadow. It was an illusion, deceiving, blocking out harsh reality. The river shimmered in the background.

They walked back to Bitsy's and through the darkened house up the stairs to Ruby's room. Neither of them spoke but the silence was charged with an energy they couldn't deny.

Nate watched spellbound as Ruby unbraided her hair and let it hang loose. Then she slowly unbuttoned her blouse.

Without touching, they mirrored each other's movements as they let clothes drop to the floor. For a moment they stood naked. Brazen. She stepped into the silver light, offering him everything. Nate's eyes touched every part of her body and Ruby felt him as surely as if his hands were caressing her.

Finally he took her in his arms and kissed her long and deep. "Yes," she whispered. She took his hands and moved them over her body. "Yes." That one word was what he had longed to hear. With that she gave him permission to please her in every way he knew how. He carried her to bed and pulled her to him, lost in the heat of her body and the cinnamon smell of her skin.

Yes, she told herself. Open yourself to this man, take him in, and let him love you. They moved in slow motion. She wanted to close her eyes, but she also wanted to watch everything he did. To see it and to feel it was electric.

Nate had never known the passion of having a woman whose body sought his touch. When they finally came together, Ruby held nothing back. At that moment the outside world disappeared. They were together and nothing else mattered.

CHAPTER TWENTY-TWO
(Waterproof)

Nate Houston wasn't the only person who was up most of the night. Hines Lomax was just leaving the newspaper office, when he saw Bud Garvey driving through town and stopped him to get the latest from Angola. Bud filled him in on the search and Hines got to work. After years of reporting engagement parties and 4-H cattle judging, he finally had three major stories on his desk at one time. Three! The hurricane, with pictures, and the search for Arlan would go above the fold. Bud posed with the hounds, so Hines had a picture to go with that story too.

And finally there was a follow-up story on the rogue judge. Hines had cropped a picture taken during the trial to show a close-up of Stub Swetman's snarling face. For at least once, the *Chronicle* was going to look like a big-time newspaper.

Without knowing it, Hines shared a fondness for Mark Twain with Nate. In his case, it wasn't the river boatman he admired, but rather the newspaper man. A quote from Twain was yellowing on his bulletin board. Hines believed that like Twain, his job was to keep folks "thoroughly posted concerning murders and street fights, and balls, and theaters, and pack-trains, and churches, lectures, and school-houses, and city military affairs, and highway robberies, and Bible societies, and hay wagons, and a thousand other things which it is in the province of local reporters to keep track of and magnify into undue importance for the instruction of the readers ..." To that end, Hines slowly rolled a clean sheet of paper into his battered Underwood and started to type.

Local Youth Sought in Prison Break

Arlan Walker, a local youth who was sentenced to 15 years in Angola in a case that is currently under appeal, was the subject of a massive man hunt at Angola State Penitentiary. After hours of searching in the wind and rain, the posse fished a bloody shirt out of the Mississippi River. The warden identified the shirt as a recent issue, probably belonging to Walker.

Due to the late hour and the lack of a body, the posse was dismissed. Searchers included Sheriff Nate Houston, Bud Garvey, the State Police, and law enforcement officers from surrounding parishes. In all, more than 100 men on horseback spent over 12 hours searching the Tunica Hills and the banks of the Mississippi River. They were authorized to shoot the escapee on sight, but Walker was not found.

In addition to the picture of Bud and the dogs, Hines had taken some storm damage pictures on his way in to work. He developed those in his darkroom and they were now drying on the big drum machine in the back office. He'd engrave the plates later.

The rogue judge story had actually been fun to write. Following up with Neil Hebert about the appeal, had turned up some breaking news. Hines deliberately buried the lead. He started by referring to Stub Swetman as "the rogue judge," and recounting his misconduct at the trial. The picture helped drive the point home. Then he dropped the bombshell about the decision of the Judiciary Commission.

Attorney Neil Hebert, who defended young Arlan Walker, presented a mountain of evidence of previous and continuing misconduct by Swetman to the Judiciary Commission of Louisiana. Although they usually move very slowly, the extensive publicity by this and other newspapers throughout the state caused them to take swift action.

The Commission has a wide range of disciplinary actions available to them and they imposed as many as legally possible. First there will be a public reprimand, then a mandatory psychological examination, the results of which are to be made public. As its final act, the Commission issued an order to remove the judge from office.

EDITOR'S NOTE: It is a great tragedy that the news of the judge's removal came too late to save the life of Arlan Walker, who attempted to escape from Angola during the hurricane and is now presumed drowned.

One of the drawbacks of running a small-town newspaper and print shop was that the owner was the reporter, editor, typesetter, composer, proofreader, and truck driver. After writing the story, Hines had to set the type. He was reasonably proficient on the linotype machine, but by no means an expert. He knew some men who actually *composed* their stories in lead, but he preferred making his mistakes on the typewriter.

He set up the three stories and decided to leave making up the page until he'd had a couple of hours sleep. He'd finish the whole thing on Sunday and have the paper ready to deliver early Monday morning.

***

Most Waterproof residents spent Sunday cleaning up after the hurricane. Although storms can cause enormous damage, on the outer edges, the wind and rain can help to spruce up the

173

landscape. Dead leaves and branches are blown out of the trees and everything is washed clean. The rest of the housekeeping is left to the residents.

As Nate drove through town, he realized the storm had also done some rearranging. Lawn furniture, garbage cans, screens, children's toys, yard tools, barrels for burning leaves, had all taken flight. He scribbled some notes on a pad he kept in his pocket.

```
Hurricane

The screens are in the trees
Left there by angry winds
They hang and sway and rust.

The screens are in the trees
Sharp angles, out of place
With nature's plan.

The screens are in the trees
But not for long
The wind that put them there
Will claim them soon enough.
```

In an unprecedented move, Mr. Blacky opened his hardware store on the Sabbath and sold almost every chainsaw in stock. Never one to miss an opportunity, he held one back, which he gladly rented by the hour—for reasonable rates, of course. For anyone who might decide to take offense, he posted Luke 14:5 as justification for "pulling the ox out of the ditch on the Sabbath."

Bitsy figured what was good for Blacky was good enough for her, so she decided to open the Cafe too. Terry was already in the kitchen when Bitsy arrived. He had been cooking for her long enough to know that Sunday or no Sunday, she wouldn't miss the chance to feed hungry folks and to swap hurricane stories with her customers.

Bitsy hadn't seen Ruby before she left that morning, but the minute Nate walked in the door, she knew that something was different. She squinted to bring him into focus—no way she was going to wear glasses at her age—and then rocked back on her heels, crossed her arms under her ample bosom and yelled, "Oh my God, you did it!"

Nate crossed the room as quickly as he could, "Bitsy, keep your voice down and I don't know what you're talking about."

"You are by far the worst liar I've ever seen and I've seen some! You can't deny it, Sheriff. There's enough energy comin' off you to light up New Orleans." She laughed. "*Oh my God!* I *knew* it was gonna happen. It was just a matter of time. Well, how do you feel?"

"Exposed," Nate muttered under his breath and headed for the door.

"Yeah, I bet you were!"

He heard Bitsy still laughing as he let the screen door bang behind him. He wanted to be angry, but Bitsy was right. He felt ten feet tall and invincible. The world was a wonderful place and in spite of everything that was going on, he couldn't remember a time when he had felt better. To top it off, a hint of cooler weather was in the air.

Get a grip Houston, and wipe that silly grin off your face. You're supposed to represent law and order around here.

Apparently Luther decided it was a workday too. His new bike was parked outside and he was making coffee when Nate walked into the office. Nate kept his eyes down and tried not to look too pleased with himself.

Luther brought him his coffee and then sat down in the chair by his desk. "Sheriff, you look ... different. Kinda, you know, better. You heard any news from Angola?"

"No, nothing yet."

Just then, Carrie and Miss Laura burst in the door. Now that the storm was past, everyone seemed to be invigorated. "Hey, Dad. I thought maybe I'd walk around and see what damage the storm did, if that's OK with you. Luther, you wanna come?"

Before Nate could answer, Luther spoke up. "Yeah, I wanna go, but lemme ask y'all something. Don't you think the sheriff looks different this mornin'? You know, better."

Carrie passed it off, but when Miss Laura's eyes met Nate's, he knew she could read him like a book. "Oh my God ..."

"Don't you have some other place you need to be?" Nate asked her.

"Well," Miss Laura said innocently, "I might walk over to the café and chat with Bitsy."

"No! Somewhere else. Not with Bitsy."

"OK. Maybe I'll just stop by the library. Reckon Ruby's gonna open up today?"

Nate started to respond, but instead he headed out the door.

"What was that all about?" Carrie asked her grandmother.

"Oh nothing. It's just a little joke between your dad and me."

Carrie and Luther exchanged puzzled looks. They left to check things out and Miss Laura walked over to sit on her favorite bench in front of the courthouse.

CHAPTER TWENTY-THREE
(Waterproof, Chicago)

So, Nate had finally fallen in love and better yet, he'd done something about it. Miss Laura smiled. She knew what that kind of passion was like, although her present family would probably be shocked if they knew her story.

The night before she had taken a shoe box of old pictures down from the top shelf of her closet. She hadn't hidden it because there was no need. She was just Carrie's grandmother, no one suspected her of having secrets.

She now took one of the pictures out of her purse and looked at it closely. It was faded and ragged around the edges. It showed three young women, their hair tied back with big satin bows, their high-topped, button shoes just visible under their long white summer dresses. Her cousins Etoile and Edna. They were sixteen and eighteen. She was twenty, well past marrying age.

Perhaps to improve her prospects, Laura's parents sent her to spend that summer in St. Louis with her aunt and her two female cousins. What a shock. Laura found there were people who *did not* go to church every time the doors opened. Instead they went to teas and parties and dances and picnics. The girls went horseback riding and *did not* ride sidesaddle. They met young men their parents *did not* know. They cared as much about good times as they did about good manners. They sat with their legs crossed, played with their pearls, tapped their feet to ragtime music, and one of them even taught her how to whistle. It was glorious.

At a picnic in August, she met Matthew Lathum. He was twenty-two and visiting from Chicago. He was tall, with dark wavy hair, deep blue eyes, and a sophisticated air about him. Laura was smitten. He was a man who knew what he wanted and apparently he wanted her.

When he told Laura he was going back to Chicago after Labor Day and asked her to go with him, she readily agreed. Her aunt was against the whole idea, but Laura's mind was made up.

By way of a compromise, she and Matthew agreed to be married before they left. Laura wrote her parents, who came for the wedding. It was a simple ceremony and when it was over, Laura hugged her aunt, said goodbye to her cousins, kissed her parents, and never looked back.

She and Matthew left for Chicago on the Illinois Central at midnight. When they arrived, they rented an upstairs apartment in a townhouse on Prairie Avenue. Their landlady, Mrs. Harper, who stood ramrod straight in her old-fashioned black dresses, announced on their first meeting that she was related to the Fields of Marshall Field's Department Store. "Second cousin, twice removed, on his wife's side." It was a little hard to follow her conversation at first, because she spoke in capital letters. The Store, The Clock, The Fire, The Fair.

She was properly impressed when she learned that Matthew was working at The Store on State Street. "Although The Store is extremely elegant, those of us in the family all know it is the warehouse store on Franklin Street that makes all the money. Six times as much, actually. Sells bulk merchandise to little stores all over the country. *That's* what makes Mr. Field the richest man in Chicago."

The motto for Marshall Field's was, "Give the lady what she wants," and although Matthew was just a trainee, he vowed to devote himself to that end where Laura was concerned. Needless to say, that resulted in his being late for work on more than one occasion.

Matthew and Laura, like everyone else in town, got caught up in the excitement of the Chicago World's Fair celebrating the 400th anniversary of Columbus discovering the New World. The Fair was dedicated in 1892, but it didn't actually open until 1893. Along with thousands of other people, they paid their fifty cents and were on hand to see President Cleveland touch a golden lever and light up the fairgrounds.

Memories. Down at the bottom of the box holding the pictures, Laura had found a piece of petrified Juicy Fruit gum, introduced by Wrigley at The Fair. Some further looking also turned up a small stack of cards held together by a melted rubber band. The Quaker Mill Company had issued them as souvenirs. Eleven of the cards showed each of the steps from planting to distribution of Quaker Oats. The last card showed the American Cereal Company Pavilion.

So long ago. They had been so young and so happy. In another picture, Matthew's handsome face smiled up at her. He was standing under The Clock at Marshall Field's on the corner of Washington and State Streets.

Near the bottom of the shoebox she had found a formal portrait. It took her a minute to realize it must have been Mrs. Harper, although why she had the picture, Laura couldn't remember. She did remember the old lady proudly telling stories about The Store. One of her favorites was about how the employees were so loyal, that during The Fire (the Great Chicago Fire of 1871), they worked through the night to rescue expensive merchandise and store records, with the happy result that, although the building had burned to the ground, The Store was back in business in three weeks.

Mrs. Harper considered it her duty to visit The Store every Wednesday. "Mr. Harper worked there for thirty-five years, did I tell you that? Well, he always said Wednesday was a slow day, so I do my bit to add to the festivities by at least the power of one. And now that you are here, my dear, we shall be two. And as your family grows, which I'm sure it will in time, we shall become more." Laura could almost hear her voice.

Mrs. Harper's visits had a precise schedule and a prescribed route. She and Laura, dressed in their Sunday best, left the house at exactly 9:20 and arrived at The Store shortly after it opened. Marshall Field's was a five-story building. They always enjoyed the elegance of the main floor and then visited one floor each week for the rest of the month. At precisely 11:30, the ladies presented themselves at the Tea Room. The Store was one of the first to offer a restaurant for shoppers. They ate a light lunch and returned home for an afternoon nap. They rarely ever bought anything.

Living in Chicago was like living on another planet. Matthew and Laura rode the "El" that made the loop around the downtown area. They marveled at and bragged on the twenty-two-story Masonic Temple, a true skyscraper. They went to the Grand Opera House to hear Oscar Wilde and see Edwin Booth perform. They even saw Buffalo Bill's Wild West Show starring Annie Oakley.

Laura had been raised in a small town, with small town values, and with small town expectations. Never in her wildest dreams did she envision herself living such a fairytale existence. Her world was perfect. She was married to the love of her life, she lived in one of the world's most exciting cities, and they celebrated the beginning of a new century with the birth of their son, Matthew Junior.

By the time he was six months old, Mrs. Harper had incorporated young Matt into their weekly excursions to The Store. However, now she spent most of her time looking for a rattle, a soft toy, a cap, or some other trifle to buy for the baby.

One Wednesday, Laura went downstairs to tell Mrs. Harper she and Matt wouldn't be able to go shopping that day. Matthew had stayed home from work the previous day with a severe cold and now he was running a high temperature. The baby had been fretful all night and Laura was afraid he might be coming down with it too.

Mrs. Harper immediately insisted they call the doctor. When Laura hesitated, the older woman got angry. "Do not wait! This is how it started with my Henry. We thought it was just a cold, we had never heard of the Spanish influenza and had no idea what living through an epidemic would be like."

"Influenza?! No, I'm sure it couldn't be that. If there were anything like an epidemic going on, surely we would have heard about it."

"Laura, listen to me. Do not take chances. This sickness happens so very quickly. No one knows what causes it, no one knows where it starts, no one knows how to treat it. Old people, babies, people in their middle years, no one is immune. I am telling you, people get sick, and days later, they die."

Mrs. Harper called her doctor and within the hour he knocked on her door. She took him up to Laura's apartment. He took a look at both Matthew and the baby. "How long have they been sick?"

"My husband wasn't feeling well on Monday, but he went to work anyway. Then he stayed home yesterday because he had a fever. He and the baby took a nap in the afternoon and when they woke up the baby started coughing …"

The doctor looked worried. "It's not widespread like it was during the epidemic, but influenza has never completely gone away. There are pockets, isolated cases. As a matter of fact, this is the third one I've seen in this neighborhood in the last week. I'm afraid ..." his voice trailed off without finishing the thought. "I'll leave you with some sulfa drugs, they are sometimes helpful. Cut the tablet into quarters for the baby. Mash up a quarter and then mix half of that in some orange juice and see if you can get him to swallow it. The dosage for your husband is on the box. I'll come back tomorrow. Mrs. Harper, I suggest that you stay away."

"I nursed my husband, I'll stay to help."

And so in less time than Laura could ever have imagined, both Matthew and the baby were gone. Neither she nor Mrs. Harper showed any signs of getting sick.

Laura got in touch with Matthew's family and they arranged for their son and grandson to be buried in Blue Island where they lived. She stayed with his family several days, then came back into the city to pack up their things.

Miss Laura sighed. Memories. Even now, fifty years later, she had no idea how she managed to get through that awful time. She vaguely remembered buying a ticket on the Illinois Central line and heading south.

The train went from Chicago, to St. Louis, Memphis, Jackson, Mississippi, and on to New Orleans. She had thought of going back to her aunt's, but St. Louis came and went and she didn't get off the train. The same thing happened at Memphis. For no particular reason, when the train stopped at Jackson, she got off.

It was like stepping into another world. When she left Chicago, people were shivering in the cold. Jackson was basking in a Southern spring. The air smelled clean, azaleas and wisteria were in bloom everywhere and people were going about their normal lives.

Laura realized no one in Jackson knew her. No one would ask about Matt and Matthew.

I won't have to tell anyone they're dead. No one will ask. I can hold them safe in my heart and keep them alive just for me.

So she started over at thirty. She found a boarding house and moved in. She told the landlady she was recovering from a loss and let it go at that. Little by little she made friends and eventually, with the help of several of the other female tenants, she got a job at the local telephone company.

She was a lot older than the other girls she roomed with, but some of the women at the phone company were her age and raising families. That's what she would have been doing if things had turned out differently.

The girls she knew from the boarding house, went to dances on Friday nights and always asked Laura to go, but she declined. Music and dancing and fun brought back too many memories of Matthew and the gaping hole his death left in her life.

Sometimes when she was alone, she would open the shoebox and look at the pictures. In the beginning she could almost hear Matthew's voice. Now it seemed as if her life in Chicago had belonged to another person.

Normally, the boarding house didn't accept men, but when several of the girls moved out to get married, the landlady changed the rules and Wayne Webster moved in. He was an older man. He had a quiet, easy manner and he taught Laura to play Whiskey Poker which in polite circles was becoming the new rage, but they called it Gin Rummy.

They usually played cards on Friday evenings, but gradually they started going out to the picture show or maybe to a musical concert at the nearby park. Two years later he told her he was moving back to Louisiana to take care of a small family farm.

In his formal way, he explained that he had fallen in love with her and hoped that she would do him the honor of becoming his wife.

It was such a gentle, sweet proposal, Laura accepted. Shortly thereafter she found herself living in a small cottage in Waterproof. Several years went uneventfully by until one morning she realized she had been feeling queasy for some time. Her first thought was the flu. She didn't even consider the alternative. Much to her complete surprise and enormous relief, the doctor announced that she was pregnant.

Laura was a little afraid at first, but the pregnancy went well and Wayne was delighted at the prospect of having a family. He was so protective, she had to laugh. "I'm just having a baby, I'm not going to break. As I understand it, women have been doing this for centuries. Don't worry."

So shortly before her 40th birthday, Laura gave birth to a healthy, eight-pound baby girl. Eunice was a happy, inquisitive child, who easily wrapped her father around her little finger. She was fearless and once nearly burned the house down when she decided to melt old candles and Crayolas to make new candles.

It was not unusual to see her trailing along behind her father, content to be involved in whatever he was doing. All too soon, Eunice was grown. As everyone expected, she and Nate were married and a year later Carrie was born. Shortly afterwards, Wayne passed on.

Once she made the decision in Jackson all those years ago, Laura never told anyone about Matthew or her son. Now there was no one left alive who knew about her life in Chicago.

She smiled and slipped the picture back into her purse. Laura considered herself a very lucky woman. Even now, with all she had lost, she thought she was pretty lucky. She closed her eyes and relaxed in the warmth of the sun. For some reason, her thoughts turned to Ruby.

She was obviously good for Nate and Laura was glad to see them together. For a long time she had felt Nate needed a woman in his life. But something told her she might not be the only person with a secret life. Laura suspected Ruby had secrets she wasn't willing to share … at least not yet.

CHAPTER TWENTY-FOUR
(New Orleans)

New Orleans had been especially hard hit by what was officially being called the Fort Lauderdale Hurricane. It eventually extended from the Gulf Coast diagonally northwest across Louisiana and into parts of Texas. A front-page story in the *Times-Picayune* Sunday edition reported that the storm "killed at least 51 people in its path through the Bahamas, Florida, Mississippi, and Louisiana. The damage was initially reported as light, but the magnitude of the surge disaster in Metairie soon became apparent. Portions of Gentilly, Moisant Airport, and eastern New Orleans were all flooded. The water spilled over the nine-foot Orleans Parish Seawall and spread over nine square miles, leaving some of the streets in Metairie submerged waist deep in muddy water."

Tony hired someone with a pirogue to take him through the flooded streets to the Scapesi compound. He found the house standing in several feet of water and managed to get his mother and sisters into the boat. No one had seen the don since before the hurricane when he left the house "to take care of some business that couldn't wait."

To be on the safe side, Tony suggested his mother and the girls visit her family in New Jersey. That way they'd be out of harm's way and the don would know where to find them when he came back.

In the meantime, the don's people took precautions and went into hiding in various apartments around the city. Rumors were already circulating in the underworld. Some said the don was hiding out in Florida, some said he was waiting for the crime investigations to weaken the other families, then he'd come back to take over. Some said he was dead. If his father were dead, Tony knew it was only a matter of time before gang members started defecting to join rival factions.

Although he wasn't strictly part of the Scapesi organization, Tony left his apartment on Tulane Avenue and moved into a seedy little place on South Rampart Street. There was no telling what the other crime families might do now.

Assuming that his phone was tapped, Tony took the same precautions his father had always taken. He stopped by the bank to stock up on quarters. The rule was to always use pay phones. Each man memorized the number for the pay phone nearest the don's known hideouts. At a specific time each day, someone in his organization would be standing by to answer if a call came in. It was the only safe way to communicate.

CHAPTER TWENTY-FIVE
(Waterproof)

When Nate left his office, he had hardly gone half a block, before Hines pulled up in his old Ford and came running across the sidewalk. "Sheriff, I was putting the finishing touches on the paper just now and I decided to check with the warden at Angola to see if there was anything new. Nate, they found Arlan's boots down river and they've called off the search. They still haven't found his body, but the warden issued an official statement saying that Arlan is dead."

Nate was shocked by Hines' news. "Officially dead" had such a final, hopeless ring to it. Nate forced himself to analyze the significance of what he'd just heard. There was still no body, which meant they didn't really know any more than they had known before. The fact that they'd called off the search meant if Arlan was still alive—and Nate continued to believe he was—then he was no longer in danger of being shot.

So, the only real difference now was the official notice. Unfortunately, that was what most people would consider to be true. Nate knew he had to drive out to the Walker's and tell Martha what he knew before the paper came out and some misguided soul told her first.

Before he left, he went back into the office but no one was there. He called Ruby and asked her to relay the news to Luther,

Miss Laura, and Carrie. He made a special point of explaining that it was in the warden's best interest to declare Arlan dead, rather than having to admit he might have actually escaped. Without finding a body, no one could be certain of anything. "Arlan might have made it, we just have to hold on to that possibility for the moment." The more he repeated those words, the more hollow they sounded, even to him.

So, Nate drove to the Walker's while the rest of the town went about putting itself back together after the storm. Bud took the dog cages off the back of his truck and offered his services to pick up tree limbs and branches. Folks made piles of twigs and leaves, waiting for them to dry out enough to burn.

Carrie and Luther were still checking out the town for storm damage. After making a quick survey of the main street and the ferry landing, they decided to do some further exploring. "Let's go down to Thompson Creek and see how high the water got."

"OK," Luther said, "but we gotta be real careful of the quicksand down there. I heard Mr. Blacky and them talkin' about how a whole cow got stuck in there and the more she tried to get out, the deeper she sunk, 'till she was plumb gone.

"You know, Carrie, if you ever get stuck, you're supposed to just lie back, don't try to fight it. Once you lie back, then you move your legs real slow and little by little they'll float up to the top. When your legs get unstuck, you can kinda drag yourself over to the bank and get out. The most important thing is not to struggle. That's the worst thing you can do."

"What about what Mr. Blacky said?"

"Ah Carrie, you know better'n to believe what you hear from that bunch."

Armed with that useful survival information and a more-than-ample supply of teenage curiosity, they set out. Carrie and Luther were familiar with the lower part of Thompson Creek because in lieu of a proper swimming pool, the deeper parts were a favorite place for local kids to gather in the summer. Sometimes church groups came to swim—not the Baptists, of course, because they didn't believe in mixed bathing.

Sure enough, Thompson Creek was out of its banks and still moving fast. They followed the path of the creek, staying on the high side. Eventually the creek joined the Mississippi. Not too far from there, they came across a huge pine tree that had come down across the water. Logs, branches, and sticks were backed up behind it nearly six feet high. As they made their way down the bank to get a closer look, they stopped in their tracks.

"It looks like something's stuck in all that stuff," Luther whispered. "Maybe it's an animal. Let's get a limb and see if we can snag it loose."

Without hesitation, Carrie joined in. It took several tries, but finally they managed to hook on to the bundle and pull it toward shore. "Oh my Lord, it's a body, Luther! A human body."

They scrambled into the water and pulled the body up on the bank. "Turn it over, turn it over, maybe it's.... "

"Arlan!" Luther said. In total shock they stood looking down into the face of Arlan Walker, escaped convict.

"You think he's dead?" Carrie asked.

"Only one way to find out." Luther knelt beside the body and pressed his hand over the spot where he thought Arlan's heart should be.

"Try up around his neck," Carrie said as she knelt beside Luther. "That's what they do in the movies." They both started feeling around Arlan's neck until Luther said, "Wait! I think I feel something. Put your hand here, you feel that?"

It was faint, but it was definitely a pulse. "He's cold as ice; we need to warm him up." They started rubbing his arms and legs and nearly died of fright when Arlan moved. He rolled over and coughed up muddy water. His eyes were bloodshot and his teeth were chattering, but he was alive. They flung their arms around him and rocked back and forth laughing and crying at the same time. Arlan was as limp as Carrie's old Raggedy Ann doll.

Carrie took off her sweater and tried to put it on Arlan. Even though the boy had lost a lot of weight, it was still too small. "Put it on backward," Luther said. That way it covered Arlan's arms and part of his chest, but left his back bare. Luther took off his heavy jacket and they put that on to cover Arlan's back. Wearing both pieces of clothing, their leftover body heat started to warm him. Arlan tried to talk, but his throat was too raw to make a sound.

They sat in the wet leaves along the creek bank. Arlan didn't look anything like the big, strong farm boy they remembered. He was skin and bones. His face and arms were covered with scratches. His skin was brown from working in the sun, his hair was matted and dirty. It was clear they needed to get him to safety. He needed dry clothes and food. "Let's take him to the office," Luther said.

Carrie immediately shook her head. "No. We can't do that. If my dad knows he's alive, he might have to take him back. We've got to hide him and we can't tell anybody he's here."

The question was where to put him so he wouldn't be found and yet be close enough so they could take care of him. "I know," Luther finally said. "We can hide him in that old shed out back of our house. There's nothing in it but junk and nobody ever goes out there but me. We could get some quilts and take him some food and water ..."

Throughout this conversation, Arlan sat with his arms wrapped around himself trying to get warm. His head hurt, he was hungry, and although he was with his friends, he was scared. He could still be found and arrested. He had already decided that if he were caught, he'd fight. They would have to shoot him because there was no way he was going back to Angola.

The immediate problem was what to do with Arlan until it got dark. They couldn't leave him there and they couldn't walk through town with him. "We can at least go get some food," Carrie volunteered. "I think Miss Laura is still in town, but if she's home I'll say we want to go on a picnic. Everybody's so busy cleaning up from the hurricane, they're not going to pay any attention. Luther, you stay here with Arlan."

She got up and gave Arlan a quick hug. "I'm so glad we found you and that you're all right. Don't worry, everything's going to be OK." The boys watched her go.

Carrie had never moved so fast in her life. When she got home, the house was empty. She breathed a sigh of relief and started to gather up everything she could think of. She found a pair of her dad's khaki pants and a shirt hanging on the line in the back yard. She also grabbed some underwear and a pair of old rubber boots.

Then she went into the kitchen. She found a big old picnic basket and stuffed in half a pan of cornbread, a Mason jar of canned tomatoes, some Velveeta cheese, a jar of peanut butter, and a quart of milk. She was careful to wrap the glass jars in the clothes and pack them so they wouldn't break. Then she grabbed a quilt from on top of the chifforobe and walked as fast as she could back through town, praying that nobody would notice her. As soon as she was able, she cut through the woods and started to run holding the basket tightly to her chest.

When she got back to the boys, Arlan was sitting up. Luther had removed the leaves from a small pool so Arlan could get a drink. It might not have been the cleanest water in the world, but they'd been swallowing water from Thompson Creek all their lives with no ill effects.

Carrie unpacked the picnic basket and turned her back so Arlan could take off his wet clothes. When he was dressed, she put the quilt around his shoulders and Luther stuffed the dirty clothes in the basket so no one would find them.

Arlan grabbed the milk and drank half of it at one time. Then he dug his fingers into the peanut butter and ate that with a handful of cornbread and more milk. Carrie and Luther watched in shock. It was scary to see somebody eat like that. Arlan tried to say thank you, but all he managed was a hoarse whisper.

His work boots were long gone and his feet were badly swollen. The rubber boots Carrie found were made to be worn over shoes, so they were big enough for Arlan to wear without too much pain. They had to wait until it started to get dark, and then Luther led the way. Arlan followed and Carrie brought up the rear.

They very carefully stepped in Luther's tracks so they left only one set of footprints. The going was slow, but they made it to the shed behind the Castles' house. It was getting late and, as much as she hated to leave, Carrie had to go home for supper. She didn't want Nana to worry and start asking questions.

Once she left, Luther piled up a bunch of burlap bags to make a soft bed. With food in his stomach and the quilt wrapped around him, Arlan immediately fell asleep. Luther took the prison pants, put them in the barrel where he usually burned leaves, and set them on fire. Then he went into the house.

When Carrie got home, Nana and her dad seemed to be enjoying some kind of grownup joke, because when she walked into the kitchen, they suddenly stopped talking. Carrie made a beeline for the bathroom to clean up before they noticed the mud all over her clothes.

During supper, Miss Laura mentioned there were some things missing from the kitchen. "Did you come by here this afternoon?"

Carrie swallowed hard. "Yes Ma'am. Luther and I decided to have a picnic, so I packed up some things."

"Did you find anything along the creek?"

Carrie's head jerked around to her father. "The creek?" She didn't remember telling him they were going to the creek. "It was still running a lot faster than usual and the water had come almost all the way up the bank. Some trees had fallen over," she said breathlessly.

"They lost some trees in town too. Miss Nell lost a huge oak in her back yard. She was lucky it didn't hit her house. By the way, did you happen to notice anything going on in our back yard? I'm sure I left some work clothes hanging on the line and now they're gone."

"Maybe the storm blew them away," Carrie said. She was ashamed of herself for lying, especially to Nana, but she knew she would probably have to tell a lot more lies if she and Luther expected to keep Arlan safe.

CHAPTER TWENTY-SIX
(Waterproof)

Since no one ever expected Luther to know anything, he had never had the occasion to lie, so he wasn't exactly sure how to go about it. Should he make up a story beforehand, or just wait and try to think up something on the spur of the moment? The Hardy Boys always figured out who was lying and that's how they solved the mysteries. Luther didn't want that to happen to him. He finally decided one big lie was safer than sitting in the office all day trying to come up with lots of little lies. Once he decided that, he called the sheriff and told him he was feeling really bad and asked for the day off.

Luther's main concern now had to be Arlan. He made sure the coast was clear and went to see how his friend was doing. Arlan was still asleep, so he left him alone and went in search of food. There were never many leftovers in the Castle household, but Luther managed to find some cold biscuits and a jar of crystallized honey. He filled a gallon jug with water and left it inside the shed.

Luther really wanted to find out how Arlan had ended up on Thompson Creek, but his mamma always said sleep was the best medicine, so he stayed away from the shed. Since he couldn't talk to Arlan and he couldn't go to work, he didn't know what to do with himself.

He needed to think, so he climbed up into the ancient magnolia tree in the back yard. It was his favorite place. Not only were magnolias the best for climbing, they were good for hiding too. Pine trees had needles, live oak leaves grew in patches, like mange on a hound dog. Magnolia leaves were big, stayed green all year round, and were thick on the outside of the tree, which made the branches near the trunk almost invisible.

Luther found a comfortable place to straddle a sturdy branch and leaned his back against the trunk. He always thought better up high.

He knew hiding Arlan was wrong. But turning him in was wrong too. Lying to the sheriff was wrong. But telling him the truth might also be wrong. He wasn't sure about taking food from his house. That was probably another wrong, but since it was for a good cause, maybe it didn't count. Usually Luther saw things in a straight line, but now everything was all mixed up and that was giving him a terrible headache.

Luther was back on the ground in time to meet Carrie when she came by after school. Arlan was awake by then and had eaten almost all the food and drunk about half of the water. His voice was raspy, but at least he was able to talk and that's when they heard the story of his escape.

He reminded them about the guard who couldn't count and how he used pebbles to keep track of inmates. "I knew if there was one pebble missing, he wouldn't realize anyone was gone and I'd be safe unless they turned everybody out to do a general headcount. I got lucky and they musta put it off 'till the next morning."

Since Arlan had worked on the levee before, he knew the lay of the land when he was sent to work there during the storm. "It was real dark, it was raining to beat sixty, and we were all covered with mud. I thought if I could get to the barge, maybe I could hide there. I just needed to get away from the work gang. I didn't really have much more of a plan at that point.

"Anyway, it was pretty easy to slide down the muddy bank and then I waded into the river holding on to a rope on the side of the barge. The river was moving so fast, it nearly swept me away. I kept hold of the rope and I found this kind of sill around the outside of the barge so I managed to wedge myself up onto it. By that time, I had worked my way around to the back, you know, the river side, so nobody could see me."

"I don't understand how getting to the barge was going to help you escape. Nobody was going to take the barge out in the middle of a hurricane." Carrie looked puzzled.

"Like I said, I didn't exactly have a plan. I just knew I had to get away from the guards while I had the chance. I was soaking wet and getting cold and the overhang on the barge gave me a little protection. I guess I fell asleep and some time later I heard this awful crash. It jarred me awake and then the barge jerked loose and the next thing I knew, it was out in the middle of the river and movin' real fast.

"I've never been so scared in my life. I wrapped the rope around me and managed to find a handhold and I just hung on for dear life. I saw another barge real close by and I figured it must have hit the one I was on. I don't know how long I was out there, it seemed like forever. I tried to watch along the bank to see if I recognized anything, but it was raining too hard to see.

"Then the barge in front of me hit something and the one I was on slammed into the side of the first one. Somehow my barge got turned around, and headed toward the bank. When it stopped, I pulled myself up on top of the deck and ran across the tarp that was covering whatever it was hauling.

Anyway, when I got to the side close to the bank, I jumped as far as I could. I landed in the water and got caught up in a pile of brush. That's when I lost my shirt and I got scratched up pretty bad, but I made it out of the water."

Carrie and Luther sat motionless as Arlan went on to describe working his way slowly along the river's edge, holding on to anything to keep from sliding back into the water.

"At one point I saw water coming in from a side stream. I knew it had to be a creek from somewhere, so it wouldn't be as fast or as deep as the river. Anyway, I took it. I thought maybe I'd see something that looked familiar, but I never did. And that's where you found me."

For a moment, nobody spoke. "Wow!" Luther said.

"Yeah, I can't believe you made it," said Carrie. "But you did. You got to Thompson Creek. You made it home!"

Arlan looked dubious. "Well, I made it this far, but now what? Are they still looking for me?"

Carrie and Luther exchanged glances. "The posse that the sheriff was riding with found your bloody shirt and they found your work shoes. The warden up at Angola thinks you drowned. That's what it said in the paper."

"The sheriff was up there with a posse?"

"Oh yeah," Luther answered. "They called in sheriffs from all the parishes around here and the state police, and volunteers. Sheriff Houston said there were nearly a hundred men and dogs lookin' for you. He was there when they found the smashed up dock where the barge broke loose. Nobody paid much attention since it didn't belong to Angola."

The teenagers sat still for a while, then Arlan looked up suddenly. "What about my mamma? And Possum and the kids? Do they know what happened? Do they all think I'm dead too?"

Carrie explained that her dad had gone out to talk to Arlan's family. Everything seemed to hinge on the fact that no one had found a body. "Dad's been saying all along that without a body there's no way to be sure exactly what happened. We've all been holding out hope that somehow you made it and that you'd turn up alive."

Arlan stood up abruptly. "I've got to go see my mamma and tell her I'm not dead."

Carrie and Luther both pulled him back down. "You can't do that. You can't tell anybody you're alive and neither can we. If anybody knows, they might arrest you and take you back to Angola."

"They might catch me, but I'm not going back!"

That brought the conversation to a halt. It was obvious Arlan couldn't stay in the shack forever and he couldn't go home. Little by little, the weight of what they had done began to sink in. Saving Arlan was the right thing to do, they knew that. But now, no matter what they decided, the consequences were likely to get them all in more trouble.

"We've got to tell the sheriff," Luther said.

"No!" Arlan and Carrie both looked horrified. "If my dad knows, he might have to turn Arlan in. He might not have a choice. It's the law."

"The law didn't work out so good for me the first time. I'm not gonna take a chance on that again," Arlan said.

"Well, you can't run away," Luther pointed out. "You can't leave and let your mamma go on thinkin' you're dead forever. Besides, where would you go? How would you get there? What would you do for money?"

"Oh Luther, for Pete's sake, shut up. We don't need any more questions, what we need are answers," Carrie said.

Luther stood his ground. "I'm telling you, we've gotta tell the sheriff. He's not just the law, he's your daddy, he's my boss, and he's Arlan's friend. We gotta trust him. I'm tellin' you, it's the right thing to do."

CHAPTER TWENTY-SEVEN
(New Orleans)

Tony had always feared his father. He couldn't wait to be out from under the old man's thumb. But now that there was a chance his father was gone, he realized living in a world without the don's protection was a very dangerous place. The other families would be looking to move in on the Scapesi's territory and that made him a liability. Actually, he was more like a piece of trash getting in their way.

Sitting in his depressing room on Rampart Street, Tony tried to weigh his options. He could stay out of sight for a while, but sooner or later, he had to take care of that woman. Like the don always said, loose ends got people in trouble. So, the first order of business was to get rid of her and that might not be all bad. Once he'd eliminated her, he would let the rumor get around that he'd killed a man and he'd gotten rid of the witness. More to the point, he'd done it without the don's help.

The trick was in the timing. Metairie might be flooded, but that really didn't mean anything. Tony had seen his father survive worse things than a Category Four hurricane. The best thing to do was to be careful. Go slow. Lay low. Stay out of trouble. That was going to be the hardest part. He was isolated. He couldn't visit any of his usual haunts, he couldn't call friends. He'd never been part of his father's crew, so they weren't going to take him in. Moreover, he suspected there were government agents looking to question anyone connected with Don Scapesi and the New Orleans Mafia.

Get a grip, Scapesi. So you're on your own, you can handle that. How many times have you heard the old man say the hardest part of hiding out is patience? You just need to make a plan. Get some food, get some booze, find some woman to take your mind off things for a while. Be a man.

Tony decided he needed to wait a week, maybe two, to see how things settled out. Then he'd make his move. After all, the witness wasn't going anywhere. Fate had dumped her right in his lap and the best part was, she didn't have any idea he knew where she lived. He breathed easier. He'd wait and when the time was right, he'd be ready.

CHAPTER TWENTY-EIGHT
(Waterproof)

Although the town had been outraged by Arlan Walker's trial and relished the fact that Judge Swetman had gotten his comeuppance, the news that Arlan had drowned trying to escape from Angola wasn't too surprising. It was a well-known fact that nobody ever escaped from Angola.

Once the *Waterproof Chronicle* published the official version of Arlan's death, most people took that as gospel and moved on to other things. The adults who had been involved in Arlan's fate from the beginning still held on to the slim hope that somehow he had survived.

Carrie and Luther were the only ones who knew the truth and their main concern was keeping the secret from their elders at all costs. They worked out a routine to visit and take food to Arlan every day. They had discussed taking him his school books, but decided that might be a little too risky.

While the kids were worrying about Arlan, Bitsy was consumed with curiosity about things going on right under her nose. She couldn't help herself. She loved excitement. Having two monumental events coming so close together was almost more than she could handle.

They had all survived the hurricane *and* Nate had finally made his move. Bitsy congratulated herself for playing a major role in bringing that about. However, if she had expected to hear all the juicy details from Ruby, she should have known better. Lord knows, she had given Ruby every opportunity to share. Her invitation to "tell me all about it" didn't get anything but a sly—and satisfied—smile. As usual, Ruby wasn't talking.

Luther and Carrie weren't talking either. They had agreed that telling the sheriff about Arlan was the right thing to do, but they realized that just because something was *right* didn't make it easy.

They kept putting it off because of the nagging fear that the adults might not understand and Arlan might end up back in Angola. They knew what that meant and neither of them was willing to take a chance. In addition, they could only assume that when Arlan said he would never go back, he meant it.

As the days went by, they realized harboring a fugitive was not only illegal, it was hard work. Carrie volunteered to take food every day because she knew Luther wouldn't be able to manage that. She just took small portions from home because she was afraid Nana might realize things were missing. Although she had initially thought it was a bad idea, Carrie gave in and took Arlan a couple of books she checked out of the library.

For his part, Luther was responsible for everything else. He and Arlan loosened some boards facing the woods so Arlan could get out to go to the bathroom without being seen from the house. Luther also took him an old Sears and Roebuck catalogue. In his mother's rag bag, Luther found a bath rag and an old towel that nobody would miss. He added a bar of Lava soap and hauled in a couple of buckets of water every day.

They managed to keep things going for a while and then one afternoon after school when Carrie came by, Arlan was lying all balled up and said his stomach hurt. Carrie felt his forehead like

Nana always did when she said she was sick. Arlan was burning up. That did it. It was time to ask for help.

Carrie went straight to the sheriff's office. Luther was there, but she didn't see her dad. "Is my dad around somewhere?"

"No, he said he was going over to the library. What's the matter?"

"Arlan's sick."

Rather than picking up the phone—which would have been the logical thing to do—they took off for the library. They burst through the door just as Nate and Ruby stepped away from one another. "Dad, you gotta come quick."

"What's the matter? Is it Miss Laura?"

Before she realized what she was saying, Carrie blurted out, "No, it's Arlan. He's sick."

"What!?"

Carrie ran to her father and threw her arms around his waist. "I'm so sorry, Dad. I didn't mean to lie to you. Please don't send Arlan back to Angola. He's over at the Castles' and he's sick. We gotta go quick."

The urgency in Carrie's voice made it clear this was a time for action. Nate's questions—and there were plenty of them—would have to come later. They all piled into the patrol car and on the way to the Castles' place, Luther told Nate and Ruby the whole story. When they got there, Luther went in to tell his mother they were just picking up some stuff from the shed to take back to Mr. Blacky. He didn't want her to barge in by accident.

Ruby, who had nursed her brothers through every non-fatal illness kids were prone to, took over. It looked like a case of food poisoning, not surprising considering what Arlan had been eating lately. Old mayonnaise was probably the culprit.

They managed to get Arlan as far as the car. Nate, Carrie, and Luther got in the front seat. Ruby sat in the back with

Arlan's head in her lap. Without thinking, Nate headed for home. When they got there and helped Arlan out of the car, he glanced at Miss Laura. If she were shocked to see Arlan, she didn't let on.

To say Arlan was a mess was an understatement. He stank to high heaven. He hadn't had a proper bath in weeks. Miss Laura suspected he had diarrhea and judging from the front of his shirt, he had been throwing up. He looked a little green around the gills, but now there was nothing left but dry heaves. She got him to drink a cup of strong black tea with lemon and no sugar, her tried-and-true remedy for diarrhea. Then she sent him in to take a bath.

"Leave your clothes in the hall. All of them." She scooped them up with the end of a broom handle and held them at arm's length. "Phew! Those look suspiciously like the work clothes that went missing from the clothesline in the back yard. Luther, would you please take these out and burn them?"

She gave Carrie a we'll-talk-about-this-later look. "Right now, Arlan's gonna need something clean to wear. Carrie, go get another set of your dad's khaki work clothes. And on your way by the bathroom, hand Arlan that tube of Prell shampoo."

Sometime later, Arlan came out of the bathroom, barefoot. They had shaved his head at Angola and his hair was growing back in all directions. He had made a valiant effort to slick it down with Brylcream. He was grinning from ear to ear.

The way Nate's clothes hung on him, he looked like one of Carrie's paper dolls. He wasn't as tall as Nate, so he'd rolled up his pant legs. The real problem was that he'd lost so much weight, he was having a hard time keeping the pants up.

"You had better sit down now before you lose those pants altogether," Miss Laura said, trying not to laugh. "Do you feel like you could keep a little something on your stomach?" Arlan nodded. "Fine. Here, drink this. It's kettle tea, just a little honey, milk, and hot water. I fixed you some buttered toast. It'll help settle your stomach. Now!" she said folding her arms and looking around the room, "*Somebody* better tell me what's going on."

They all sat at the kitchen table and first one and then the other started to tell parts of the story. Nobody knew all the details, so there was a lot of telling and asking and retelling until it was all laid out from Arlan's first day at Angola to his last hours in the shed. By that time, several hours had passed and it was nearly suppertime. "Lord-a-mercy, that was quite a story," Miss Laura said. "It's hard to believe you actually survived all that and yet here you are." She reached over and patted his knee.

Skin and bones, I swear, that boy is nothing but skin and bones, bless his heart.

"Arlan, how's your stomach feeling?" Miss Laura asked.

"Better, Miss Laura."

"You reckon you could eat a little chicken and dumplings? Not much else to offer. Luther, you stay too. Go call your mamma so she knows where you are."

When they sat down to eat, the "not much else" had turned into the Biblical loaves and fishes, enough to feed a multitude. In addition to the chicken and dumplings, Miss Laura had found some pickled beets, some leftover macaroni and cheese, carrot and raisin salad, cornbread, and half a blackberry cobbler. Apparently whatever had caused Arlan's discomfort was gone. He tried his best to take only small portions, but it was by far the best food he had eaten in months and he was ravenous.

After a good meal, conversation usually flowed easily but instead, nobody knew what to say. It was Luther who finally said what they were all thinking. "What are we gonna do about Arlan?"

"Dad, you aren't going to send him back to Angola, are you? You just can't do that." Everyone turned their attention to Nate.

Nate shook his head but took his time before answering. "No. I can't do that. But he can't stay here." Hurriedly he corrected himself. "I mean he can stay here at the house for a while, but he can't stay in Waterproof permanently. Somebody would be sure to see him and if word got out ... Well, we don't want to take a chance on that happening.

"Still, we can't let his mother and Possum keep on thinking he's dead. On the other hand, if his whole family knows the truth, it's just a matter of time before one of the kids lets something slip. It's asking too much to expect them to keep that big a secret. We have to make sure the wrong people don't find out."

Again it was Luther who spoke the obvious. "If you're worried about the kids, then don't tell 'em. I know that may sound kinda mean, but I think we better just let his mamma know what's going on. She'll keep his secret sure enough."

They spent another hour or more trying to come up with some place for Arlan to live. Miss Laura finally said, "I don't think we can do this on our own. We need to get your mamma involved, Arlan. She has to have a say in this."

Nate nodded. "You're right. Miss Laura, why don't you take the car and go pick her up? If somebody sees me out there, they might ask questions. Nobody will think twice if you go. I know you'll figure out some way to tell Martha about Arlan, kind of prepare her so it's not such a shock when she walks in and sees him."

"I'd like to go along," Ruby said. Miss Laura happily agreed and the women left.

Luther took charge. "Since Miss Laura fixed us such a nice supper, let's do her a good turn and clean up the kitchen before she gets back." Since Nate lived with two women, he escaped the daily dishwashing chores. The boys, however, were both used to pitching in to help their mothers.

In no time, they had a system going. Arlan ran the plates under cold water, then put them into a sink full of hot soapy water. Luther washed, stacked them on the drain board, and rinsed them with boiling water heated on the stove. Nate dried and put them away while Arlan cleaned up the stove and wiped off the table. They had just finished when Arlan heard the car in the driveway. Instinctively he smoothed down his hair. "Do I look OK?"

Nate hardly had time to assure him he looked fine before Martha Walker pushed open the back door, ran across the room, and threw her arms around her son. They hugged and kissed and laughed and cried and even when everyone went to sit in the living room, she couldn't keep from touching him. It was as if he might disappear if she didn't hold on to him.

Arlan had to go through the whole story again, but for his mother's sake, he left out the bad parts. Finally they got around to talking about the problem at hand. What to do now.

Martha was normally a shy woman, but when it came to her son, she wasn't about to let anybody else decide what was to become of him. "My brother, Anderson, lives in Port Arthur. You remember him, Arlan? Him and his family come to visit once. His oldest, Dean, is about your age. Port Arthur's not too far away, so we could still visit from time to time. Important thing is, it's in Texas. Getting Arlan out of the state would be a good thing, wouldn't it, Sheriff?"

"It couldn't hurt."

It took some time to work out the details, but in the end, it was decided that Martha would call her brother to make sure he was willing to have Arlan come live with him. He was. To cover their tracks, they planned to drive to Baton Rouge and put Arlan on a Greyhound bus there. In the meantime, he would stay at the sheriff's house.

Knowing that Martha wanted to spend as much time as possible with Arlan before he left, Miss Laura came up with a scheme. "You tell your kids that you're gonna be working here for the rest of the week helping me with some canning. Fact is, I want to put up some sauerkraut and I could use some help. Then on Saturday, we'll all take a trip down to Baton Rouge."

They stayed up talking for a while and then Nate took everyone home. Luther first, then Martha, and finally Ruby. When he parked in Bitsy's driveway, they sat for a while. After all the talking that had gone on, it was relaxing to have a few moments of peace and quiet. "I know you're going to want to tell Bitsy, but you can't do that. She's a good friend, but Bitsy couldn't keep a secret if her life depended on it. In this case, it's Arlan's life I'm worried about."

"Yes, keeping secrets can be hard."

"You know, you don't ever need to keep a secret from me, Ruby. Not about anything. I want you to know everything about me and I want to know everything about you."

Ruby kissed him and went into the house.

You have no idea how much I want that to be true, Nate Houston. You have no idea at all.

CHAPTER TWENTY-NINE
(Waterproof)

The following week, Nate picked Martha up each morning and brought her to his house where she and Miss Laura made sauerkraut. They cut off the tough outer cabbage leaves and saved them. Then they quartered the heads, removed the core, and chopped the cabbage into narrow strips. That done, they put layers of cabbage in each of two large crocks and sprinkled them with salt. They repeated the process layer upon layer until the crocks were almost full.

Finally they covered the salted cabbage with the outer leaves and weighted the whole thing down with bricks. It would take a couple of days, but once the fermentation started, Miss Laura would remove the bricks and skim off the scum every day. It was all she could do to finish the job before Carrie got her fingers in the crock to eat the salty cabbage.

Arlan and his mother weren't big talkers. It seemed to be enough for them to be in the same room together. It was clear they had lots of experience working together in the kitchen. He saw what needed to be done and did it without being asked.

Saturday morning early, Nate, Carrie, Miss Laura, Martha, Arlan, and Luther piled into the car and headed to Baton Rouge. Nate drove, of course, and Carrie sat in the middle with Miss Laura by the window. Martha sat in the back seat with Arlan on one side and Luther on the other. They put Arlan's small suitcase in the trunk along with the shoebox Miss Laura had packed with food.

Nate remembered the last time he had been in the car with Arlan headed to Angola. Then he had been doing the right thing, but it had turned out very wrong. Now he was doing the wrong thing and he hoped to God it was going to turn out to be right.

An hour later, they pulled into the bus station on Florida Boulevard in downtown Baton Rouge. They parked in a lot adjacent to the station. Nate went in to check the schedule and discovered they had enough time to eat at Woolworth's lunch counter before Arlan's bus left. "I ain't never been in a bus station before, never ate at no lunch counter either," Martha said with a trace of both sorrow and wonder in her voice.

"Me neither," said Arlan. "I'm sad to be leaving home, Mamma, but I'm kinda excited too. Is Uncle Anderson gonna be there to meet me? What'll I do if he's not? Reckon he'll know who I am? Tell me again what he looks like."

Nate assured Arlan everything was taken care of. He handed the boy an envelope, "Now here's your ticket. Don't lose it. And here's some money so you can get something to eat when the bus makes a rest stop. The driver will tell you how much time you have. Just keep your eye on him and when he gets up to leave, you follow him. Make sure to get back on the bus on time 'cause you don't want to get left."

"Miss Laura's packed me a lunch, Sheriff. I don't need any money."

"You keep it. You don't ever want to travel without at least a couple of dollars in your pocket. By the way, just in case you need it, your uncle's name and address and phone number are on the back of the ticket envelope." Nate hesitated a minute, trying to decide whether to hug Arlan or not. Instead, he shook his hand. "Don't worry, Son, you'll be fine."

"I put in a piece of paper with all our addresses on it so you can write to each one of us, not just send one letter to my dad's office," Carrie said. "And when you write to us, don't forget to give us your address so we can all write back."

Five of the big silver Greyhound buses were lined up ready to depart. Each one was taking on passengers at the front of the coach and belching out black exhaust at the back. The air under the shelter was thick with fumes that made it hard to breathe.

Nate looked at the passengers. He saw one young girl traveling alone with a tag pinned to her thin jacket. She looked cold. An old couple stood holding hands. A man in a business suit was standing next to an old farmer wearing overalls. Nate wondered what secrets each of them carried. Were they running away from something or running to a new adventure? In a way, he envied them.

The bus driver took Arlan's suitcase and stowed it in the luggage compartment at the side of the bus. Then he took his ticket. It was time. Martha hugged her son once more. She had tears in her eyes, but she wasn't crying. Arlan was holding the shoebox and Luther handed him a shopping bag just as he stepped on the bus. "Books from Miss Ruby," he said.

The driver called all aboard, took his seat behind the big steering wheel, and closed the heavy door. The loud hiss from the air brakes sounded like the bus relaxing after holding its breath for a long time. They all stood and watched as the Greyhound pulled out of the station. Arlan was gone and slowly the five of them got back in the car and headed for home.

***

With no more big news stories, Hines was back to writing about high school football games, spelling bees, and who had guests visiting from out of town. The only thing in the next two weeks that broke the tedium was the delivery of a new Coca

Cola machine at the bus station. For as long as anyone could remember, a boxy old red cooler sat in the corner. It stood about waist high, opened from the top, and the Co'Cola bottles hung by their necks from a series of metal rods.

A nickel dropped into the coin slot activated a breaker bar, which slid back to allow the customer to slide an icy cold bottle off the rack. Sometimes the system didn't work quite right, so Leon Harvey left a screwdriver and a hammer on a shelf nearby. Everyone old enough to buy a Coke knew where to place the end of the screwdriver and how to hit it with the hammer to free up the breaker bar. It was a nuisance, but folks learned to adapt.

Leon's best customer was Junior Leggett. He was the town handyman. He worked on everything from tractors to cars to houses to gardens. Junior wore size fourteen work shoes and moved slowly, partly because he was never in a hurry and partly because he weighed nearly 300 pounds.

He always wore Oshkosh overalls with a long-sleeved undershirt in winter and a short-sleeved T-shirt in summer. It was a well-known fact that Junior drank more Co'Colas than anybody else in West Feliciana Parish.

When the Coca-Cola Company came out with a new dispenser, Leon decided to spruce up the bus station and have one installed. It was a beauty. It stood upright, had a shiny red finish and it was all electrified. No more reaching in to serve yourself. The new machine took your nickel, made some internal grinding noises, and spit the bottle into a compartment at the bottom of the machine where the customer could easily retrieve it. However, since it *was* a machine, naturally sometimes it didn't work.

But now, rather than customers being able to take care of the problem themselves, Leon had to come over with a key, open the door, and get the conveyer belt moving again. Kids lucky enough to be around when that happened were in for a treat.

Instead of bottles hanging on metal bars like in the old cooler, the inside of this new Coke dispenser had a series of channels filled with bottles lying on their sides, with the caps facing outward. The mechanism zig-zagged back and forth inside the machine and when it was activated, all the bottles moved down the line to the next free space and the last one was deposited into the space at the bottom of the machine.

The new apparatus was a big success and it did increase Leon's business, but not for the reason he had anticipated. It turned out that now he had two games of chance available, the slot machine and the Coke machine. Each one took customers' nickels and each one paid off, occasionally.

In the case of the Coke machine, Leon wasn't always available to open the door when it didn't work. So by trial and error, customers discovered that hitting the machine on a spot about four inches to the left of the coin slot usually got things moving again.

The one person the trick didn't work for was Junior Leggett. From the first day Junior dropped a nickel into that machine, the contraption seemed to take a personal dislike to him and never, ever gave him a Coke. Junior tapped it, hit it, and threatened to open it up and rip its insides out, but the machine stood firm.

No more Cokes for Junior unless he found Leon and asked him to open up the machine. The problem was that Junior didn't like having to ask for help. He was used to fixing things on his own. So it became a daily battle. Man vs. machine. Junior often went away empty-handed, while the machine proudly wore the dents from Junior's brogans.

Like most small towns, Waterproof didn't have much public entertainment other than the picture show. It was only a matter of time before folks caught on to the heavyweight contest going on at the bus station. People saw Junior headed in that direction and by the time he dropped his nickel into the slot, a crowd had gathered to watch and cheer him on. There were rumors of bets being placed, but Leon denied all knowledge of that.

Sunday afternoon Nate and Carrie stopped by the bus station to pick up the *Times-Picayune* because it had the best funny papers. They were about to leave when Junior walked in, strode over to the Coke machine and dropped in his nickel. Nothing happened.

"Dad, Dad! Watch. Mr. Leggett's gonna fight the Coke machine. Look!"

But Junior didn't do anything. He simply walked out to his pickup and for a minute Carrie thought he was going to leave. Then she turned around and saw Junior walk back in carrying a double-barreled shotgun. This attracted attention. The few folks in the bus station took cover and those outside gathered to get a better view of the action.

Carrie was sure she felt the floor vibrate as Junior lumbered over to the Coke machine and pointed the gun at its heart. "Hand it over, you worthless, cheatin' pile of junk."

Unfortunately, the Coke machine ignored Junior just once too often and he let go with both barrels and blew the machine wide open. Coke bottles fell on the floor and rolled away in all directions. Without a moment's hesitation, Junior reached into the machine, gathered up four Co'Colas, put one in each overall pocket and left the bus station.

There was a moment of stunned silence, then the crowd broke into applause. "It's about time somebody taught that damn machine a lesson. Listen, Leon, when you dispose of the body, reckon you could get our old machine back?" The crowd laughed and helped themselves to the Cokes rolling around the station.

Leon sputtered, "Sheriff, what're you gonna do about this? Junior Leggett is crazy as a loon. He's a menace. You seen what happened. You gotta do something. Arrest him."

"What do you want me to charge him with, Leon? Coke machine murder?"

That was enough to give Hines an idea for a front-page story. After all the serious news in the past months, he decided to have some fun and entertain his readers at the same time. He got his camera and took pictures of the victim from every angle.

The crowd was eager to get in on the fun. This was shaping up to be a better show than they had expected. "Sheriff, we all seen it happen and I think Junior was just takin' care of business. After all, that machine provoked him, we all know that." General agreement. Hines treated the situation with great seriousness and took formal statements from the witnesses.

"Hey, Hines, put this in the paper," one bystander called out. "I think maybe Junior did the whole town a favor. How many of y'all lost nickels to that machine?" Every hand in the room shot up. "See there, maybe you oughta start a campaign to give ole Junior a medal. Have a ceremony and everything. That'd make a great story."

"Now wait just a minute," Leon said. "I want you to put my side of this in there too. I think it's a crime that the sheriff is probably gonna let Junior go free. I tell you there is no justice in this town. Now you be sure to put this in there too, Hines. The next election, maybe we'll find ourselves a sheriff who'll take some real action."

Nate had seen enough action and he wasn't the least bit afraid that someone would run against him. For good or bad, he knew nobody else wanted the job. Truth be told, he was relieved not to have to deal with anything more serious that an assault on a Coke machine that clearly had it coming.

CHAPTER THIRTY
(New Orleans)

Metairie had been flooded for over a month. In an effort to get rid of the standing water, breaches were made in the levee to drain the water back into Lake Pontchartrain and pumps had been working for weeks to dry out the low-lying areas.

In all, 5,000 homes were flooded and the death toll was officially set at fifty-one. No one had seen or heard from the don. However, since each Mafia family was autonomous, the Scapesi organization had a system in place to take care of such emergencies.

Tony had fantasies about becoming the head of the family, but he knew in reality that wasn't going to happen. The don earned his place as the boss. Following a time-honored tradition, Giuseppe Scapesi appointed an underboss to keep the capos, the managers, in line and to take over temporarily if he was ever imprisoned or otherwise missing. That's where the real power now lay. It was the underboss's job to keep the organization running smoothly while the don was away. It was not his job to look out for Tony.

The only person Tony felt he might be able to turn to for help was the *Consigliere*, his father's advisor. Not only was he the family lawyer, he was also their stock broker and Tony knew his father trusted him. As it happened, the two men had known each other since they were children in Palermo, Sicily, and they were close friends. Even so, Tony resisted the urge to make contact.

So far, Tony had done pretty well on his own. He hadn't called any of his old friends and he'd stayed away from the bars he usually frequented. However, it was about time to make a move. He could almost hear his father saying, "Finish the job. Don't leave loose ends, they're bad for business. I know a lotta guys got tripped up by loose ends."

Tony would have liked to call on the organization to provide the muscle to do his dirty work, but he had no access to the men. And even if he reached one, he knew they would refuse. He had never bothered to show proper respect when he spoke to a *mafioso* in his father's gang. Now his superior attitude was catching up with him.

The Mafia family worked because everyone knew his place and followed the rules. As a civilian, Tony was on his own. He realized he would never take over the business, but still, he was Giuseppe's son and he had a certain reputation to maintain.

There was no getting around it, he had waited long enough. So without telling anyone his intentions, Tony left New Orleans to take care of business in Waterproof.

CHAPTER THIRTY-ONE
(Waterproof)

Boredom might have suited Nate, but not Bitsy. She was truly sorry to hear about Arlan, and she always enjoyed a big funeral and a proper wake, but she understood that the Walker's didn't have that kind of money and, when you got right down to it, you couldn't have much of a wake without a body.

Junior's run-in with the Coke machine had provided a laugh or two at the Firehouse, but the customers had wrung about all the juice out of that one.

In the past, Bud Garvey could usually be counted on to do something stupid, but now it seemed even he had settled into a life of respectability, or at least inactivity. So Bitsy was on the lookout for a little excitement.

So far, she had been extremely patient with Ruby about her encounter with the sheriff. She had waited politely, but now her patience was running out and second-hand excitement was better than no excitement at all.

That night when Bitsy got home after closing up the Firehouse, she got a pot, added a little cooking oil, poured in the popcorn, and turned the gas burner up high. As the corn popped, the smell filled the house and pretty soon Ruby walked into the kitchen. Bitsy smiled. Never failed. "Want some popcorn?"

Bitsy asked as she added a generous amount of butter. "The beer's in the icebox."

They took a big bowl of salted popcorn into the back room and Bitsy made idle conversation for a while. Then she got down to business. "I've never seen the sheriff looking so good. It's like he's a whole new man and high time too, if you ask me."

Ruby took a swallow of beer but didn't respond. Bitsy tried another approach. "You know, from the first minute I saw the two of you together at the Firehouse, I knew sparks were gonna fly. It was just a matter of time and I for one am real glad it happened."

No response.

"I remember what it was like when my second husband and me first got together. Lord, Lord, it was Katie bar the door! We couldn't keep our hands off each other. Know what I mean?"

Ruby smiled, but didn't rise to the bait.

Bitsy put down her beer. "Ruby, let me just say this right out. After all the trouble that I went to getting the two of you together, you know, you working at the library and the sheriff on the library committee and all, it just seems like you could share a little about what went on between you two. You know, girl talk."

"It was nice."

"Nice!!?? Ruby, Sunday school socials are nice, God knows I should hope making love was better'n that." Bitsy sighed in exasperation and took a gulp of beer. "Listen, I know you're not a big talker, but you gotta give me at least something." Ruby just smiled. "I'll tell you what, you give me one word, just one well-chosen word about what happened."

Ruby looked at Bitsy and took her time to consider her response.

"Well???"

"More," Ruby said. Her voice was low and husky. Then she looked Bitsy in the eye, smiled and nodded slowly, "More." She got up and brushed off her hands. "Thanks for the popcorn."

Bitsy was stunned. Then she started to laugh. True, Ruby's account wasn't long on details and it left a lot to the imagination. And that was just fine because Bitsy prided herself on having a very good imagination.

Later in the week, Bitsy came home one night and found Ruby reading in the living room. "We've gotta talk." Ruby started to protest, but Bitsy stopped her. "No, not about that." Ruby knew by the tone of Bitsy's voice, this wasn't just her usual chatter.

"It's been over a year since you got here and I've never asked you where you came from or why you're here, 'cause I didn't really care. But there was a guy stopped in the Firehouse today asking about you. He had Orleans parish plates on his car and it's not the first time somebody from down there has been nosing around.

"First time I didn't make too much of it 'cause it was just the guy who collects from the slots. But this guy was different. Expensive clothes, shiny shoes. Tall, dark, and handsome. A real lady-killer if I ever saw one."

Ruby cringed at Bitsy's choice of words. "What did he want?"

"You. He said he was a friend from New Orleans and he just wanted to say hello. Wanted me to tell him where you lived."

"What did you tell him?"

"I told him I didn't know anything about you except that his description sounded a little like a woman I'd seen getting in a car over at the bus station. He was charming, but he just wouldn't let it go. It was like he *knew* you were here. What's going on, Ruby? Are you in some kind of trouble?"

Very slowly Ruby put down her book. She made a great effort to stay calm on the outside, but her heart was pounding and her mouth was dry. The description could have fit one of Scapesi's men, but in her heart, Ruby knew it was Tony. For a moment, she saw his face again. His eyes burning, his lips drawn back in rage. The knife in his hand. The smell of blood. It all came back.

One way or the other, it was clear he had found her. Ruby looked at Bitsy. "Would you call the sheriff, please, and ask him to come over. This will involve him and I don't want to have to say this twice."

Ruby was white as a sheet. Bitsy had been mildly worried before, now she was getting truly scared. She called Nate and filled him in as much as she could. She didn't know what Ruby was mixed up in, but she was sure it was a lot more serious than running away from a no-good husband.

When Nate arrived fifteen minutes later, Bitsy met him at the door. Nate saw his own fear reflected in her face. He walked into the living room, Ruby stood, and he hugged her. "Don't worry, whatever it is, it'll be all right."

"You better hear the story first," Ruby said quietly.

Bitsy brought out a pound cake, whipped cream, and coffee, hoping that good food would be an antidote for the bad news she knew was coming. No one touched the food, so Bitsy had to make do with pouring coffee for everyone.

Finally, Ruby told them the whole story beginning with her family in Mississippi. She explained how the company sold the land, which meant she and her father had no place to stay, no work, no money. She told them about meeting Henry Bladder, falling in love, coming to New Orleans, and getting stranded. She quickly explained that their marriage had turned out to be a sham, and how she had met Minnie Tucker and gone to work for her.

"You worked in a whorehouse!?" Bitsy blurted out before she could stop herself.

"They call them sporting clubs, and yes, I worked there as the *bookkeeper*, that's all."

How dare she assume I was a prostitute?! And what if I had been, she has no right to judge me. I wonder if that's what he thought too? God, will this nightmare ever be over?

Ruby took a deep breath and went on with her story. She didn't bother to try to explain how much she liked Minnie or how she had enjoyed the company of the women at the house. Instead she got quickly to the night of the murder. She described hearing Lola scream followed by the scuffle in the hall.

"I opened my door just as Tony stabbed the guy. We were this close," she held her hand about six inches in front of her face. "I'll never forget the look in his eyes, cold and angry. I realized I was actually the only one who had seen what he did and I knew I had to get out of there." She looked at Nate. She wasn't sure, but she thought what she saw on his face was sadness.

Ruby was anxious to get it all out in the open. She explained that to avoid suspicion, she took only what she had with her when she arrived on Basin Street. "I left the house while everyone was asleep. I took a bus across town as far as it went, then I started hitchhiking. I made it as far as Airline Highway and just after dawn an old couple picked me up. That's how I got here."

"So you think the guy who talked to Bitsy is the same guy you saw stab a man?" Nate asked gently.

"Yes. His name is Tony Scapesi. He's Giuseppe Scapesi's son," Ruby said as if that were explanation enough.

The name meant nothing to Bitsy, but Nate recognized it right away. Everyone working in law enforcement knew Scapesi was head of the ruling Mafia family in New Orleans. He was involved in loan-sharking, numbers, bookmaking and, if the rumors were true, he also controlled a number of well-placed politicians and the upper echelons of the police. He was known to be a gentleman in public and ruthless in business.

Nate explained the significance of what they were dealing with. Bitsy looked puzzled. "I don't understand why he's here. Seems to me like he'd want to stay as far away from you as possible."

"He's here," Nate said, "because Ruby can identify him. She's a loose end and he's come to … tie up loose ends. You think his father ordered this?"

"Probably. I saw the don at the house from time to time. He and Minnie were friends. He was polite and a big tipper. Tony was different, mean and arrogant. Treated everybody like dirt. Minnie put up with him because she didn't want to offend his father."

"Did you tell Minnie where you were going?" Nate asked.

"I didn't *know* where I was going, and I didn't tell anyone anything. I have no idea how he found me."

"Maybe it was the guy who services the slots. Could he have told him?" Bitsy asked.

"I don't see how. Tony is the only one who knows what I look like …" Ruby stopped short and all the color drained out of her face. "Oh my God, the papers, the trial. That must be it. I remember seeing myself in the crowd in that picture of Possum throwing the gavel. It was in the Baton Rouge paper, maybe it was in the New Orleans papers too."

Bitsy turned to Ruby, "Any possibility that we're making too much of this?"

Nate cut her off. "No! He's killed a man and now he needs to get rid of the witness."

"So arrest him," Bitsy said.

"First of all, I don't know where he is. You said he left town."

"Well, I guess he did. I haven't seen him around anywhere. But he said he'd be back, and it sure sounded like a threat to me."

"There's another problem. So far, there's no official report that he's done anything illegal. I haven't seen any report about a murder in the French Quarter last fall and, as far as I know, there's no record of a warrant for his arrest."

"I haven't seen anything about the murder either," Ruby added, "and I checked the papers every day for weeks. The fact that it was never reported shows you how the Scapesi family controls New Orleans."

"I guess that rules out calling the police down there for help. If they're in bed with the Mafia, that would do more harm than good." Nate sat thinking a minute. "The first thing we have to do is get Ruby out of sight. Go pack up your things and come home with me."

"No. That would put your family in danger and staying here does the same thing to Bitsy." Ruby hesitated, "Maybe I could move into the library. He'd never think to look there. If I had a cot, I'd be fine."

Neither Nate nor Bitsy thought much of the idea, but they couldn't come up with a better suggestion. Maybe the library would work, it was easy to overlook the little brick building and Ruby knew from experience that other than Nate, no one but Luther and Carrie ever came by.

Reluctantly, Nate gave in. "All right, we'll do that. There's a cot and some bedding at the office. Luther used it when he was staying with Arlan. Let's go pick that up and then we'll get you settled in."

Ruby went upstairs to pack and grabbed some blankets out of the closet. Bitsy raided the icebox and threw food into paper bags. When they were ready to leave, Bitsy hugged Ruby. "I'm sorry if I made you mad. I didn't mean anything. You call me if you need anything and please be careful." After they were gone, Bitsy smoked the last cigarette in her pack and went to bed. The house felt oddly empty and quiet.

Nate and Ruby drove over to his office to pick up the cot and Nate got his toolbox. Thanks to Luther's new-found passion for putting things in their proper places, he found a deadbolt lock—miraculously filed under the L's. Nate had bought it for the office when he first took the job, before he realized locks in Waterproof were superfluous.

When they reached the library, Ruby turned on one small desk lamp. They unloaded the cot and the bedding. Ruby set everything up in the back room and put the food in the icebox while Nate installed the new lock.

When he finished, he locked the door from the inside and put one key in his pocket. He gave the other one to Ruby. Then he sat on the couch and pulled her down beside him. Several hours later, he kissed her good night, let himself out, and locked the door behind him.

CHAPTER THIRTY-TWO
(Waterproof)

Tony was not happy. He had expected to charm the information he needed out of the gaudy old waitress. She should have been flattered by his attention. Instead, she turned out to be a tough nut to crack. Well, no matter, he just needed to come up with a new tactic.

He'd noticed a roadhouse about five miles out of town. That was more his style. He knew "nice" people in little towns didn't go to roadhouses, so he wasn't likely to be spotted. Still, he needed to do this right. He'd had the good sense to take one of the cars his father kept in the city for emergencies. His new sporty coupe in this hick town would surely have been a dead giveaway.

His expensive suit had to go too. And the Italian shoes. In the trunk of the car, he found an old pair of pants and some scruffy loafers. Better. Finally he grabbed an LSU baseball cap. Go Tigers! That was more like it.

Tony was at home in bars. He'd learned that spreading money around made him instantly popular. But it also drew attention. So no buying drinks for everybody this time.

I need to think like my old man. What would he do? He'd sit and wait and they'd come to him. They always did. I never have understood why that worked, but I guess it's worth a try.

The roadhouse was smoky, dark, and smelled like stale beer and cigarettes, with just a hint of vomit to make it complete. Tony took a seat toward one end of the bar.

"What can I get'chu?"

"You got Jax?"

"Sure." The bartender reached into a cooler behind him, pried off the cap, and put the bottle on the counter. He didn't offer a glass and Tony didn't ask for one. He drank slowly and surveyed the room in the mirror behind the rows of bottles. Not many men around, but it was early yet.

He was into his third beer when he signaled the bartender. "Reckon I could get a hamburger? No, make it a cheeseburger and load it with everything." Eating gave Tony an excuse to hang around a while longer. The order took a while and he was just about to ask why it was taking so long when the bartender slid the plate across the counter. The burger was surprisingly good and the fries were spicy. "You got some Creole hot mustard?"

"Yeah, Zatarain's."

Tony recognized the familiar New Orleans seasoning. "My mamma figures she can't have a crawfish boil without a bag of Zatarain's."

The bartended smiled, "Yeah, mine too." It was Louisiana, and family and food were guaranteed to start a conversation anywhere, anytime, with anybody.

Tony and the bartender talked about oyster po-boys in La Place, muffalettas in the Central Grocery in the Quarter, a Creole-Italian restaurant in Thibodaux, and crawfish etouffee in Houma. Everybody had their favorites.

Tony said he was looking to buy some local property. That gave him an excuse to drive around town for a couple of days without raising any questions. By the end of the evening, he had been offered access to a room on the second floor of the roadhouse and had set up a time the next afternoon to go look at some property along Thompson Creek. He marveled at how easy it was to dupe people.

The hard part was working out how to find the woman. He'd seen that kid who worked at the sheriff's office riding his bike all over town. He might know where she was. That brought him to the real problem. Once he'd done the job, how was he going to get rid of the body? That was crucial. No body, no crime. He'd heard his father say that often enough.

But you couldn't just walk around town carrying a body. He had the car, of course, but he'd still have to get the body from wherever he killed her to the car without being seen. And once he did that, he had to make sure the police couldn't identify the car. So he needed to steal a license plate. But that required tools, and he needed to find a car where no one would see what he was doing.

Hell, I'll just rub some mud on the plate I've got. Once I cover up Orleans parish, I'll look just like everybody else.

So, he could use the car, assuming he was able to get it close enough to transfer the body without being seen. Then he'd head for New Orleans. There were plenty side roads, bayous and swamps along the way. He'd just dump the body and count on the alligators to get rid of the evidence.

The whole operation involved a lot more planning than he had initially thought. Tony was beginning to realize why his father paid his soldiers so well. Killing people was a lot more complicated than it looked on the outside.

***

Ruby was alone again. She was surprised to find she actually missed Bitsy's chatter. She had gotten out of the habit of being by herself. Now she found that too much quiet filled up the space like water and made it hard to breathe. She tried to read, but couldn't sit still long enough to get involved in a book.

It was the Dewey Decimal System that saved her sanity. She meticulously arranged books until she literally couldn't see straight, then she dusted shelves. Finally she changed the sign on the front door to read "Temporarily Closed for Repairs."

Her one link to the outside world was the telephone. She couldn't even *see* outside. Since the original front windows had been bricked in, the only windows left were those along the sides of the building and they were partially hidden by privet bushes.

Being locked in was totally different from coming to work each day and sitting alone at her desk. She missed being able to leave the front door open. Thank God Luther came by late every afternoon to bring food from the Firehouse. Nate and Bitsy stayed away.

Although Bitsy hadn't seen him lately, Tony was still in Waterproof. He was being very careful and he limited himself to one circuit through town at a different time each day. He'd heard that folks in small towns kept track of their neighbors by watching whose car went where and was parked for how long at what address. God, he missed the city.

It was just by chance that Tony was driving by the library and saw Luther park his bike, and unload books and a large shopping bag. When the boy got to the door, instead of going in, he knocked, and a few minutes later the door opened and he disappeared inside. Strange. Nobody locked up a library.

Tony parked directly across the street so he could read the sign on the door. That was strange too. If the building were closed for repairs, why was anyone going in? Even with an arm full of books, that made no sense. And if he wasn't mistaken, he'd seen "Firehouse" on the bag. So someone was there, someone who was hiding and needed to have food brought in.

Tony knew a lot about hiding. He smiled and drove slowly around the block.

Ruby met Luther as he struggled to balance the books and not spill the food Bitsy had packed. "I'll put this in the icebox, you know where those books go back in the stacks." Luther left to return the books he'd read and Ruby walked into the back room to put the food away.

Tony waited a few minutes then walked up to the library door and pushed. It was unlocked. The woman was in the back room standing with her back to him, putting away groceries.

This was his chance. Quietly he took the switchblade out of his pocket and opened it. Half a dozen quick steps brought him within striking range. He grabbed the woman around the neck, pulling her back against him, and reached around to plunge the knife into her abdomen.

Then everything went black.

It happened so fast, Ruby didn't have time to cry out. She looked down and saw Tony lying on the floor, unconscious. Luther was standing over him holding the Virgin Mary. There were traces of blood on the base of the statue. Luther put it back on the work counter.

"That him? Did I kill him?"

Ruby looked more closely. "That's him, but I think he's still breathing."

"I don't think we oughta be here when he wakes up," Luther said as he reached for Ruby's hand. She stepped over Tony and the two of them ran for the door. Once on the street, they headed for the sheriff's office. It was getting dark, but the street lights hadn't come on yet.

Luther burst through the door with Ruby right behind. "We got him Sheriff! He tried to kill Miss Ruby, but I hit him with the Virgin Mary and knocked him out. He's in the library."

The three of them got in the car. Nate hesitated, thinking he should take a gun, but at that moment, he couldn't remember where it was. Hell, Luther had probably filed it, but he didn't have time to ask about it now.

The library wasn't far and Nate parked on the sidewalk and sprinted up the steps. He was fishing in his pocket for the key, when Luther pushed the door open. "Come on, he's in here."

They headed into the back room, but when they got there, it was empty. "Where?" Nate asked. "Where did you leave him?"

"Right there," Luther pointed to a spot near the icebox.

Clearly there was no body, but Nate did see a drop or two of blood. "All right, he's gone. Ruby, lock the door, then you two tell me exactly what happened."

Ruby did as she was told then sat down on the couch and immediately started to shake all over. Nate had seen it happen in combat. Soldiers caught up in the heat of battle showed no fear. It was only after the threat was over that their emotions betrayed them. He sat down and put his arms around her. That's when she started to cry. Luther disappeared into the bathroom and returned with a handful of toilet paper. "Didn't see no Kleenex."

Ruby nodded her thanks and blew her nose. "It's my fault. I unlocked the door for Luther and I forgot to lock it back. I'm so sorry."

Nate covered her hands, which were holding the balled-up toilet paper. "It's all right. The important thing is you're both OK." As he said it, he suddenly realized how close he had come to losing her.

Oh God no! I can't let this happen. I've got to keep her safe no matter what it takes.

"Luther," he reached over and grasped the boy's shoulder, "thank you."

Luther suddenly realized what a really important thing he had done. He'd saved Miss Ruby's life! He straightened his shoulders and smiled. "Yes Sir, you're welcome." He hesitated a moment, then continued proudly. "I was putting up books in the stacks when I seen what was goin' on. I just picked up the first thing I saw and hit him. You don't think the Virgin Mary's mad at me, do you, Sheriff?"

"No Luther. I think she'd be proud of you."

CHAPTER THIRTY-THREE
(Waterproof)

Tony had a splitting headache. He had a bottle of bourbon in his room and he stopped to buy a bottle of aspirin on his way to his room. When he got to the roadhouse, he took the back stairs up to his room over the bar. He didn't turn on a light because the glare made his head hurt worse. In the dark, he managed to find a glass, pour the bourbon, and swallow a handful of pills.

The bump rising on the back of his head made it impossible to lie on his back. Instead, he curled up on his side, whimpering, and feeling sorry for himself. This was supposed to be just business, tie up loose ends, and get out of town. Now that damn kid had made it personal.

Well, fine, if they want a fight, I'll give 'em a fight. They don't know who they're messin' with. When I catch that kid, I'll give him a whole lot more than a bump on the head.

CHAPTER THIRTY-FOUR
(Waterproof)

Before they left the library, Nate called Bitsy to make sure she was home. He told her what was going on and said he was going to bring Ruby and Luther to her house. When they got there, all the shades were drawn, the porch light was off, and the front door was locked. Nate knocked. "It's cold out here. Why'd you lock the door, Bitsy? I told you we were on our way."

"You also told me there was a crazy fool runnin' around out there with a knife. Locking the doors just seemed like the logical thing to do." She reached out, pulled them into the hallway and locked the door behind them. Then she hugged Luther. "I swear, Luther, you're an honest-to-God hero." Still holding on to Luther, she looked over at Ruby. "Are you all right, Honey?" Ruby nodded.

Predictably, they all ended up in the kitchen. Bitsy couldn't help herself. She made a fresh pot of coffee, and put what was left of two pies from the Firehouse in the oven to warm up. When everyone was seated around the table, she started making grilled cheese sandwiches. "There's nothing like getting the shit scared out of you to build up an appetite. Beers are in the icebox, so dig in." They did.

"I can't figure out where he's staying," Nate said, "but it's clear the guy has been hanging around town long enough to figure out Ruby was at the library. It's also clear that as long as he's here, she's in danger."

The question wasn't so much how to keep Ruby safe, but *where* to keep her. They ate the sandwiches and nibbled their way through the remainder of the pies as they went through a list of possibilities.

Nate volunteered to take her to his house, but that idea was quickly vetoed because, as Ruby had already pointed out, having her around put both Miss Laura and Carrie in danger.

The Walkers clearly owed the sheriff a favor, but asking Martha to take Ruby in when she hardly had enough to feed her own family made no sense. The same was true of Luther's family.

Bitsy suggested her sister's house. At least Ruby would be out of town, but then she'd be isolated and that didn't seem like a good solution either. Nate wondered how Scapesi, who didn't know anyone in town, had found a place to stay when they couldn't come up with a safe place for Ruby to hide.

"I guess I could ring up some of the church ladies and see if any of them has a room they'd be willing to rent. But on second thought, that means we'd have to come up with some kind of story and that bunch—from Baptists to Catholics—are the worst gossips in town.

Finally, Ruby spoke up. "I know where I can go. Back to New Orleans." That brought a chorus of objections. "It's the one place Tony won't look. I could call Minnie ..." More objections.

"I can't let you go back to that place," Nate began.

Ruby bristled. *"That place?!* That place and that woman gave me a home and a job when I needed one. Don't you dare say anything against her!"

Nobody moved. Nobody spoke.

"People judge and they shouldn't. Most of the time they don't know what they're talking about." Ruby's voice was hard and angry.

Nate apologized, "I'm sorry, I spoke out of turn."

Luther looked from one face to another. "What place?"

Ruby waved off his question. Very quietly she explained that if she stayed in Waterproof, she was putting everyone close to her at risk. Tony was obviously convinced she was in town, so the smart thing to do was to get *out* of town and the only place to go was back to Basin Street. "I'll call Minnie and see if I can stay there until ..."

And that was the sticking point. Until what? Until Tony got tired of looking and went home to New Orleans? Until the sheriff arrested him for attempted murder? And if that happened, how long would it be before the don showed up to rescue him?

Luther listened to the discussion and realized they were doing it again. That thing that adults did. They couldn't get the right answer because they never asked the right question. How were they gonna get rid of Tony? That's what they needed to be talking about. They shouldn't be wasting time trying to figure out what he was gonna do to Miss Ruby, they should be deciding what they were gonna do to *him*. Luther knew they wouldn't listen, so he'd just have to wait. Usually they figured it out after they wasted a lot of time doing other things.

Ruby picked up the phone and called information for New Orleans, Minnie Tucker, on Basin Street. She got the number and dialed. It was nearly 9:00 and Ruby just hoped she'd catch Minnie in her office not out in the parlor talking to clients.

"Hello?"

"Minnie, it's Ruby ..." Suddenly she couldn't remember what her last name was supposed to be. "It's me, Cinnamon."

It took Minnie a minute to put two and two together, "Ruby Canelle! Where are you callin' from, Cher? Are you all right?"

In as few words as possible, Ruby explained why she left the way she did, how she'd gotten to Waterproof, and what Tony was up to. "As long as he's looking up here, I'll be safer down there, unless the don's looking for me too."

"You don't have to worry about the don. It's not like they gonna put it on the front page of the newspaper, you know, but the gossip is that Giuseppe Scapesi was one of those unfortunate people what got drowned in the hurricane flood. Anyway, what I hear is that the underboss took over the Scapesi family and he's running things now. You reckon Tony knows that?"

"I don't know, Minnie. What does that mean exactly?"

"Well, again I'm not for sure about this, but Tony was never part of the family business. The don had big plans for him, you know, go to college, be legit. But now that the don is gone, Tony … well, I think he's pretty much on his own. He was always a hothead, a problem. The don was always gettin' him out of trouble. Now that the business is under new management, I don't think they're gonna welcome Tony back with open arms.

"Anyways, you are welcome back here any time you wanna come. My accounts are in a mess and I don't think there's an honest bookkeeper in the whole state of Louisiana, 'cept you, of course.

"Remember what we say down here, *Lache Pas! Lache Pas la patate.* Don't give up! Keep it up! That's good advice, Cher, don't drop da potato."

Ruby had to smile at the memory of her first night on Basin Street. She hung up the phone and related the news about the don. With him out of the way, they agreed that going to New Orleans might be the best solution after all.

Luther just shook his head. Getting out of town might keep Miss Ruby safe, but they still hadn't gotten around to asking the right question. What were they going to do about Tony? He was still out there and they were wasting time.

Bitsy called the bus station to check departures to New Orleans. There was a bus headed south just after midnight. Bitsy helped Ruby pack while Nate and Luther waited. When Bitsy came back downstairs, she rummaged around in the kitchen closet until she came up with a shoe box. She lined it with waxed paper and filled it with sandwiches for the trip. She handed the box to Ruby and gave her a quick hug.

Then Nate and Luther got their coats and took Ruby to the bus station. Nate kissed her good bye and watched as the bus pulled out of the station.

So while Tony nursed his throbbing head, Ruby escaped. Again.

Luther's bike was still at the library so he rode along and waited while Nate stopped at the office. Initially, Luther sat in the car, but when the sheriff didn't come right back, he went to investigate. He found Nate hunched over his desk cleaning his rifle.

Nate looked up. He seemed to have forgotten Luther was waiting for him. "Tomorrow morning, Luther, I want you to get on the radio and see if anybody out in the parish has seen this guy."

It sounded like the sheriff was headed in the right direction, but he hadn't gotten there yet. Normally Luther would have sat back and waited for him to figure it out, but they had already wasted way too much time. "You gonna shoot him, Sheriff?"

Nate had been asking himself that very question. He almost smiled. Leave it to Luther to get to the heart of things. Nate hesitated a moment, then looked at Luther. "I'll give him a chance to surrender."

"And if he don't?"

"If he resists, then I'll do whatever I have to do to protect Ruby."

"Finally!" Luther whispered to himself.

It was very late when Nate took Luther by the library to pick up his bike. Then he headed for home himself. He was surprised to find Miss Laura still up. "Bitsy called earlier to tell me what went on at the library and that y'all were headed over to her house. I can't believe that feller was actually gonna kill Ruby. Thank goodness Luther was there. So, I guess you worked something out. Where's Ruby? She with you?"

All Nate could do was shake his head. "She's gone. But this isn't over yet, not by a long shot."

CHAPTER THIRTY-FIVE
(Waterproof)

The next morning, Luther talked to all the sheriffs on his list and gave them what little information they had on Tony. Two days went by with no responses. Nate spent his time talking to everyone in Waterproof who might have seen anything. It was as if Tony had dropped off the face of the earth.

The only bright spot in what was turning out to be a frustrating, dismal week was a letter from Arlan. Carrie opened the one delivered to the house and read it out loud.

Dear Carrie, Miss Laura, and Sheriff Houston,

I am doing fine. Uncle Anderson, Aunt Madeline, and their whole family met me at the bus station. Their son Dean is my age, then there's David, Diane, Dale Anne, Doris, and Daniel. Dean and I are both seniors and I made the football team. The high school here is real big. It's got a chemistry lab, and a big gym, and even a stadium. That's because they get a lot of oil money. Every which way you look around here you see oil pumping machines. They look kind of like a big hammer balanced on top of a ladder.

They make us study "petroleum" in school. Y'all may not know this, but it was an engineer from Louisiana who drilled the first big gusher, called Spindletop. (That's how people talk around here.) Uncle Anderson works in the Humble Refinery, it's part of Standard Oil like in Baton Rouge. Their house has three big bedrooms. All the boys sleep in one room, all the girls in another room. Uncle Anderson and Aunt Madeline have their own room.

I'm a little behind in school, but I'm catching up. The hardest part at first was just finding my way around. The school building is so big I kept getting lost and that was kind of embarrassing. I'm doing better now.

I hope everybody is doing good. Don't worry about me. Mamma, I've got a job after school and I'm saving money to send to you so you can come visit. It is suppertime so I have to go.

Love, Arlan

"How come he's talking to his mamma in our letter and why is the writing all blue?" Carrie looked puzzled.

Nate examined the letter. "I think Arlan just wrote one letter and made carbon copies. His mother probably got the original. Sounds like he's doing fine." Nate's first impulse was to pick up the phone and share the good news with Ruby, then he realized she was gone.

Strange that a person who had been in Waterproof only a relatively short time could leave such a void when she was gone. Bitsy missed her friend. Nate missed his lover. Luther missed the only person who ever told him he was smart.

Nate told Carrie that Miss Ruby had decided to leave town for a couple of days. When his daughter left for school, he walked into the kitchen where Miss Laura was washing breakfast dishes. He hadn't shared Ruby's story with her before, thinking Ruby might not want everyone knowing her personal business. But now he realized there was no way to explain where Ruby was without revealing the whole story.

Over a second cup of coffee, he backed into the story because he didn't know whether Miss Laura would be more shocked finding out where Ruby had been living or that she'd seen a murder. He decided to go with the murder first and then changed his mind.

"Before Ruby came here she was living in New Orleans. Do you know anything about Storyville?"

"Sure. It was the red-light district they set up in the French Quarter right after World War I, but it's long gone now." She saw Nate's surprised expression. "For heaven's sake, I haven't lived in Waterproof all my life, you know. What's that got to do with Ruby?"

"Well, when she lived in New Orleans, she worked for a woman who has a house on Basin Street. Don't worry, she didn't do anything but ..."

"Why is it every generation thinks they invented sex? We had sex. If we hadn't, none of you would be here. So just tell me what you're trying to say."

Nate took a deep breath and told her the whole story, about Minnie Tucker and the house and the girls and the bookkeeping and finally about the murder. "That's why she left. The man she saw is the son of Giuseppe Scapesi, the head of the Mafia in New Orleans. Ruby was the only witness and now the son, Tony, is here to get rid of her." Nate couldn't bring himself to say "kill her." Saying the words out loud, even in the safety of his own kitchen, made the whole nightmare too real.

243

"So why in the world did she go back to New Orleans?"

"She called Minnie Tucker, the landlady, and it turns out old man Scapesi has been missing since the hurricane. Rumor is that he drowned in the flood. The way Ruby sees it, New Orleans is the one place Tony would never think to look for her."

"So, have you got a plan to catch this gangster guy?"

"I'm working on it."

Nate left for the office anxious to see if Luther's calls had turned up any information. Just as he was getting out of the car, Neil stopped him on the street. He hadn't seen the young lawyer since the news report about Arlan's death.

"I've been meaning to call and tell you how sorry I was to hear about Arlan. We got rid of the judge, but it wasn't enough, it wasn't nearly enough."

"I appreciate that," Nate said and added with a slight smile, "we just have to believe that Arlan is in a better place." He and Neil talked for a moment longer and then parted. Nate opened the office door, but since Luther wasn't in yet, he decided to head down to Blacky's to see if any of the men sitting around there had seen Tony.

Luther saw Nate drive away just as he parked his bike next to the door. He went through his usual routine, straightened up, made coffee, and then got on the radio to check in with his list. He was confident that, even if he didn't want to, the sheriff would take care of Tony when he found him. The problem was, they couldn't find him.

When Luther lost something at home, his mamma always said, "Go look in the last place you had it." That would be the library so after he got off the police radio, he searched the sheriff's desk until he found what he thought was the library key. He jumped on his bike and went to do a little snooping around on his own. When he got to the library, he was in luck.

The key slipped into the lock and the door opened easily, but it didn't feel right.

It sounded empty, and it didn't smell like lemons anymore. It smelled like sweat and something metallic. Miss Ruby would have had a fire going. Now there were only ashes. Luther didn't want to go in, but if that's what it took to keep Miss Ruby safe, he'd do it. He searched carefully, but he didn't find anything useful so he went back to the office to report to the sheriff.

"It was a good thought, Luther." Nate's rifle lay within easy reach on the side of his desk. Hunting was a normal part of life in Waterproof. Men hunted ducks, or deer, or squirrels or sometimes even possums. From an early age, kids were taught that guns were not toys. Fathers, uncles, older brothers, someone in the family initiated the younger boys into the proper way to handle a gun. However, Luther knew when the sheriff picked up this gun, it wouldn't be to hunt game.

"Sheriff, would you really shoot that feller dead?"

"Not if I can help it. I just want to bring him in and let the law take care of him."

"Yeah, but that don't always work out, does it, Sheriff? With the law, I mean."

"No, Luther, it doesn't. We'll just take this one step at a time and hope for the best." At noon they walked up to the Firehouse to get something to eat. Nate talked to Bitsy and sent Luther across the street to talk to Leon at the bus station one more time. If Tony had a car, he was going to have to buy gas somewhere.

Bitsy said she hadn't seen Tony since the last time he came around asking about Ruby. That puzzled Nate. "It's like he's here, but he's not here. If he's not buying gas at the bus station, where is he buying it? Nobody out in the parish has seen him anywhere. If he's not coming here to eat, where is he eating?

The Firehouse is the only place around here to get a meal. It just doesn't make sense."

Bitsy thought a minute. "He struck me as too much of a fancy-pants to be livin' in his car, so that means he's found himself some place to stay. And if that's so, he could just be buyin' groceries and eating in his room out of sight. But I don't know of anybody who's got a room to rent."

That gave Nate an idea and that afternoon Luther put out the call asking other sheriffs to double check grocery stores. Nate did the same with the two stores and the fish-bait stand in Waterproof. Nothing. Frustrated, he called it a day.

As she was closing up for the night, Bitsy had a thought. Although she found it hard to believe that a city slicker like Tony would go there, maybe he was eating at one of the roadhouses or the juke joints out in the parish. She made a mental note to call the sheriff about that.

After Nate left, Luther got his jacket and headed for home too. It was getting dark and his mamma had warned him about riding his bike on the highway after the sun went down. Unlike his old bike, this one had a headlight and taillights, but they weren't very bright.

Luther was almost home when he heard a car coming up behind him. Just to be on the safe side, he pulled onto the shoulder and stopped to give the car plenty of room to pass. But instead, he realized the headlights were coming straight at him. He heard the crunch of metal at the same moment he felt the impact and went sailing over the handlebars. His last conscious thought was, "Oh no! Not my new bike!"

CHAPTER THIRTY-SIX
(Waterproof)

When he came to, he was in a cramped, dark place that smelled like oil and gas. A car, he was in the trunk of a car going down a bumpy gravel road. Luther tried to touch his head and realized his hands were tied behind his back. That's when he broke out in a cold sweat. He was scared.

Several minutes later the car stopped. He heard a door open and close. Then the trunk lid flew open and someone shined a flashlight in his face. Tony pulled him out of the car, threw him on the ground, and kicked him hard in the side. Something snapped and Luther screamed.

"Scream all you want, you little punk, nobody's gonna hear you. Now get up." Luther tried, but the pain in his side made it impossible. "I said get up!" Tony grabbed Luther's jacket and dragged him to the base of a tree. Then he untied his hands, but before Luther could bring his arms around to cover his chest, Tony yanked them backward around the tree and retied them. "Now we're gonna have a little talk and you're gonna tell me where that woman is."

Tears ran down Luther's face. "I don't know."

"I think you do," Tony said and hit him in the face. Blood spurted from Luther's nose. He'd scuffled with his brothers, but he'd never been hit in the face before. He was surprised how much it hurt.

Luther kept telling Tony he didn't know where Ruby was, and Tony kept hitting him. "I got all night, Boy, and I'm beginning to enjoy this. So if you wanna live to see tomorrow, you better tell me what I want to know right now."

Luther tried hard to be brave, but he was cold and scared. He knew no one would be looking or him. He hurt all over and there was no way to dodge Tony's fists.

Finally, he broke down and told him where to find Ruby. Tony laughed and hit Luther once more just for good measure. Then he left. Luther struggled against the ropes, but the pain in his side was too much. He passed out.

The next thing Luther felt was something rough and wet on his face. "Leave him alone, Rutledge." Bud Garvey used his flashlight to see what the dogs were into. "God damn, Luther, is that you? What the hell happened to you, Boy?"

Bud tied the bloodhounds to a tree and laid aside his hunting rifle. Then he stuck the flashlight in his mouth so he could use both hands to untie Luther. "Come on, I'll help you up. My truck's over yonder, not too far. Can you walk?" Luther made an effort to answer between sobs, and he tried to stand, but his knees buckled.

"I gotcha." Bud half carried Luther to the pickup and gently helped him into the cab. "Just hang on a minute 'till I get the dogs locked up in the back." Once he untied them, the dogs followed him obediently to the truck and waited to be helped into their cages. Then he went back to get his rifle and the flashlight.

Bud climbed into the cab and closed the door. Before he started the engine, he reached over to the glove compartment, took out a bottle and handed it to Luther. "Here, this'll help." Luther took a swallow, coughed, and drank again. Then he put his head back and closed his eyes. "Attaboy, you just lie back and try to relax."

Bud wasn't sure exactly what to do. It was getting on toward midnight and he didn't want to wake Lucy Castle up and have her seeing Luther looking like that. It was pretty clear the boy needed a doctor. Still, maybe he ought to take him to the sheriff first. Then again, if he was really hurt bad, he might die. That settled it.

Bud drove as fast as the pickup allowed, trying to avoid the ruts and holes in the road. Once they were on the highway, it was smoother riding. He pulled into the doctor's driveway, walked around back, and pounded on the door. It seemed like forever, but finally the doctor appeared. Bud explained the situation and he and the doctor got Luther out of the cab and into the examination room. Through his badly swollen eyes, Luther squinted at the bright lights.

"Lord help us, what happened?" the doctor asked when he saw the extent of Luther's injuries.

"I ain't got no idea. I was out possum huntin' and I heard him moanin'. The dogs found him all bloody, tied to a tree. That's all I know. Can you fix him, Doc?"

The doctor examined the cuts and bruises on Luther's face and gently pressed along his side. "I think he's got a couple of broken ribs, and his face is lacerated, but he'll live. I'll fix him up best I can. You probably ought to call his family. You can use the phone on the desk in the front office."

Bud made a call, but not to Lucy Castle. He called the sheriff, told him they were at the doctor's office, and explained what little he knew about what happened. Nate told him he'd be there as soon as he could.

Fifteen minutes later he walked into the office and Bud went through the story again, explaining how he had been possum hunting down along Thompson Creek when he heard Luther moaning and how the dogs found him and started licking his face. "If they hadn't got some of the blood off, I don't think I'd have known it was Luther. He was beat up pretty bad, Sheriff."

Just then, the doctor came into the waiting room and told them they could come back to see Luther. The boy was sitting on the examining table. His nose was all out of shape and his eyes were swollen almost shut. A long line of black stitches held a gash on his cheek together. His face looked like a Mardi Gras mask, bright orange from the mercurochrome mixed in with the blue and purple of the bruises that were already beginning to show. His shirt was open and they saw the bandage wrapped tightly around his chest. In spite of the cuts on his lips, Luther tried to smile.

Nate walked over and gently put his arm around Luther's shoulder. Then he thanked Bud and the doctor and said he'd take Luther home and call his mother. "Miss Laura and I can take care of him tonight and I'll take him home in the morning."

Clearly, walking was painful, but they managed to get Luther into the sheriff's car. "I've given him some pills for the pain, so he may be a little groggy. Just let him sleep if he can. That's the best thing we can do for him now." The doctor handed Nate a small box with some additional pills. Nate thanked Bud again and they each headed for home.

"It was Tony and he..." Luther tried to talk, but the pills kicked in and he nodded off. Nate's heart went out to the boy. "We'll handle it tomorrow, Son. You've had enough excitement for one day."

CHAPTER THIRTY-SEVEN
(Waterproof)

Dawn was just breaking when Nate and Luther got home. Miss Laura got Luther settled as comfortably as possible in the spare bedroom. Then she pulled the shades so the morning sun wouldn't wake him. The boy looked so vulnerable, she reached out to touch him but drew back her hand afraid she might hurt him. Tears came to her eyes as she leaned over him. "You rest now, Luther. You're safe here, nobody's going to hurt you. It'll be all right." She kissed him gently on the forehead and tiptoed out of the room.

When she came into the kitchen, she was crying softly. "How could anybody do that? Oh Nate, he looks so broken ..."

By that time, all the activity had awakened Carrie who came into the kitchen in her robe. Miss Laura made her a cup of coffee-milk and Nate told her what happened. She wanted to see Luther, but Miss Laura put the kibosh on that. "No, you're going to school, and you are not to say *one thing* about this to anybody yet. You understand? We need some time to think this through before everyone starts gossiping about it." Reluctantly Carrie agreed.

It was after supper before Luther finally woke up. He had been asleep more than twelve hours. When he shuffled into the kitchen wearing one of Nate's old robes, all conversation stopped. He looked both better and worse. The swelling had gone down some and his face was almost its normal shape again, but the color of the bruises had intensified. All in all, he was still a pitiful sight.

Carrie immediately started asking questions. "Hold on, Missie. Luther needs to build up his strength. Food first, then questions," Miss Laura ordered.

She hard boiled a couple of eggs and mashed them up in a plate of grits with lots of butter and salt and pepper. It was nourishing, but nothing that required any chewing. Luther drank three glasses of water and a glass of milk before he started to eat. Every time he started to talk, Miss Laura pointed to the food. "Eat. You can't heal if you don't eat."

"You sound just like Miss Bitsy," Luther managed to say. When he finished eating, he pushed his chair away from the table very carefully. It was as if someone had turned down his volume. All his movements and his facial expression were very slow and tentative.

"Can you tell us what happened?" Nate asked. Luther took a deep breath and slowly recounted his story. When he described how Tony hit him, Miss Laura and Carrie both cried, but no one interrupted. Toward the end of the story, Luther hung his head and almost in a whisper said, "It hurt so bad I just wanted it to stop, so I finally told him."

Nate waited a minute trying to understand. "What did you tell him, Luther?"

"I told him where to find Miss Ruby."

"You told him she was in New Orleans?"

"No. But he kept saying I better give him an answer or he was gonna keep hitting me, so I gave him one. When I figured out I was down by Thompson Creek, I told him about the fish camp down close to where it runs into the river."

"Luther, I think you may still be a little woozy from the pain pills. You know there's no fish camp on Thompson Creek, and down close to the river there's nothing but ... there's nothing down there but ..."

"...Quicksand," Carrie finished the sentence for him.

"Yeah, everybody knows that," Luther said and smiled shyly.

It took Nate a minute or two to thoroughly process this information. "So you sent him down there on purpose. Why'd you do that?"

Luther was pleased. Finally an adult who asked the right question. "It was the right thing to do." He could tell by the look on Carrie's face that she understood. Obviously he needed to explain it to the adults.

"It took me a while to think it through while he was hittin' me, but I finally worked it out. He wanted an answer about Miss Ruby, I wanted him to stop hittin' me, and you wanted to catch him, but you didn't want to shoot him. So the right thing to do was to send him down the creek. He'd get good and stuck in the quicksand and then we could go back this morning and get him. That way, you wouldn't have to shoot him or nothin'."

Try as they might, Nate and Miss Laura couldn't help but laugh. "It was a good plan, Luther, but it didn't exactly work out that way. The morning you're talking about has come and gone. You've been asleep all day. The grits and eggs you just ate weren't breakfast; that was supper. I'm guessing Scapesi doesn't know much about how to deal with quicksand. By this time he's probably ..."

With some effort, Luther patiently explained. "Sheriff, the quicksand's not gonna swallow him up. I know that's what folks tell stories about, but my daddy says that only happens in the movies. If what's-his-name had moved real slow and just laid back on the surface, well, he might have got out."

"Luther, he's a city boy. Living down there in New Orleans, I don't think he's had much experience with quicksand. By now he's most likely … Do you think you could locate the place he took you?"

"Yes Sir, I think I can."

"All right. We've got a couple of hours of daylight, let's drive down there and see what we can find."

Of course Miss Laura and Carrie wanted to go along, but Nate pointed out that this was police business. More to the point, he wasn't sure what they might find, but he was sure it wouldn't be pretty. Luther got dressed and he and Nate bundled up and got in the car. They took a few wrong turns before they found the gravel road leading back through the woods to Thompson Creek.

About half a mile from the highway, they discovered Tony's car. The trunk was still open. They saw the tire tracks from Bud's pickup and the tree where Luther had been tied.

Luther started to shake. "It's all right. You're safe now," Nate said. "Stay in the car. I'm going to have a closer look." He found the ropes at the base of the tree and saw blood splattered on the nearby bushes. He walked back to the car. "I'm going to follow the creek and see what I can find. You don't have to come if you don't want to."

Luther opened the door and got out carefully. "No, I'm feeling better and I want to go." As a precaution, Nate insisted they find two sturdy walking sticks. He hardly ever used his cane anymore, but he thought they could both use a little extra support.

The sticks had a second and more important function. "We don't want to fall into the same trap you set for Tony." From experience they both knew that although sand might look solid, if there was water seeping up or if they saw slight ripples on the surface, they better tread carefully. Better to test the ground with the sticks before they tried to walk on it.

As they made their way slowly down Thompson Creek, they found a number of areas of quicksand, but no sign of Tony. "You reckon he got out, Sheriff?"

Nate didn't have a definite answer although it didn't seem likely. He had a pretty good idea about what probably happened. Not knowing where he was going, Tony wandered into the quicksand and panicked. Cold and alone in the dark, he struggled, and the more he fought against the suction of the quicksand, the faster and deeper he sank. When the quicksand surrounded his chest, the pressure would have made it extremely hard to breathe. What happened after that was anybody's guess.

"I don't see how, but without a body, you never know. Let's just keep looking a while longer." They continued to search until Luther said his side was really hurting and asked if they could rest. They found one last patch of sunlight and sat down. Nate lit a cigarette. From their vantage point, they could see where Thompson Creek flowed into the Mississippi. "Is this where you and Carrie found Arlan?"

Luther looked around. "Yeah, it was right after the storm and limbs and branches were all piled up. He was caught in all that stuff. At first we thought it was just a pile of old rags or a dead animal. Wasn't 'till we fished it out of there that we discovered it was Arlan. Liked to have scared us both to death when he moved. But we sure was glad to find him. I'm gonna go take another look."

Before Nate could stop him, Luther got up and carefully shielding his broken ribs, waded across a shallow spot in the creek. Nate watched as he took his stick and poked around the debris from the storm that hadn't been washed away yet. "Sheriff! Look what I found."

In his excitement, Luther splashed back across the creek holding something in his hand. When he got close to shore, he put the object on the end of the stick and held it out for Nate to see. The muddy blob turned out to be an LSU baseball cap. "It was stuck in all that stuff. Tony was wearing it. I remember that." Luther looked a little shaken. "You reckon he could have gotten out of the quicksand?"

They stood together looking at the cap and the swirl of water where the creek flowed into the Mississippi. "I guess it's possible," Nate said, "but if he did, it's kinda like jumping out of the frying pan into the fire. I wouldn't worry about it." Nate took the cap and shook some of the mud and water off. "Either way, let's go home, Luther. I think we've done enough here."

The sun was going down and the woods were quiet except for the sound of birds and the squirrels chattering high up in the trees. The men kicked up leaves and inhaled the loamy smell of rich soil.

As they passed Tony's car, Nate tossed the cap into the open trunk. "Go Tigers," he said softly.

CHAPTER THIRTY-EIGHT
(New Orleans)

Once again, Ruby was part of the household on Basin Street and the rhythm and excitement of New Orleans. Waterproof had been her haven, but with the threat of Tony in the background, she began to enjoy the city again.

The girls were glad to see her and Minnie was ecstatic. She had been right, the books were in a mess. Ruby got to work trying to make heads or tails out of Minnie's notes. Keeping her mind occupied meant she didn't have much time to worry about what might be happening in Waterproof.

However, it didn't take Ruby very long to realize that notwithstanding the laws of nature, it was possible to be in two places at one time. Physically she was in New Orleans, but mentally she was with Nate in Waterproof. She could follow his steps throughout the day, knew when he'd be at the café for pie and coffee. Although he'd never been to the house on Basin Street, she knew he was with her there too.

She and Nate had decided the safest thing was to have no contact until the business with Tony was resolved. But not knowing meant her imagination was running wild. She knew both men had killed, although under completely different circumstances and for different reasons. She also knew Tony couldn't give up and neither could Nate. A confrontation was inevitable.

Why in the world did I decide to leave? I should have stayed. I might have been able to do something. At least I would know what was going on.

After closing one night, Minnie knocked on Ruby's door and walked in. "Listen, Cher, I think we need to talk. What I mean is, *you* need to talk. Half the time you seem OK and the other half seems like you're carryin' the weight of the world around. No good is gonna come from that, I'm tellin' you. So, talk to me about that Waterproof place and that sheriff man."

"He's tall."

Minnie let out a sigh loud enough to be heard two streets away. "*Mon Dieu!* I was hoping maybe you'd learned to talk while you were out there in the sticks with nothing else to do. Now, I want to hear the whole story and I mean with all the details. Talk to me."

So Ruby did and, as usual, Minnie was right. Just being able to tell someone about Nate and everything that had happened since she left, helped. It didn't solve anything, but it did help.

Minnie left shaking her head. What a mess. She had long since learned not to get too close to anybody. People were the core of her business, but that was it, they were just business. Minnie sympathized with Ruby, but she had problems of her own to deal with. Since Ruby had been gone, the world of the Mafia in the city had changed and that had Minnie worried.

Because of the disappearance of Giuseppe Scapesi, New Orleans was in danger of an all-out gang war and that was having a profound impact on Minnie's business. She counted on the patronage and support of the underworld and the out-of-towners who liked the perceived danger of rubbing shoulders with them.

The greater population of the city had no idea what was going on. Most residents went about their lives completely unaware of the Cosa Nostra's presence. As long as they could eat at their favorite restaurants, watch their favorite entertainers, drink their favorite booze, buy the imported goods they wanted, and gamble with impunity, they were happy.

As a rule, the Mafia functioned like a well-run corporation. But in fact, it was made up of factions and feuds that went back generations. Provincial grudges imported from ancient mountain villages in the old country.Underneath all the polish, it was still a feudal society.

The rumors on the street were thick as gumbo. Don Scapesi was a victim of the Fort Lauderdale Hurricane. Don Scapesi was hiding out in Florida, or New York, or Memphis, or St. Louis. Take your pick. Don Scapesi had been detained by the Feds. The truth was, he could just as well have been encased in cement resting at the bottom of Lake Pontchartrain. No one knew. The fact that Tony was also missing was curious, but not significant.

Minnie had heard enough talk in her parlor to piece together her own version of what was going on. A lot of it went back to the Havana Conference the year before. According to one of her secret sources, Lucky Luciano had arranged the meeting to discuss mob policies, rules, and business interests that affected them all. Representatives from all the major crime families met to decide who was to control what rackets.

It didn't take a genius to figure out that the mob needed to come to some agreement, because nobody wanted a shooting war. Since not much changed as far as Minnie could see, she guessed that the Scapesi organization kept control of the numbers, bookmaking, loan-sharking, and smuggling in south Louisiana.

The other families were left to fight over prostitution, the enforced protection racket, and narcotics. That seemed fair to her, but apparently not everybody was happy about the decision. Now with the don out of the picture, no one was sure who stood where. Talk on the street said the smart money was on Carlos Marcello to end up as head of the New Orleans crime family.

Frankly, Minnie didn't care who won. She just wanted things to settle down and business to pick up.

CHAPTER THIRTY-NINE
(Waterproof)

The ice house in Waterproof was powered by a huge motor that sounded like the lub-dub rhythm of a giant heart. It could be heard all over town and no one ever noticed it until it stopped. Nate, Miss Laura, Carrie, Luther, and Bitsy had been living with fear and tension so long they didn't realize the pressure they were under until it disappeared. Then they straightened their shoulders and breathed a collective sigh of relief.

The first thing Nate did was to call Ruby. Since they knew Luther was going to be all right, he left out that part of the story. "As far as we can tell, Tony's gone. We found his car abandoned down in the swamp along Thompson Creek, but we haven't found a body yet. I don't think you should come back until we're absolutely sure. Give me a few more days. In the meantime, I don't want to put you in any danger with more phone calls. I'll be in touch as soon as I can, so please take care of yourself." It wasn't until he hung up that he realized he hadn't asked how she was doing. He hadn't told her how much he missed her. He hadn't said he wanted her to come back.

Stupid! You've done it again. You're gonna have to let yourself be a man first and then be a sheriff. If you keep on like this, you're gonna mess this up.

Having decided that, he went back to being a sheriff. As he drove to the office, he took stock of where they were at the moment. Arlan was in a better place. Luther was planning to come into the office for the first time. Miss Laura and Carrie had settled back into their normal routines. Ruby was safe in New Orleans.

Then there was Tony. What had really happened to him? Was he dead? Drowned? Scared off? Nate wanted to believe it was over, but he knew better than to take anything for granted. When he got to the office, he found Luther on the radio calling off the search. "By the way, there's a message from Miss Bitsy on your desk." Luther's speech was still a little slurred, but it was getting better every day.

Nate read Bitsy's message with interest. She suggested he check out the roadhouses in the parish. Since there was only one such establishment within ten miles, Nate decided to start there. When he described Tony, the bartender said yes he had been staying in a room upstairs while he was looking for property along Thompson Creek.

Don't say it! Do not tell that man Tony may have found a place to put down roots.

They went upstairs to have a look at the room. Everything was in order. The closet was empty and there was an envelope on the dresser with $50 inside. "I wasn't charging him anything, but I reckon he left that to pay for the room. Nice feller, but it doesn't look to me like he's planning to come back any time soon."

"You're probably right," Nate said and thanked the man for his time. Before he went back to town, Nate drove over to Thompson Creek to do a more thorough search. He found Tony's car and went through it carefully. He took all the papers out of the glove compartment and stuffed those in his pocket.

In the trunk, he found a duffle bag with a suit, a fancy pair of shoes, a white shirt, and some dirty laundry. He also found the LSU cap. Nate stuffed everything into the bag and set it aside.

Then he removed the license plates. While he was at it, he lifted the hood and pulled out a handful of wires. That done, he put the car in neutral, released the brake, and pushed it farther into the underbrush. Finally, he covered his tracks and left the car to the tender mercies of the heat, humidity, and any wildlife looking for a home.

Nate picked up the duffle bag and threw it into the trunk of his patrol car. While he was there, he grabbed his cane and changed from his shoes to his Army boots. He took a deep breath and started walking slowly along the creek toward the river. When he got there, he slid down the embankment and waded along the edge of the water poking at any pile of debris that looked suspicious. Thirty minutes later and about half a mile downriver, he found it.

As if the river understood what needed to be done, it had already started to dispose of the body. Trying not to look at the disfigured face, Nate emptied Tony's pockets and removed the watch and anything else that might identify Scapesi. Then he waded out into the river as far as he could and pushed the body into the current.

Nate nodded to the river. "Thank you for your help, my old friend. I'm counting on you to keep my secret," he said as the river rolled Tony's body over and took it away.

Nate avoided the highway and took the back roads on his way into town. Before he got there, he burned the duffle bag and its contents. With that, he watched the last of Tony Scapesi go up in smoke.

***

It was only a matter of time before Hines showed up at the sheriff's office to interview Nate and Luther about what happened. The official story as Nate related it to Hines was that Luther had surprised a man threatening Miss Ruby and had knocked him out. When the man came to, he hunted Luther down, ran him off the road, and beat him in retaliation. Nate had arrested the man and it turned out he was wanted out-of-state, so he had been shipped off to another jurisdiction.

It wasn't exactly accurate, but it contained enough truth to satisfy Hines and the readers of the *Waterproof Chronicle*. Luther declined to be interviewed, but he was only too happy to pose for pictures. "You better watch out now, Luther," Hines said with a smile, "once the paper comes out, you're gonna be a hero and all the girls are gonna be after you." Luther smiled, but he didn't put much stock in that prediction.

Nate had a serious talk with Carrie and impressed on her the importance of sticking with his official story. If folks knew what really happened, it would raise questions about Ruby and open a very nasty can of worms. However, gossip was already rising like heat waves from the sidewalks and everybody at school knew Carrie and Luther had been friends forever, so there were bound to be questions.

"Does that mean I can't tell them about Luther hitting the guy with the Virgin Mary?" Carrie was clearly disappointed.

"Oh, I guess you can tell them about that. Just don't mention Thompson Creek. If you talk about Luther being run down on his bike and how bad he looked when we brought him home from the doctor's, that should be enough gore to keep everybody happy," Nate said. Carrie reluctantly agreed.

After Carrie left for school, Miss Laura walked over to the Firehouse to relay their cover story to Bitsy. The safest thing to do was to concentrate on Luther's role as the hero and leave Ruby out of it as much as possible. And so the story was told and retold. Folks listened, commented, and then moved on to other more immediate matters.

If anyone had had a bird's-eye view of Waterproof that night, they might have suspected a genie had cast a sleeping spell on the town. For the first time in months, the principal players in the drama all fell into a deep, peaceful sleep.

CHAPTER FORTY
(Waterproof)

And then they waited. Waited for Miss Ruby to come back. When that didn't happen, they waited for Nate to make his move. When that didn't happen, they were puzzled. Then they got annoyed. Finally they got angry and decided to take action.

When Carrie and Luther approached Nate about the situation, he put them off with a lot of talk about not understanding women. Since they didn't get the right answer, Luther figured they had asked the wrong question.

Bitsy took a more direct approach. "When's Ruby comin' back?" She didn't get any satisfaction either and worse than that, Nate didn't come in for his usual pie and coffee for two days. Bitsy let it go for the moment.

It was Miss Laura who finally ambushed Nate and demanded an explanation. "What's going on with you and Ruby?"

"I don't know," Nate said sheepishly.

"What do you mean, you don't know? Have you talked to her?"

"No."

"Well for Pete's sake, why not?" Miss Laura's voice went up a couple of notches.

"I'm afraid of what might happen. You know, hiding out in Waterproof was one thing, but living here, that's altogether different. One lesson I've learned from Luther is to make sure you ask the right question. What if I ask her to come back and she says no?"

"What if you don't ask her? Reckon that's gonna get you the answer you want?" Nate looked so miserable, Miss Laura took pity on him. "Sit down, I'm gonna tell you a long story and I don't want you to interrupt until I'm done.

"When I was twenty my parents thought I was going to be an old maid, so they shipped me off to an aunt in St. Louis to 'improve my prospects.' Well, I met a boy from Chicago. He was twenty-two. I knew him for six weeks and when he asked me to go home with him, I said yes. In less than a week, we were married and I never looked back. We moved to Chicago, had a son and for nearly nine years, I had a perfect life. Then both my husband and my son died of influenza and I came back south to Jackson, Mississippi.

"That's where I met Wayne Webster. He was a lot older than me, but he was kind and gentle and after a while, we got married and I came here to Waterproof with him. When I was nearly forty, Eunice was born. Now both Wayne and Eunice are also gone.

"I have had two wonderful men and two precious children in my life and I don't regret anything. I decided a long time ago I might not get into heaven for sins I committed, but I sure wasn't going to hell for sins I *didn't* commit.

"Now, I'm not trying to tell you what to do. You have to decide that for yourself." Her story complete, Laura patted Nate on the shoulder and left the room.

Nate was stunned. He had never thought of Miss Laura as anyone other than his mother-in-law, Carrie's grandmother. Clearly there was much more to this woman than he had given her credit for. She had a past! Separate and apart from anything he knew anything about.

He had to admit she was right about going to hell for sins you *didn't* commit. And Luther was right about asking the right questions, if you wanted to get the right answers. Nate started to go to bed and changed his mind. He lit a cigarette, then put it out. He thought about going to the office, but discarded that idea too. He finally decided to walk down to the river. On his way out the door, he grabbed the car keys.

CHAPTER FORTY-ONE
(New Orleans)

"Miss Minnie, come quick! You're not gonna believe who's out there in the patio. See I was walking through the park and he was just sittin' there big as life with his horn case and I recognized him right off, so I introduced myself and I told him where I worked and I asked him if he'd like to come by for a while and he said yes and he walked over here with me and now he's sittin' out there in your patio!"

Tee Jean was talking so fast Minnie could hardly separate her words. "Tee Jean, who are you making such a fuss over?"

"Him!"

Minnie looked where Tee Jean was pointing. "*Mon Dieu!*" She recognized his round face, the big diamond ring on his left hand, and his wide toothy grin.

"Lord God, it really is him!" Minnie whispered. "Louis Armstrong is sitting in my patio!" As quickly as she could, she gathered her wits and went to greet her guest.

"Evenin,' Miss Minnie, isn't it?" If there had been any lingering doubt, the man's raspy voice clinched it.

"Welcome to New Orleans, or I guess I should say, welcome home. You back to stay?" Minnie asked.

"No just visiting. Chasin' memories. I grew up not too far from here, you know. Me and three other boys used to sing on the street for money. I was the one who knew all the best corners 'cause I delivered coal to the houses in Storyville. Got to know all the landladies.

"They'd give me food and sometime they'd let me come in and listen to the music." Armstrong paused for a minute, lost in memory. "You ever heard of a place called Pete Lala's? It was a dance hall. I met King Oliver there. Good times. Real good times."

Ideas were running through Minnie's mind so fast they were tripping over each other.

I'll invite him to stay for supper. Then maybe with a little help from Our Lady of Assumption who protects all Cajuns, he'll play a note or two.

"I was just about to have some supper, will you join me?"

Louis smiled. "I wouldn't want to put you to any trouble, but you know what I really miss living up there in New York City? Hot tamales. Wrapped in corn shucks, spicy enough to make your eyes water. Can't get 'em anywhere but down here."

Tee Jean had been standing by listening to every word. "I'll get 'em, Miss Minnie. There's this guy got a cart down on Toulouse." Before Minnie could respond, Tee Jean was on her way.

Like feathers blowing in the wind, the news that Louis Armstrong was at Minnie's spread through the Quarter. Of course, there was no guarantee that Louis would play, but nobody was going to miss the opportunity, just in case.

As Minnie entertained her guest, she could almost feel the house filling with people. It would be standing room only, but there would be no business upstairs tonight. She didn't care. She knew the story of Louis Armstrong's visit—whether he played or not—would bring customers to her house for years to come.

Minnie was never one to rush a good thing. Tee Jean was back in no time with three dozen hot tamales wrapped in several layers of newspaper. Minnie couldn't remember the last time she had seen Tee Jean move so fast.

"Louis, what can I get you from the bar," Minnie asked. "A Jax, maybe?"

"Sounds nice, but I'd really like a big glass of ice tea. Cools things off after the tamales. Did you know they don't know how to make ice tea up north? They try to put sugar in it when it's cold. Half the time they don't add lemon juice at all. Terrible! It's a sin and a shame to call that stuff ice tea."

Minnie didn't even bother to look in Tee Jean's direction. She knew Louis only had to ask and his every wish would be fulfilled. Sure enough, Tee Jean brought a big pitcher of tea and when Louis invited the girl to join them, Minnie thought the child was going to faint.

The three of them ate tamales until tears ran down their faces. Then they cooled things off with proper Southern ice tea, sweet, tart, cold, and strong. "Lord, Lord I miss the food down here," Louis said. "You can get better tastin' food at almost any fillin' station in Louisiana than you can get at a lot of those fancy restaurants in New York City."

Louis was mopping his bald head, Minnie was fanning herself and Tee Jean was about to explode with excitement. Minnie stood up, "Shall we?"

"We shall." Louis offered her his right arm and escorted her into the parlor. Just as she had expected, the downstairs was full. The air vibrated with expectant conversation, like the moments in the theatre before the lights dim and the curtain goes up.

It took a few seconds, but when folks saw Minnie walk in on Louis' arm, all conversation instantly stopped. And when the assembled crowd realized Louis was holding his trumpet in his left hand, applause exploded like fireworks. Every eye in the room followed Louis as he walked to the piano and raised his horn to his lips.

Ruby was there, but it wasn't Louis she was watching. All she saw was a tall man with a cane who made his way through the crowd, smiled and held out his hand to her. "Let's go home."

It was a night no one who was there would ever forget.

Bio for Grace Hawthorne

Grace Hawthorne is an award-winning author. Her first novel, *Shorter's Way,* won an Independent Publisher Award for best regional fiction. *Waterproof Justice* is her second novel.

She began her career writing business and industrial news for the Baton Rouge *State Times/Morning Advocate.* She has written everything from advertising for septic tanks to lyrics for Sesame Street and the libretto for an opera.

She was born in New Jersey, grew up in Louisiana, lived in Germany and in New York City. She and her husband, Jim Freeman, now live in Atlanta, Georgia.

CPSIA information can be obtained at www.ICGtesting.com
Printed in the USA
LVOW06s0205130315

430373LV00001B/37/P